THEA,
THE WATCHER
Passion personified. In her, savagery and majesty live again.

JASON,
THE BUILDER
On the run from his destiny—to create that which cannot be surpassed.

KEVIN,
THE BLOODLETTER
After untold discord and disharmony, the world would lie at his feet.

Also by J. Edward Lord
Published by Ballantine Books:

ELIXIR

INCANTATION

J. Edward Lord

BALLANTINE BOOKS • NEW YORK

Library of Congress Catalog Card Number: 87-91482

ISBN 0-345-34072-8

Manufactured in the United States of America

First Edition: November 1987

For something over 6,500 years, images of the scarabaeus beetle have been held sacred by mankind. Representing Khepri (Khepera, Kheperu), the charms symbolize this god of the dawn, the renewer of life, and the idea of eternal existence.

Prologue

THE ROOM WAS BARE, EXCEPT FOR THE SMALL LAMB-
skin rug upon which she stood. Her head was inclined upward. She appeared to be held, caught by
something in the distance. Her stance did not change when,
after long minutes, she spoke.

"My love, what a heavy price upon our happiness . . ."

She began to pace, pursued by the demons of memory.
Madwoman, queen—perhaps no one would ever learn the
truth of her, and so would she wish it. She paused now,
and faced the bedeviling past.

The air in the room became dull, heavy, as before an
electrical storm.

"I remember.

"I live that memory, I breathe that day.

"I had known what portended. But you, like the others,
sought comfort in procrastination, in denial."

She paused, a slight tremor entered her voice.

"The wind blew harder than usual that day. How dry and blistering it was. What a fair, delicate world there had been, the night before. What brilliance! That day, we awakened drugged, benumbed, as madness struck the land. The gate holding evil at bay was forced, and in spilled a killing rage."

She hurled words in rapid-fire cantos.

"Proud and valorous reign, fallen victim to greed and hate. Disintegration, unchronicled, occurred in so short a time. A legend or two, with all we were and all we attained forgotten, is all our labor won.

"It cannot be envisioned, that which blew in with the morning breeze. That which crazed, depraved, and destroyed. The earth did not quake nor tremor. There was no change in the river, nor in the sun's path. Nay, the desolation of the two lands was wrought by human wrath. Servants, innocent at daybreak, by midmorning were forced to cut the throats of children who slept with trust. Loyal partisans lay dead, or dying. Priests killed and maimed randomly.

"Some few were wise, quick to know, and sipped sweet-tempered poison, lest they live and watch the horror grow. The peace of playrooms adorned with pastel imagery—with vases of flowers and toys dangling from string—was blasted by shouts of savagery. Savagery fulfilled in the dagger's flowing ring of blood.

"I heard the screams and chaos. Helpless, I could only pray as my Egypt fell to that day's means. I ran outside my chamber to seek help, to restore order. But, the sickness . . . was upon every creature, as if dripping from the very leaves.

"One lazy budding day . . . when madness dawned and insanity led the way. Our way of life—ourselves—and what we had molded our world to be, would perish by dusk. Without conscience or remorse, human killed human. The worst horror, that whelp of my sister frothing with bestial glee . . .

"Two decades of purpose erased in less than two days."

2

She turned around, shook her head slowly. "All I had known and loved, strewn at frantic mania's demand, caused . . . my heart to dissolve . . ."

She paused, battled the trembling of her shoulders, denied the tears upon her cheek.

"From the East, in those days, were imported slender tubes of smokey glass—long cylinders used for surgical purposes."

Her voice became implacable.

"You were my chief advisor, an upstart in the view of many, and my lover. Thus, a special treatment was reserved you. They took one of those cylinders and thrust it in your member. Slowly, and with gruesome purpose, they broke it in place after place. Even now, I hear your cries, your rasping throat after you could cry no more.

"I did not see this, though I heard it. How loud excruciation must be before it can penetrate walls of stone. Then, after they dispensed with that preliminary, the torture began. On you, on our child, on the others.

"It happened yesterday, as far as time goes. Time is an illusion, a twinkling, a bird's fluttering. Did it take an hour for you to die, my love, or an eternity?

"And now, the hour of my revenge is come. Upon this earth walk many who were the principals in that lost drama. *You* live again. My cursed nephew lives. Others . . . It may be that only I remember fully. So shall it be. It will be enough.

"There were three great queens of the ancient world," she said softly. "I was but one. Each faced a similar problem—a man incapable of coping with that final chimera, self-honesty.

"Yea, though it be ten thousand years, each one must face himself.

"The nephew who took my lands to war mere days after desecrating my world has not evolved with the passage of time. He is yet a man who seeks the pleasures of power, of wealth. He is but part of my life to come. For the present I nurture him, though he knows it not. Understanding shall not be in him until he lies at my feet.

"For, imagination is the strongest power. An incantation can unleash ten-score terrors.

"But thee, my love. Thou art changed, stronger in thy fashion. I accept this and approve it. Yet this I say: ye shall be mine."

Beauty spoke:

"I will have thee!"

"Does it please you, Mistress?"

Expert hands massaged the lower back of a woman resting atop a tufted leather lounge. A heavy smell of myrrh drifted through Moorish doors. Willow blinds shut out all but thin shafts of sunlight. Wicker furniture, pushed against arching walls, encircled the two women. The blues of the mosaic floor were a sharp contrast to white-tiled walls. An aroma of cinnabar emanated from the oil being gently rubbed into the nude female.

"It informs me." The woman replied in a rich contralto, soft and suggestive.

The masseuse paused, then pulled back the thick black hair with care. Firm arms turned the woman until she lay face up. Piercing olive eyes, undisturbed by the movement, looked past the ceiling fan turning slowly overhead.

"Does the information bring you pleasure?"

"It brings satisfaction."

"I would not have lost him for you, Mistress."

"I know. And, there is the other . . ."

The woman closed her eyes and set a placid look on the very face of perfection, a loveliness derived from some ancient wellspring. Here reposed a calm not of civility, but of power, of archetypical pagan beauty—beauty fit for invoking both passion and terror.

ONE

Ṡāt

I AM PHARAOH.
I AM YOUNG.
FROM MY HANDS
THIS FORTUNE'S WRUNG.
I AM PHARAOH.
I SHALL GO.
I SHALL SEND
THE SEEDS TO SOW.
I SHALL BE
THE ONE TO GROW.
I SHALL HARVEST
AND I SHALL KNOW.
THEY MUST SEE
IN THOSE YEARS
FROM ME
WHEN DYNASTIES
ARE NO MORE
AND PHARAOHS ARE
BUT LORE
THAT THIS DYNASTY
IS ILL-CONTENT
WITH CRUELTY, WASTE,
AND WAR'S LAMENT.
MY FATHER IS DEAD.
HE DIED WELL-FED.

THE PEOPLE HOLD DREAD
AND DIE UNSAID.

—Hymn to Hat-shepsut,
from *Shadow of Khufu*,
Cecil Rupert-Lewis, 1894

THE SONG PURSUED HIM. TELDARIS THREW HIS HEAD back and swerved through a tight curve, his face becoming a stony expression of contempt. The car pulled from a dangerous swerve. The unsanctioned inner sound intensified, then crested. He chuckled bitterly in self-abnegation, but the song remained with him.

The mountain roads were narrow, and Teldaris deliberately took the curves with too much speed. The DeLorean didn't protest, except for a squealing of tires. The car itself seemed to beg for more. It growled sensuously, as though pleading to be the agent of his destruction.

He floored the accelerator, narrowly making another sharp turn past a sheer canyon drop. After several more such turns, his agitation lessened.

He slowed. Below, a small stream made violent by melted snow and late spring rain beckoned. He pulled to the side of the road, left the car, and descended to the water's edge. He knelt and plunged his hands into it, then splashed his face repeatedly, running wet fingers through dark hair.

Cold, he thought, but not too cold. He stripped to his underwear and entered the water. It was less than a foot deep, but had a powerful flow. Teldaris leaned back, feet braced against smooth stones, enjoying the icy pleasure.

He forced himself out when his muscles began to cramp. He took off the soaking briefs, hung them on a dead branch to dry and reclined on a warm boulder, but his mind refused inaction any longer. It roused, but did not come fully awake.

Teldaris stretched and rolled over.

He squinted his eyes, seeing the sun through the trees. He loved the mountains as he loved the sea. They were tangents of the same reality—earth. They expressed identical themes: majesty and calm remorselessness. He'd lived on the beach less than two months before, but already he missed the sea. . . .

He stilled his restless thoughts and listened. The wind blew faintly in the treetops above. An instant later, he grabbed his clothes. Leaning beside a large fir, he pulled on his pants, then ran for the silvery sports car.

He sped off within a minute, escaping but not eluding.

Beauty pursued him again. He had heard her song.

Kevin Adderson scowled, shoved a lurid newspaper account of the recent rash of cattle eviscerations into a trashcan, and turned his attention to an end-of-month sales report. The phone interrupted his concentration halfway through the first page. He frowned in irritation, and answered the phone with undisguised ill-humor.

"Kev, I got it! I actually did it!"

Adderson's pale eyes widened, and took on fresh intensity.

"Speak carefully, Deb." He glanced around to see if any fellow workers could overhear.

"It was like you . . . we discussed." The sound of a passing truck blurred his wife's elation.

"Go on, tell me!" he pressed.

"At first he didn't want me, so I did the tits and ass bit, came on as Miss Animal Lover, and it worked! The old lech—"

"Forget that," Adderson hissed. "Are there any other vets?"

"No," she replied, "just him." Deborah Adderson stood on her toes without realizing it. "Kev, our luck is turning around. I'll be closing the clinic every night. Can you believe it? I'll be the last to see the animals each day . . ."

Adderson swiveled back in his chair, smiling.

Susan walked near the edge of the lake. Near, but not too close; her gaze was bolder given the perspective of a few yards of solid ground.

The surface of the lake was flawlessly smooth. It looked more like a gigantic irregular mirror than a body of water.

Five hundred yards across from where she stood, trees gave mute testimony to the treacherous nature of the water. Aspens and pines that came too close to the edge had bare roots exposed to the elements. They would not live long, by a tree's reckoning. Only the little yellow and electric-blue flowers could dare the lake's shore with impunity, and they would die soon of their own accord. Summer was a fleeting thing in the Colorado Rockies.

That's all right, she thought, they'll come back next year. They'll always come back, and they'll be beautiful for a month or two.

Susan adjusted the fur around her neck. Wind, even summer wind, chilled her at these heights. Yet, she felt sustained by this solitary resistance. Alone, enjoying the solid aloneness that combined melancholy with tranquillity—this was luxury. In summer, she retreated to the lake when disturbed or tired. Some inner compulsion was satisfied. She belonged at this altitude, in these mountains.

A secret smile crossed her lips. The sheer angles of rock, wind murmuring among aspen, and the placidly dangerous water drew her magnetically.

She leaned over and looked. The shallow bottom by the lakeshore was brown and featureless. From the cold surface, someone gazed back at her. A woman with graceful, attractive features regarded her solemnly. Striking features, but not classic beauty. Light hair heralded middle age with a generous sprinkling of ash among the brown.

Her eyes narrowed. The eyes were as gray as the stone beneath her feet. Intelligently perceptive, they saw and assessed everything.

She jerked back. No introspection today. Her brother, that's why she'd come. Serious consequences impended. She must do something, before someone got hurt.

Susan sat on the stone, trailing her hand in the arctic water. She had gravitated here at other troubled times. A day after high school graduation, she'd borrowed her mother's ancient Chevrolet to drive up the steep winding road. Her feelings of discontentment had frightened her. On the night of college graduation, instead of celebrating with friends, she'd returned in her party dress. Confused, she'd looked out on the lake searching for some meaning, some message. Nothing could be seen on its surface but a doubly polarized image of the moon. She had run back to the car.

Years later, the divorce became final and again she returned. It had been an unhappy end to an unhappy marriage, but she'd found relief, of a sort. The lake seemed to soothe her feelings of failure. No answers or clues were forthcoming, only relief.

For these twenty years, the mountain lake remained unchanged. Laughing, taunting its mystery, refusing to yield or to comfort.

She stood suddenly, frightened. She retraced her steps. Lighting a cigarette behind the automobile's closed windows and locked doors, Susan exhaled bitterly. The lake had won again.

"This is Third Eye Enterprises. Please leave your name and number at the sound of the beep. Mr. Tyler will promptly—"

Vern Tyler clicked off the answering machine in disgust. No response was at least better than the obscene messages he often got. Thoroughly miserable, he stopped by an oval hallway mirror and spent several minutes combing his hair. His swarthy features did not meld into appealing looks, but fate had given him an abundant supply of cleverness in compensation. And cleverness, in his opinion, outclassed handsomeness in every way.

He wandered into the tiny duplex kitchen, opened a can of food for Peck. Tyler looked beneath the table, found the cat curled on the floor by a closed furnace vent. Peck returned Vern's look. The enormous tiger-striped tom had lived with Tyler since kittenhood. Each used the other for certain necessities. Peck got food and shelter, Vern got a living conversation piece and mouser. There was no other commerce between them, and the arrangement suited both.

Tyler left the kitchen, aware that the cat wouldn't eat until left alone. He looked out a side window. It was a beautiful summer morning for Denver. To the west, the mountains stood in crystal definition—smog hadn't set in yet. He pushed back an intruding reminder of his sister when he saw his aging Toyota. He resented Susan, and begrudged the fact that he worked for her. Someday, he swore to himself for the thousandth time, someday he would be able to get out from under her thumb.

* * *

Kevin pulled himself forward on his elbows until he made eye contact with the caged rabbit.

"Tobias, who am I? Tell me."

The rabbit sniffed expectantly.

"Tobias, you're not listening. Who am I?"

The rabbit stared blankly through the wire, patiently awaiting the whim of its owner.

Adderson stuck out his tongue. He darted it in and out of his mouth rapidly. "I am a reptile. Repeat, Tobias, I am a reptile." The rabbit continued to stare.

Adderson repeated the chant several times, then fished a wilted bit of lettuce from his pocket. He tossed it into the animal's cage and watched Tobias eat it languidly.

He rubbed his eyes, glanced at the mantel clock. One minute after midnight. He rose to his feet. How much longer would Deb be at the vet's? He opted for a long hot shower instead of heating up leftovers. He grabbed a beer from the refrigerator. As he sipped, Adderson tried to recapture an elusive thought. The furious barking of his German shepherd reminded him. How many days had it been since he'd fed Wolfgang? Two, three? Surely not four . . . ?

He drained the last of the beer and mechanically crushed the can.

"I am a reptile," he said again. Kevin turned on the hot water tap, which quickly transformed the bath into a sauna.

He went back into the living room, opened the cage, pulled his wife's pet out by the back legs.

"Who am I, Tobias?" he demanded, as the hare squirmed to be put down. Adderson whistled. "You blew it, Toby." Tobias quit struggling.

Adderson strolled to the garage, where the dog had been penned all week. He opened the door a crack and tossed the bewildered rabbit inside. Deftly, he slammed the door shut and sauntered back to the steaming bathroom, accompanied by the sound of Tobias being torn to pieces by the frenzied hound.

"The hell with it." Susan threw down the pencil, dizzy from hours of close work. Account books were strewn across the table. "I'm going for a walk," she announced to the empty room and rose stiffly from the dining room chair. Though she would have been loath to admit it, this break in routine had become an almost daily ritual for her during the last few years. A better-than-average businesswoman, she actually enjoyed the work incurred by the four laundromats she'd inherited from her father. She'd some time ago hired such good managers (using Vern as her main overseer on day-to-day problems) that she could concentrate almost entirely on the financial side of the business, including managing a modest investment portfolio on profits.

She left her apartment, walked a few blocks to Cheesman Park, and paused to watch the antics of two squirrels. They scampered over to her, sat on their back legs, forepaws in the air, tails twitching. She shook her head, chuckled, walked on. These animals were always out, even in winter, indulging their gluttony rather than enjoying a warm nest. Susan wondered why they didn't burst. With few exceptions, they were fed by older people whose loneliness was a tangible thing.

Susan refused to feed the squirrels, afraid that in doing so she would slip over into the ranks of the lonely and hopeless. That fear manifested at other detested sights: two-wheeled carts used by old women to carry groceries, pampered dogs who became surrogate children. She didn't want those things. And wouldn't, she hoped—ever.

A figure in a safari shirt and slacks appeared in the corner of her eye. Susan walked on. The man paused, then headed toward her. She sighed, more annoyed than afraid, and turned toward the botanical gardens. She could hear him behind her, but willed herself not to walk faster.

She walked faster anyway, her heart beginning to accelerate.

"Hey, wait up." He was a few steps behind.

"I've got mace," she lied without breaking stride.

She had no time to plan her next move. He dashed around and blocked her path. The modern high rises and Victorian mansions surrounding the park would be an odd setting for daytime rape.

"Listen, I'm not a mugger. I just want to ask a question." His dark hair flew in all directions with the wind. He seemed to have difficulty in catching his breath.

Susan was startled by the exotic good looks of the man. She immediately assessed him: not a mugger, upper-middle-class, possible psycho. Too young, too pretty, too married.

"You're unzipped!" She pointed.

Instinctively, he checked.

She breezed past him and dashed across the street into the safety of the botanical gardens building.

Deborah's mouth pulled down at the corners. The sounds of Wolfgang being punished by her husband did nothing to improve her mood. She wiped her glasses with a dishtowel and turned to her potful of simmering tamales. Her stomach had gotten queasy.

"That's enough, Kev!" she shouted. A moment later she repeated, "Ke-*vin*, that's enough!" She went to the drainboard to chop lettuce for a salad.

Her husband came in, threw the whip on the floor, and headed for the refrigerator.

"Get me one, too. I could use it!" she called without turning around.

Adderson obeyed. He stole up behind her and planted a

kiss on her neck. He held the opened beer next to her mouth. She wasn't friendly.

"Okay, so you have to work nights. Poor baby." He took a sip, waiting. A minute passed. He shook his head and pulled a tall stool up to the counter.

"And weekends."

"Double poor baby."

Deborah hit the chopping board a little harder with the butcher knife.

Kevin ignored her, sat, and became serious. "Deb, you know it's worth it." She pretended not to hear.

"Look, I'm twenty-four. You're no younger. How long can we afford to wait?"

She paused, and scratched the back of her hand with the knife.

"How did Tobias get in the garage?" She turned to face him.

He shrugged.

"How did Wolfgang get in the house?"

He shrugged again.

She went back to the salad. "Where were the empty cans if you fed him?"

Adderson stood. "Would it help if I bought you another goddamn rabbit?"

She dished up tamales without replying.

"Name your pet, and quit your bitch, for god's sake!"

"How about something that won't bleed?" she said. "I'm so sick of blood . . ."

Adderson took her in his arms and squeezed tightly. "It'll be worth it, Deb, you'll see."

"Oh, Kev, I hope so."

Adderson looked at the cramped kitchen. "It won't always be like this, dandelion." He stroked her yellow hair and gently removed her glasses. "It'll get easier."

"Poor Tobias," she murmured.

"I know," he whispered. "I know."

* * *

Susan sat at the park's edge, across from an impressive Tudor-style mansion, taking her daily break.

Inevitably, her thoughts returned to Steven. She'd refused to call him Steve, like everyone else. He'd appreciated that, but she never found out why. A year and a half was all the time they had together. After the miscarriage, she'd blamed him, though she hated herself for doing so. No one had been at fault, but she could not help condemning him. He'd refused to accept that and had left eleven years ago . . .

"Hello again." A voice surprised her.

She recognized him immediately, but stubbornly refused to leave when he sat beside her.

Her eyes roamed over his forest-green jogging suit. Up close, he appeared thirtyish. Susan was caught by his eyes, which were chestnut brown, and disturbingly intense.

God, she thought, you *are* a lady-killer, aren't you?

"Sorry about yesterday." He smiled.

"What about it?"

"The reason I bothered you is that I'm asking people . . ." He poked around in a backpack.

She waited, fidgeted with her keys, classifying him as just another salesman with another gimmick.

". . . if they've seen her." He produced a blurred snapshot of an attractive young woman.

She studied the photo. "Are you with the police?"

"No . . . but I need to find her and make sure she's okay. So, I'm asking around. She was last seen here in Denver."

Susan understood without being told: he had shown the picture to many people and held little hope of a positive response.

She shook her head. "Runaway?"

"No, not really."

"Break the law?"

"No."

She waited for something more. He was about to speak, then stopped.

"Who is she?"

"My wife. She disappeared. I want to know she's all right."

"Well . . ."

"Sorry to have bothered you."

"No bother," she replied, rather too quickly.

"Thanks." He turned away.

Susan watched him until he disappeared behind a grove of spruce trees.

Tyler hummed a Barry Manilow song, trying to drown out the ominous noises coming from the engine of his Toyota. It was a black-on-black night. No moon, clouds, or stars broke the solid vault overhead. Street and car lights were the only illumination.

He turned into a narrow parking space. Grabbing the sack of hamburgers, Tyler gingerly walked to the back door, cursing the unlit alleyway. He climbed the five steps to the back door and switched on lights before entering. He put the bag on a kitchen counter and glanced under the table. Peck was there, in his usual position.

"Waiting for your supper, are you? Must be nice to be waited on hand and foot," he grumbled. The cat didn't move a whisker, didn't even seem to be breathing.

"Don't try to spook me, old cat. Nothing is going to detract from this ambrosial dining experience." He threw the burgers onto a plate and put a straw into the chocolate shake, then walked into the living room and placed his meal in front of the television before returning to the kitchen. He put out food for Peck, but the animal didn't move toward it, didn't appear to notice him.

"What in hell's wrong with you?" Tyler demanded. "Are you sick?"

The idea of a vomiting cat was not appealing. He reached under the table and groped for the feline. Peck didn't react. His eyes seemed focused on something far away. He sat, paws curled under him, a living statue. The striped fur was raised more than usual, but Vern didn't take note. He grabbed the skin at the back of Peck's neck and tried to pull him from under the table.

The contact jolted the cat into terrible animation. Eyes widened, teeth bared in a freakish grimace, he sprang up as if burned; the hand grasping his neck didn't release him. Tyler was too surprised to let go as the claws unsheathed and Peck, hissing like a snake, attacked his arm. Vern's sleeve was shredded within seconds. He wrenched away, unaware of the shirt, seeing nothing but the maddened animal. He retreated until the counter stopped him.

Peck jumped onto the counter and paused there, with arched back and puffed tail. Every hair on his body was raised to maximum length, making him look three times his size. He hissed, spat, then issued a low, deep growl. Vern knew the cat didn't recognize him, that in a cat's rage anything that moves is an enemy. He forced himself to freeze.

The animal quieted. Tyler slowly exhaled. Then, without warning, Peck leapt at his face. He raised his hands to protect himself, but too late. A paw struck his cheek twice. He thrust the cat away, paying no attention to the damage being done to his hands. Peck yowled in a near-human voice and fairly flew out of the room, down the basement stairs. Round-eyed and panting, Vern slammed the basement door shut, then checked himself for damage. His neck felt warm and sticky. He rushed to the bathroom and inspected his wounds in a mirror. Two parallel gashes, about three inches long, bled copiously down his right cheek. Blood ran down his neck, staining his shirt. He stripped the shirt off, then rummaged through the cabinet for disinfectant and bandages.

Five minutes later, he returned to the living room and

sank into an easy chair. The incident was too fresh to bring into clear focus, but he was beginning to feel angry. If he had his way, this would end with Peck's demise. He ate the cold hamburgers without tasting them. He had to think of some way to corner the cat and get him in a box. Maybe he should call somebody for help. . . .

The lights went out. Tyler jumped. Ridiculously, his thoughts dashed to Peck. He forced a laugh. It's only another blown fuse, he told himself. He'd half risen from the chair when he heard a rustling in the bedroom.

"Jesus! How'd he get there from the basement!" he wondered.

Tyler stood very still, realizing dimly that he wouldn't stand a chance against the cat in the dark. He tenderly touched his cheek.

Then, from the basement came a long, octave-leaping howl. Peck. Yet the rustling still sounded in the bedroom. Vern shook violently, unable to move. Beneath him, in the cellar, was quite possibly a rabid cat. In front of him, in the room where he slept, there was . . . what?

His head moved from side to side in small, jerky motions. His arms and shoulders tingled. The rustling approached. Peck's cry grew in volume.

In the doorway . . . his eyes narrowed to see. There was a shadow darker than the rest. It was large, and moved toward him. Vern would've run, but could not force himself to move. The shadow paused by his side before it moved on into the kitchen. Peck stopped yowling. Tyler heard no sound, no door open or close, but he knew exactly when the thing left.

He collapsed to his knees and shook like some wet, cold beast. After a time, he calmed down somewhat and stumbled to the kitchen. Fumbling, he found matches, struck one, looked around. Peck lay on the table—dead.

* * *

Adderson thrust both hands into his back pockets, tilted his head and assumed an arrogant pose to conceal his fear.

He was cold, despite summer heat shimmering off the parking-lot asphalt. Two men were stationed behind him, two more were on either side of the old man facing him. That man was Kevin's judge and jury. Adderson was glad of the daylight, the congested downtown traffic on nearby Broadway.

"Are you sure he didn't recognize you?" the old one demanded.

"Tyler was too busy crapping himself," Kevin snapped.

"Answer my question."

"He knows someone was there. But he didn't see me. He got the message, though." Two trickles of perspiration ran into his eyes.

"A dead cat is a message?"

"It's a warning."

"You were sent to find the thing, not to kill a cat."

"I wanted to rough him up, but you wouldn't let me. I did what I could." Adderson displayed two bandaged hands. Long scratches ran past his wrists. "This is what it cost me," he said bitterly.

"You understand nothing of the simplest psychology." The old man shook his head. "If Tyler were to suffer a beating, he might just take the scarab and disappear." He advanced a step toward Kevin, flanked by his associates.

Kevin willed himself not to step back. He felt the presence of the men behind him.

"What assurance do we have that you didn't get it and decide to keep it for yourself?" His accuser squinted against the sunlight, face hardened by suspicion.

"It's too well hidden, if it's there at all. I combed every inch . . ."

The taller man behind him clamped a hand on Adderson's shoulder. "Don't waste our time with excuses!"

"I do not wish to take this thing by force. The nature of the scarab is sufficiently hidden from me that I do not

20

know the consequences of theft by violence. It is possible that we would suffer some sort of psychic backlash. You know the principle—violence begets violence. No, that is the path we must avoid, if possible. Convince this man Tyler to relinquish the thing, to give it to you. How often have I told you that?'' the old man snapped.

Once too often! Kevin thought. Anger began to nudge him past fright. He'd been tested, over and over again, taunted, told what not to do. Every time he made a decision, they disapproved.

''I'd nearly killed the cat when Tyler came in,'' Adderson defended himself. ''There was no time to write a note.''

''You should've had one prepared! Didn't you think this through before you started? How can you possibly imagine you're ready for initiation?'' The man's face twitched when he saw the approach of a parking attendent. The men separated for a moment, while the tall one dealt with the intrusion.

Kevin loosened the top button of his shirt, pulled the drenched cotton material away from clammy skin. The sun beat down oppressively, but he was still cold.

''If I had the thing you want and withheld it, wouldn't I be committing suicide?''

The old man nodded.

Jason loosened the laces of his jogging shoes in slow deliberation, then looked at the crinkled photo lying next to his soft-drink can.

He dialed a memorized number.

''I wish to send an overseas cablegram. Fourteen words, collect. Cairo Museum. Cairo, Egypt. 'Will accept offer, stop. Can complete transaction, stop. No proof yet, stop. Need cash advance, stop. Item here, stop.' ''

He sipped the cola as the cable was read back to him.

TWO

Ā Uaa

THE NEXT LIFE
FROM HENCEFORTH
SHALL BE DEPENDENT
UPON THIS LIFE.
AND HE WHO DOUBTS ME
SHALL CONSULT THE PRIESTS.
FOR THEY, TOO, SHALL
FIND BENEFIT IN BELIEVING.

CALL INTO THE NEIGHBORING
LANDS A REQUEST THAT ALL
LEARNED MEN AND WISE SCRIBES
SHALL GATHER HERE.

AND OF THOSE WHO COME,
WE SHALL BUILD
TOMBS BY OUR MINDS
FOR TERROR, MUTILATION,
TORTURE, AND WARRING.

—Hymn to Hat-shepsut, from
 Shadow of Khufu,
 Cecil Rupert-Lewis, 1894

JOY STRESSED HER ORIENTAL FEATURES BY RAISING HER right eyebrow. The man before her fidgeted.

"Who . . . um . . . what was the name to be? . . ."

"Thea Markidian."

"Would you mind spelling . . ." The portly realtor clicked his pen nervously. The stature of this woman, as well as her manner, frightened him.

"Yes." Joy smiled blandly and waited.

The disconcerted man looked up from his pad.

"Miss . . . uh . . ."

"Joy." The smile returned.

"I need to know the alphabetical spelling of your . . ." Beads of perspiration broke out upon his forehead. Something about her made him feel like a very small mouse confronting a very large cat.

"Sir, can your ear be so untrained? My enunciation is

superior to that of most American natives. Spell phonetically.'' Her expression remained pleasant.

He loosened his tie.

"No, I will not spell it for you. Continue.''

"Why . . . what did you say the house was going to be used for?'' The realtor felt outclassed by this woman, lost in the vast Tudor mansion he was trying to sell.

"An oasis.''

A quick curling movement by a slender arm stopped his question.

"What does it matter, as long as you have this?'' A deft maneuver produced crisp new hundreds held between long, lacquered nails. A free fingertip touched his earlobe gently. She could feel him shiver.

"Cash?'' he protested in disbelief.

"Yes.''

"But the price is eight hundred-forty thousand dollars!''

"So it is.''

"This is unusual. I mean, it isn't done!''

"Yes, it is.'' She opened a valise. The realtor was staggered by its contents.

Joy turned to him. "Tomorrow morning, you will bring all necessary papers and people to this house. By ten o'clock, Thea Markidian will be the owner or you will lose your commission, possibly more. Then, you may have this valise.'' She placed the case on the floor and seemed to forget it.

"Turn on the furnace.''

"But . . . it's blazing outside.''

"Do it.'' Joy slipped off one shoe.

"It'll make this place an inferno.'' He looked through the leaded windows to the park across the street, thinking of his commission.

"I know,'' she purred, content with the house. Mistress would be pleased; Joy could produce an oasis anywhere.

* * *

Tyler stormed across the hotel lobby, credit-card imprinter dangling under one arm. He barely broke stride as he entered the banquet office, though he was puffing under the combined load of cassette recorder, briefcase, and imprinter. The sales director looked up and smiled.

"Hello, Mr. Tyler. How are you?" The director noticed scratches on Tyler's cheek, but said nothing about them.

"Not too damned well, Ferguson!" Vern snapped. "My meeting's in fifteen minutes, but the room's locked, it's not on the lobby marquee, and . . . What the devil are you smiling for? Tell your setup boys to get my room ready or—"

"Or what?" the young executive asked, rising from his desk. "Or you won't pay your bill? A bill already delinquent four hundred dollars?" He stepped forward, apparently eager for the confrontation.

"What are you talking about?"

"You understand me, Mr. Tyler. You've disregarded notices from accounting, ducked my secretary, and refused to return my calls. Enough is enough!"

Tyler had no defense. His arms ached, but he refused to set anything down.

"We require payment in advance of your overdue bill, plus a one-hundred-dollar deposit."

"Deposit? I've never had to put down a deposit!" His last words were loud. A secretary looked up in surprise.

Ferguson was about to speak when a woman interrupted.

"Mr. Tyler? Is that you?" An overly groomed woman in her fifties edged into the office uncertainly.

Tyler turned around, heart sinking. "Why, Betty . . . you're early." His mind raced, searching desperately for some way out of his predicament.

"First one in gets the best seat." She laughed. When no one responded, she continued, "Where . . . which room are we meeting in today?" Janice Hughes, another member of Tyler's group, entered and peeked over Betty's shoulder.

Tyler slowly set the recorder and imprinter down on a chair. "If you'll wait outside in the lobby, I'll join you in a minute."

"Oh, you men and your important business," Betty chided, but did not leave. The other woman drew up closer behind her.

The banquet manager remained impassive, arms folded.

"I'll write you a check."

"Your last check bounced, Mr. Tyler. You know that," Ferguson replied.

Betty mumbled a quick "Excuse us," and left with Janice in tow.

Tyler was livid. "Did you have to say that in front of clients, you bastard?" he asked between clenched teeth.

"Do you wish to do business here or shall I ring for security?" Ferguson's hand reached toward the intercom.

"That won't be necessary, Mr. Ferguson." A clear voice sounded behind Tyler. He spun around.

"Susan! What are you . . ." His eyes darted to the handful of outstretched green. His sister ignored him, instead walked directly to the manager. She had been in Ferguson's reception area and overheard their angry voices.

"Will this buy Mr. Tyler his room for the day?"

Ferguson took the money, began counting.

"Do you represent Third Eye Enterprises?" he asked.

"I am his guardian, shall we say?" Susan reached in her purse.

"Susan, what on earth do you think you're doing?"

She nonchalantly pulled out a credit card and slid it into Tyler's pocket. "I'm joining your little group today. Didn't I tell you?"

"Like hell you are!"

"Mr. Tyler, I'm a busy man. If you'd rather—" Ferguson's words were interrupted by a cluster of people gathering at the door. "May I help you?" he asked in exasperation.

"We're . . . we . . ." Betty's voice faded away, her face matching her pink suit.

Tyler's head shrank into his shoulders.

"It's up to you," Susan said slowly.

A long moment passed. Tyler closed his eyes, nodded his head. He shifted his overstuffed briefcase automatically.

"I'll require a receipt for tax purposes, Mr. Ferguson. What room did you say we were in?" Susan's briskness propelled everyone into animation. Betty herded the others into the coffee shop until a room was ready.

"You'll pay for this, Susan!"

"I just did."

"Any other time . . . Sit in the back somewhere and don't say a word. Don't tell anyone we're related." He scowled at the two banquet setup men who sauntered by, seemingly in no hurry whatever to ready his meeting room.

"This is the first time most of you have attended a TEE meeting. I'm sure you are wondering what you've let yourself in for. Let me assure you that, if you've come with a skeptical attitude, you're precisely the type of person I want here. Firstly, the name of our group—TEE—is short for Third Eye Enterprises. What does it mean? The third eye is the legendary extrasensory organ that enables the human mind to perceive those things beyond the ranges of our mundane senses—sight, touch, hearing, and so on. Does the third eye actually exist? Let's find out together.

"Our TEE classes will be devoted to the study of self, of metaphysics, and of the occult. Don't let those last two put you off. Those words have been bandied about too casually for over thirty years and have become so distorted in connotation that they've become almost laughable. Metaphysics. Do you think of a near-naked Indian or Oriental man, with limbs twisted into impossible contortions, who chants 'OM' minute after minute, year upon year? When you hear the word occult, do you think of a black-draped crone stirring a cauldron and spitting vitriolic curses?

"Wrong. On both counts. Wrong. Look in a dictionary. Metaphysics is psychology. It is a mental science; it is the philosophy of self and of knowledge. Occult is a simple adjective that means hidden, or secret.

"Together, we will explore many subjects with many fanciful names—ESP, PK, astral projection, altered states of consciousness, psychometry, déjà vu, thaumaturgy and on, and on, and on. But, the most important thing to keep in mind is that we will, in reality, be studying ourselves as mankind, as a group, and as individuals."

Susan studied the room as her brother continued to speak from the podium. Just under twenty people were gathered. They seemed to represent a fair cross-section of the American middle class. Young, old, male, female, blue collar, and professional. And, importantly, they *all* seemed interested in Vern. As was she. Susan had never seen her brother so self-assured, so vital, or so knowledgeable.

"A good way to start these beginning meetings, to break the ice and get acquainted, is to introduce ourselves and give a short summary of the reasons we've come here. So, let's begin in back with Susan Tyler and work our way down front. Susan, would you start?"

She felt a surge of horror and anger at being singled out in this manner. To her, Vern's action was an attack. The respect she'd begun to feel for him in the last few minutes vanished, replaced by red ire. In effect, she'd just loaned him five hundred dollars in the manager's office. Very well, she decided, if he wanted to play hardball, she was going to get her money's worth. She rose.

"My name is Susan Tyler. I have little interest in the occult or supernatural. Most of my work deals with financial management. I am Vern's sister. I am here to find out what he is up to," she ended dryly, and sat.

Her announcement was met with utter silence. Tyler, unbelieving, had a broad grin frozen on his face. Uneasy seconds passed before the banquet-room door opened, thankfully pulling attention away from Susan.

She looked up defiantly, successfully camouflaging her self-consciousness. A man had entered. He seemed unmindful of the roomful of strangers staring at him. To her discomfort, he looked toward her. After placing a check on the registration table, he headed for the chair next to hers. He was the man she'd met twice in the park.

Person by person, the new members of TEE gave summaries of themselves. Slowly, the crimson flush left Susan's cheeks. She decided that she would slip out as soon as she could get away unnoticed. The man next to her looked her way too often, seemed more interested in her than the meeting.

Mercifully, Tyler called for a refreshment break. Everyone began to mill around. Susan headed toward the back exit, but instinct caused her to pause and turn around. The stranger was following.

She squinted, dazzled by sunlight on concrete and chrome. Susan automatically donned sunglasses.

The silence was broken by a car horn. She moved from dead center of the hotel parking lot. Susan turned toward him abruptly.

"What do you want?" she demanded.

"How about lunch?" he answered casually.

"I . . ." Susan stopped, uncertain.

He stepped forward.

"You name the place," he offered.

"I've got to take care of some business matters," she murmured.

"Fine. Some other time, maybe." He turned and walked toward a gleaming DeLorean parked nearby.

"No, really, I *do* have . . ."

"Okay, no problem. See you around." He smiled politely before he unlocked the gull-wing door. Susan made a decision, then walked up beside him.

"Why were you at the meeting? Why you, why here? Does it have something to do with me?"

He straightened, and regarded her curiously.

"You surprise me."

"What?"

"You surprise me. I don't even know your name. Are you so conceited as to think I followed you here?"

Susan flushed red.

"Well?" He waited.

"Look . . . if we're going to have a confrontation, I think at least I should know my sparring partner's name."

A look of pure pleasure came over his face.

"Jason. Jason Teldaris. And you?"

"Susan Tyler. Vern Tyler is my brother."

"I know. I was listening at the door when you made that scene."

Susan's irritation rose to anger. She found herself unable to reply, a rare situation for her.

"Don't misunderstand," he said. "I admire anyone with the spirit necessary to make an ass of herself in public."

She had slapped him hard before she realized her hand had moved. A stinging palm forced her to believe she had done it.

Teldaris fought for self-control and won. "If you ever do that again," he said calmly, "I will return the blow."

"I . . . I'm very sorry. I don't know what . . ." she ended lamely.

"You never answered my question. Why should I follow you anywhere?"

She was devastated. An urgent voice deep within her warned, This is important. You've met a man who has your own breed of arrogance. Be careful!

"I don't believe in coincidences," she said at last. "I'm very suspicious when they occur. I met you in the park twice, now here. The odds against that happening are astronomical." She felt better, now that her doubt was honestly stated.

Teldaris saw the truth in her eyes. He nodded once, then spoke. "No, Susan Tyler, I did not follow you here. How could I? But, you're making a grave error if you don't believe in coincidences. You *must* believe in them."

He got into the sports car, gunned it viciously, and roared away.

The unblinking eyes that surveyed the four-hundred-foot drop were not those of a predator bird, nor was the precipice upon which she stood some high flung aerie. Thea Markidian shrugged away her mantle and veil and stepped to the balcony's edge. The dark mantle slipped to the floor, but the veil remained in her left hand, moving softly in the breeze.

Dusk had set upon the city. From the hotel penthouse balcony, the night view was magnificent. Joy had apologized for the inconvenience of the one-night stay in the hotel suite, had explained that the temporary staff she'd hired had not readied the new house. Thea smiled to herself, sympathizing a little with the staff. They'd not precisely followed Joy's instructions, and were certain to regret their omissions. The well-being of *anyone* who crossed Joy was in doubt.

The twinkling city lights made Thea realize that she was indeed glad the house had not been ready. Gleaming, modern, in its own way beautiful, the city of Denver deserved to be greeted from this high place. Denver. A precise opposite to her native Istanbul. Fascinating, the differences . . .

Something moved in her hand. Glancing down, she realized she'd forgotten the veil. Thea tossed the black silk over the balcony edge and watched it slowly flutter to earth.

"Never again shall I wear the veil," she vowed, "save in pursuit of thee. Never."

Susan fingered her watch, crushed out a cigarette, finally motioned for the waiter. A discreet smile greeted her order for another glass of wine. She fought an overwhelming impulse to leave. That was exactly what Vern wanted, she knew, glancing toward the entranceway. When the Chablis arrived, she sipped it with slow and deliberate pleasure.

Her thoughts drifted to the kind of man she'd prefer to meet for lunch, but a shadow interrupted the flow of sunlight through the window.

She looked up, prepared to meet Vern's eyes. Instead, a blue-eyed stranger leaned over the table.

"You don't know me," he said, displaying a crooked smile. "But I know you." He sat beside her, uninvited. She studied the man and instinctively reached for her purse. His pale eyes and blondish hair did not disguise that he was not open, not honest. There was a sardonic hardness about the eyes and mouth that was unusual in a man so young.

"What a coincidence running into you like this!" He placed both hands on the table. Susan couldn't decide if the gesture was threatening, uncertain, or merely clumsy.

She flinched when he smiled again.

"*If* you know me, you are aware that I neither thrust nor parry when I'm at a disadvantage." She reached for a cigarette.

"Kev." He quickly struck a match. "May I call you Sue?"

"I was waiting for my brother, so if you'll excuse me . . ." Susan started to reach for her bag. She wondered how he knew her name.

"So was I, so was I." His arm stretched across the table. She moved her hands further from his, swallowed, but remained seated.

"You know Vern?"

"Yes. I used to be in one of his classes." He chuckled. "What he calls classes."

Susan responded with a flat stare.

"Looks like he stood us both up. Can I buy you some lunch?" he offered awkwardly, aiming for rapport.

"No, I have to leave. Another appointment."

"Yeah, right. Some other time, maybe."

"May I give Vern a message?" she asked.

"No, the message is for you." The tone of his voice let her know his sycophancy had ended.

"Me?"

"Tyler . . . That is, your brother . . . has something that belongs to me. Correction, something that I want."

"What's that got to do with me?" she protested.

"I can't seem to get through to him." Adderson handed her a matchbook with a phone number scribbled inside. A time was written beside it.

"So?"

"So make sure he gets this, Sue." Adderson stood. "Tell your dear brother to contact me, or . . . I can't be responsible."

"For what?" she demanded. "What are you talking about?"

He nodded, and walked away.

Tyler cursed as he stumbled through his living room. The insistent knocking couldn't have come at a more inopportune time. A peek out the window at the Renault out front made him aware that the caller was Susan and that she would not go away.

He opened the door and was met by a slap in the face.

"That," said Susan as she walked past him, "is for standing me up." She whirled around, slapped him again. "That was for lying to me."

Vern slammed the door shut, face crimson. "What is it now, sister dearest? Do you want something, or did you just come by to use me as a punching bag?"

She paused before answering.

"This." She held out a letter, anger unabated. "From the district attorney's office. You are being investigated."

"What the hell for!" he sputtered, and grabbed the envelope.

"Practicing spiritualism for profit without a license, among other things," she said, smoldering.

"Who the devil do they think—"

"And this"—she interrupted him, handing him a scribbled note—"was placed in my mailbox last night, probably by the man who . . ."

Tyler took the note, read aloud, " 'Only a thief may talk to a thief. Make your brother hear, or—' "

"What?" he demanded, frightened.

"*Or what* is what I'd like to know! Vern, you'd better—"

Shuffling sounds from the bedroom silenced her. A couple of dull thuds—shoes dropping—followed. Susan looked at him clearly for the first time, and saw that he was half dressed. Hastily half dressed.

She closed her eyes in embarrassment. "Oh, brother . . . ," was all she managed to say.

She walked to the door. "I'm double-parked anyway. When you're done, I expect you to phone me!"

He waited a moment, then muttered, "Like hell I will." And returned to his bedroom.

> Our products possess *no* supernatural powers.
> All items are sold strictly as curios.
> All data is derived directly from folklore.

The disclaimer was centered prominently over the entrance, above the varied credit-card emblems. Susan hesitated, bit her lip before gathering courage. A moment later she entered the occult shop, hoping no one had observed her. She would rather be seen entering a porn store.

Her eyes quickly adjusted to the darkness. The tang of burning incense assailed her. A light aromatic smoke circled gently—motion and scent combined and produced a calming effect.

A minute passed before a middle-aged woman approached from the rear.

"How do you like your tea, with or without sugar?" the shopkeeper asked without preamble.

"Why . . . that's exactly what I needed."

The other woman merely nodded. A telephone rang in the back. "Please look around, I shan't be a minute."

Susan felt at a disadvantage. She would prefer not to delve into things paranormal or supernatural. However, Vern had forced the issue by setting up Third Eye Enterprises. And the forthcoming investigation by the D.A.'s office could be serious. Therefore, skeptic or not, she'd better do some investigating on her own. Forewarned, and all that rot. Besides, she admitted, maybe she *was* just faintly curious.

Susan began to inventory the contents of the shop. Like a traveling museum, it was small, neatly compact, and loaded with seashells, minerals, statuary, swords, crystal balls, and various styles of Tarot cards. One entire wall was filled with candles, tapers of all sizes and colors, predominating in white, crimson, and black. There were also strange figure candles in the shapes of cats, sphinxes, mushrooms, nude men, and women. Susan felt a sense of unease upon seeing these, but this passed. The next wall was lined with shelves containing clear glass cannisters of powdered incense. Every color of the spectrum must have been represented. The smells crept out, a light scent of perfumed talcum. In three glass display cases made into counters were rings, necklaces, knives, bracelets, beads, and even a jeweled staff. Susan couldn't help herself; she was fascinated. She fumbled for a cigarette, then changed her mind.

Carved wooden boxes, silver trays and bowls, pewter and brass chalices were displayed in attractive arrangements. Ornamenting the walls were broomsticks and lacquered tree branches. She noticed the absence of any books on magic. The few books she saw were about herbs, gardening, mineralogy, and mythology. She brooded—not one primer on curses, cults, or hocus-pocus. There was no sign of any charlatanry. She had hoped to effortlessly dismiss this sector of life as obvious fraud. Yet . . . it was compelling.

The saleswoman reappeared, carrying a cup of spiced tea. Susan thanked her soundlessly.

The woman studied her briefly, then asked, "What is it that troubles you?"

Susan was startled, but did not answer.

A wistful look emerged on the woman's face. "Don't tell me you came in to browse. I doubt you use any of these items." Her friendly manner appeared genuine.

Susan studied her. Refined, tranquil, outwardly no more noteworthy than a shopper at a suburban department store. Her eyes made the difference. They were sharp, indefinably colored, and sparkled with hidden depths. A thought darted into Susan's mind. What if those eyes sensed more than they saw?

The woman said, "We are all telepathic to an extent, some more than others. But, anyone could read your thoughts. They're written all over your face."

"I don't believe that," Susan stated slowly, trying to calm herself.

"I know." She indicated a needleworked maxim hung above a side counter. "Those who wait, rob." The sign was in stylized Gothic script.

"Only a thief may talk . . .," Susan murmured. She recalled the note in her mailbox. Her gray eyes narrowed suspiciously. She felt overwhelmed by the shop and its contents. The exotic, which she had never permitted to enter her life, now baited and taunted her.

She apprehensively turned around, shivered, felt as if shadows were stalking her.

"I'm sorry . . . I can't believe in this sort of thing. Too illogical, too much left to—"

"Fortuity?" the woman softly interjected.

"No!" Susan nearly shouted, surprising herself. "I can't . . . I'm not . . ." She blurted a hurried apology, fled from the store, and did not look back.

"Someday," the woman whispered, touching Susan's half-empty cup, ". . . someday, you will."

The nondescript bar was one of dozens that lined Colfax, the main east-west strip of the city. On Friday and Saturday nights, this one offered a local country and western band.

Jason was grateful that the place was nearly deserted on this Thursday afternoon; there'd be no one to overhear them. He slowly sipped a draft beer while he waited.

When he saw Tyler appear in the doorway, Teldaris drained his mug.

"You wanted to see me?" Vern asked gruffly, standing over the dark-haired man.

"You're late," Teldaris chided.

"Couldn't find this . . .," Tyler lowered his voice, "dive. Why here?"

"Why not?" Teldaris motioned the other to sit.

"Let's go to the bar." Vern pointed in the direction of some empty bar stools.

"Why? This booth is fine."

Vern frowned, but apparently decided not to press the issue.

Teldaris raised a hand. Two beers were soon served.

"Does this have something to do with Sue?" Tyler asked, genuinely curious. "Did she ask you to meet me here?"

"I don't know your sister."

Tyler's jaw tensed.

They sat in silence for some seconds. Vern drank his ale quickly, then ordered another round.

"I called you because I had hoped we might do a little business privately, for mutual benefit," Jason began.

"I run TEE myself, with no outside interference," Tyler cut him off brusquely.

"This has nothing to do with your group, Mr. Tyler. Believe me, I have no desire to enter into the business end of your organization," he said dryly.

Tyler scowled. "Then what do we have to talk about? Are you telling me you want to quit the sessions? You've just started the course."

"No. That's not it at all. . . . I wanted to talk money."

Vern looked up in bewilderment tempered with interest. Teldaris had hit the right button.

"Vern, I've heard that you're quite a collector of . . . artifacts. Some of which could be quite valuable, to the right people."

Tyler's eyes narrowed. "Who said that?"

Teldaris waved it by. "Sometimes I make a little money by acting as an . . . agent, you might say, for various institutions. I scout for anthropological and historical curios."

Tyler's eyes widened. "Really?"

"I could offer a good deal of money for something that interests me. I'd like to take a look at your collection."

"What makes you think I've got anything like that?" Fear began to show on Tyler's face.

"Anything of historical value is of interest to museums."

Tyler stiffened. An image flashed in his mind.

"Anyway, I thought we might discuss it over a couple of drinks."

"I'm leaving now. I have nothing that would interest you. Thanks for the beer." Tyler rose to leave.

"This might involve a *great* deal of money, Tyler." Tempted, Vern sat again. Teldaris breathed easier.

"Where did you hear that I might have anything . . . of interest?"

"Where did you go to school?" Teldaris went on the offensive.

Tyler started, and Jason immediately sensed this was the one wrong thing to say.

"I . . . uh . . . it no longer exists," Tyler replied cautiously. "Went bankrupt. Why?"

Jason had realized minutes earlier that he was handling Tyler clumsily. Subterfuge of this kind was simply not his forte. He hoped the truth could salvage the situation.

"Frankly," he told Tyler, "I'm not quite sure myself. As I told you, I do sometimes recover artifacts. I've had a couple of moderate successes in the field. Before I decided to move to Denver, I received a fairly detailed letter concerning a certain . . . object. Its last known location was the college you attended, which had it on loan from an Egyptian museum, but the object was stolen. According to the letter, you left the school a few days later. An odd coincidence."

"So, you're a private investigator?"

"No. I'm a treasure hunter."

"Who are you working for?"

"I don't know."

"What!"

"It's the truth. The letter was anonymous. I don't know who sent it. An agent for the Cairo Museum, as far as I can find out. A bank draft followed the letter. It was large enough to convince me to come here. I wanted to anyway."

"Why?"

"Personal reasons. I wanted to find someone."

"Who?"

"None of your business. A private matter. Let's not get sidetracked. I've been up-front with you. Are you interested in opening negotiations?"

"No! I don't know what you're talking about. I've told you that I have nothing that would interest you. Leave me alone, or you'll regret your interference."

"Deceit is a double-edged sword, Tyler," Teldaris said smoothly. "Don't cut yourself."

Tyler stormed out of the bar.

Jason finished his drink. He'd frightened the daylights out of the man and confirmed his suspicions at the same time.

He rhythmically drummed his fingers against the glass.

Tyler's slight overbite was accentuated by excitement. He inhaled rapidly, almost panting in anticipation of what would come.

He closed his mouth as a remarkable transformation passed over him. The muscles of his face changed subtly, as tension shifted axis. In the dimness of his bedroom, his features changed. His body slimmed, grew more erect in profile. His slack mouth and weak chin acquired strong, determined lines. His persona underwent a similar metamorphosis. But he was not aware of this—his concentration was singularly directed to the small bundle on his dresser.

He carefully unwrapped layers of cloth. Nestled in scarlet velvet was the scarab. Flecks of gold glistened, encased in a stone greener than an emerald. His mouth curved into a smile. Any torment, he thought, would be worth this. And no power on earth could ever make him part with it.

He slowly stroked the scarab with the tip of his right index finger. He felt warmth, comfort, promise, and delivery simultaneously. Tyler could produce no ritual as intense as admiration, but what he did manage was enough. There could be no reward sweeter than the pure euphoria that flowed into his hand.

He placed the beetle within his left palm. Perspiration made his hand shine.

A shade crossed his face. His features returned to normal. He lowered his eyelids. Once more he was himself. His lips curled with deep-rooted fear. Already, two men had tried to take the scarab away. One through threats, the other with a bribe, but this was the one thing in life he wouldn't sell for any price. And, he realized, the one thing he'd defend at any cost.

"Mine," he said soothingly, stroking the necklace attached to the scarab. A flood of exhilaration coursed through him, stronger than any sexual release.

Deborah felt his pillow. It was cold. Rubbing sleep from both eyes, she fumbled for her glasses. It was four in the morning. She sat up, listened for sounds from the bathroom. There were none, nor were there any lights. She waited. Several minutes passed. She got up, shuffled to the bedroom door, started to call out, then changed her mind. Deborah thought she heard her husband, maybe with Wolfgang. She heard whispering . . . faint, faraway, but staccato in intensity. Her eyes adjusted to the darkness while she tried to locate the source of the sound. It came from the direction of the hall closet. Her bare toes touched cold linoleum gingerly. The telephone cord ran the length of the hallway.

She tiptoed toward the closet, quiet as possible. Deborah paused in recognition of the voice coming from behind the door. Why would Kevin be in the closet? Her mind darted to the beautiful auburn-haired bank teller who often dazzled him with a large smile. She approached, mouth curled downward. Whatever this was, it wasn't good. "Kevin, who is it?" she asked. His voice grew louder.

"No! I could never do that!"

"Of course, I swear . . . anything!"

"It's all I—I must have it."

"Yes, it is worth anything."

"I exist only . . . Without? No, *never!*"

Too dismayed to stand quiet any longer, Debbie crept back into bed, where she pretended sleep. After some time, the room began to get light. She went back into the hallway. The closet door was open, the phone returned to the living room. Her husband was gone.

THREE

Pet

LET THEM KEEP THEIR
LIGHTNING CHARIOTS
AND SWORDS OF STRENGTH.

WE SHALL NOT FEAR
THOSE WHO WISH AGAIN
TO BURN OUR CITIES
AND PILLAGE OUR TEMPLES,
KILL OUR CHILDREN,
RUIN OUR WOMEN,
DESTROY OUR MEN
WITH THE SEEDS OF IMMORALITY.

AND, LASTLY, TO SEPARATE
OUR WELL-KEPT SLAVES
FROM THEIR DESERVED
IMMORALITY.

—Hymn to Hat-shepsut,
 from *Shadow of Khufu,*
 Cecil Rupert-Lewis, 1894

SHE WAS RADIANT; SHE SURPASSED ALL ELSE. PERFECtion personified, or deified, he knew not which.

She looked long into his eyes. Hers were the color of two sunbows joined together. She smiled benignly, if not lovingly, at her visitor.

"You want to know." Not once did her eyes leave his.

He nodded carefully, careful enough to suppress anxious hunger.

Her eyes remained fixed. The silence droned on, intermittently interrupted by movement outside the room.

"Tell me . . . why?" She narrowed her eyes and slightly lowered the angle of her head at the same time.

He was well-prepared. Concise. Purposeful. More, he felt, than she would have expected.

But she again asked, "Why? Tell me."

"Because . . . I want to know."

Her smile faded. "You have not answered my question."

"What . . . would you have me say?"

Her lips tightened.

"That you do not deserve to know. . . ."

"Deserve?"

"At least not now . . . it is too early. . . ."

"Too early? No. As I sit here, it is too late. Too late."

Her back straightened. Her eyes appeared to glaze as she stared into the distance. After some time, her eyes refocused. He sat watching her intently.

Her eyes and face had an almost palpable look of decision, as she began to speak.

"Perhaps . . . some leniency can be shown in this matter. Yet, only a certain amount of knowledge may be imparted. As you mature, more will be added."

To acknowledge the concession, he bowed his head.

She walked to a window and gazed out.

"If you would allow . . . I am curious." He stopped. Should he ask? Did he have the courage to ask, or to receive the answer?

"Are you," he asked slowly, accenting every syllable, "The Breastless One?"

She did not answer, instead turned to face him. She was changed, but he did not know what made her appear so.

After an uncomfortable silence, he began again.

"Are you then The Bearded Warrior, Son of the Sun, Lord of the Two Lands?"

She did not respond.

"I would suggest that your brilliance is unmatched," he stammered. "Could you be, by fate, the Daughter of Amon and Ahmasi, in whom all valor and strength of the great god Amon was made manifest on earth?"

She advanced and the light grew more intense.

"I am I," she said unaffectedly. "But I am also what you make me. Does not the imagination of others hold us all in bonds?"

Saying this, she was gone.
He was sent hurtling back.

The buzzing clock was swept off the bedside table by a swipe of his hand. He sat up, blinking in confusion. Rubbing the back of his neck, Teldaris struggled to remember.

Tyler slammed his fist on the table.
Susan looked up, only mildly concerned for her china.
"I said I don't want you talking to that Teldaris again!" he said.
"And I said I was old enough to take care of myself," she replied in quiet contrast.
"He's trouble."
"I don't even know him. I met him at your meeting, that's all."
He looked at her with narrowed eyes, unsure if she was telling the truth. "And that goes for anyone else in my group, as well," he added.
"If it wasn't for me, you wouldn't have a group. The fine I paid for you this morning, plus that damn fortune-teller license, will come out of your paycheck."
"For two hundred bucks, I should be able to practice medicine, damn it!"
"Vern, quit evading my question," Susan said coldly. "Now, what do you have that doesn't belong to you? What does this Kevin person want?"
"Nothing," he muttered. "Adderson's sore because . . . I kicked him out of my group."
"Try again." She walked to the kitchen stove. "You couldn't convincingly lie your way out of a paper bag."
"None of this concerns you!" he said. "You're just mad because I forgot about our lunch date the other day. I should be the one who's ticked off, after the stunt you pulled at the meeting."

"Let's eat. The stuff you brought should be ready." She opened the oven door.

"Sue, when you try to teach people about the metaphysical, you run into all sorts. Some of them would be better locked away somewhere. Kevin Adderson is just another kook."

"I'll say."

"And this Teldaris is another one. He's after something, and it sure as hell isn't—"

"Why are you so obsessed with that man?" Susan looked at him suspiciously. "He's certainly got you worked up."

"Why are you always on my back about something?"

She served the steaming pizza, a weary look on her face. "Can we just once suffer through a meal together without an argument?"

Tyler shrugged. "Probably not." He eyed the food. "But as long as it's ready, let's give it a try."

Susan poured wine. "Then after dinner we'll resume our cat fight."

Tyler stared moodily at his glass, raised it and drained it in one gulp.

The reply from the Cairo Museum contained seventeen words. It read: "No monies forwarded until item secured, stop. Legally, stop. Official policy, stop. All further collect messages returned unopened, stop. Thank you, stop."

Teldaris wadded the telegram in anger.

Tyler glanced around his living room, pleased with the turnout. Betty and Janice were busy bringing in kitchen chairs for those who couldn't find other seating. Twelve other people either mingled or sat quietly. Betty had done well in getting them all here and organizing things. He sometimes used her as an informal secretary who took care of minor details. She relished the position—basking in the reflected authority it gave her.

He walked toward the front door, turned off the porch light, and returned to his chair.

"Great," he said, "we're all here. Let's find seats and make ourselves comfortable." Tyler noted that Janice obeyed with some reluctance.

"Can I get anybody anything?" she asked.

Tyler frowned slightly. Janice was becoming increasingly difficult to handle lately. He found that his interest in her and their intermittent affair had waned somewhat. She was getting too possessive, asked too many questions. Briefly, he thought about breaking off with her, but the doorbell interrupted his reflections.

Jason Teldaris stood in the shadows beyond the porch, dressed in a tailored shirt and pants of the same dark blue.

"Good, this is the right address. I thought I might have been lost," he said.

"What are you doing here?" Tyler demanded. After the scene in the bar, he had hoped never to see this man again.

"I assumed you were sober at our last meeting," Teldaris responded. "I never said I was quitting your classes. Betty called and told me about this meeting."

Tyler was at a disadvantage and knew it. He couldn't very well kick Teldaris out in front of his other students. He might make trouble if crossed. So, he bowed his head slightly and held out his hand.

Teldaris stepped into the room, ignoring Tyler's outstretched hand.

Vern waved expansively, in the manner of a king forgiving a recalcitrant subject.

"What's the purpose of tonight's meeting?" Teldaris asked, displaying little actual curiosity.

"The more advanced meet at my home occasionally to do special work. I'm sure you'll be a welcome addition."

"I'm flattered," the other responded with restraint. He sat down beside Betty.

"What are we going to do tonight?" she asked.

"Each of us will talk about our interests and problem areas," Tyler said. "Then we'll discuss it as a group. The interchange should be interesting."

"I'm not sure what you mean." Teldaris acted puzzled. "What . . ."

The ringing of the doorbell interrupted his question.

Tyler opened the door reluctantly. Susan was standing there with an unreadable face.

"Hi," she said sweetly. "Am I late?"

"For what?"

"For the meeting."

"I didn't expect you." He frowned.

"Betty called me."

"You're not welcome here. Please leave!"

"No. I'll be attending all your sessions and there's nothing you can do about it. I've spent over seven hundred dollars paying for your licenses and meeting-room rentals. I've a right to know what you're doing."

She walked into the living room before he could object further. She hesitated. The only vacant seat was beside Teldaris. She shrugged and sat without speaking to him.

"Thanks for reminding me of the meeting, Betty. I hope I'm not too late," Susan said smoothly. "I thought I'd be tied up all night."

"What a shame," her brother said. The irony was not lost on her. He had followed her in, grateful that the hallway partition had prevented the others from overhearing their argument. "I was about to bring up the subject of astral—"

"Travel?" she completed. "That's when the self leaves the body and goes to other places, isn't it?" she asked.

"Yes." He paused.

"From what I've read, it's a fairly common event. Dreams of different places, different times. Night flight."

"How much do you know about it?" Tyler asked, surprised.

"I've read a little on the subject. Not much."

"It's also known as the falling dream," Betty said. With no further cue, the older woman launched into a fairly detailed account of the subject.

Tyler picked up a book and called for attention before Betty had quite finished speaking.

"I want to read something to you," he said abruptly. "We'll continue this discussion later. I think this text will help to put some of our efforts into perspective for our newer members. And, it might show some direction for a few of us."

He cleared his throat and read:

I remember great cities, at least those which I knew,
I remember strange peoples, the customs, and dances they do,
I remember vital and sad and wonderfully happy times,
I remember being old and learning childish rhymes,
I remember pageants and battles and death,
I remember sweet songs, labor, and love's breath,
I remember fear and hate and honor and greed,
I remember loyalty, devotion, and fulfillment of need,
I remember surprise and hunger and laughing at humor,
I remember wealth and blunder and gladness and rumor. . . .

The words droned on. To Susan's ear, the quality of her brother's voice seemed to change, to become almost neutral. The intonations that made his voice individual seemed to diminish—leaving room only for the words. She thought them very beautiful. She felt a nearly anemic weakness in her limbs as she concentrated on them. Perspective altered slightly within her. She felt . . . smaller, as if she was looking up at the world through the eyes of a child.

She shook her head, forced herself back to the here and

now. She felt almost as if she'd been hypnotized against her will. She looked around. Apparently, no one else was affected. Vern had stopped reading. A short man was talking, everyone seemed to be listening to him. For some reason, she couldn't quite make out what he was saying.

She turned toward Teldaris, found that he was staring at her, his eyes transmitting an extraordinary feeling toward her. She felt awash in an emotion comprised of deep sorrow, fatalism, and tenderness, and did not know if the emotion originated with him or with her. She only knew they shared it.

Seconds later, the mundane began to creep back into her awareness. She watched as Teldaris pulled out a pen and hastily scribbled something. He handed her a piece of paper, stood, and walked out without speaking to or acknowledging anyone else in the room. She pocketed the slip and left the meeting within a minute of his departure.

The exchange had been noticed by her brother. He classified and cataloged the occurrence as something important to worry about.

"Hello! This is Vern's favorite genie. He's not home right now, so I hopped out of my lamp when you rang."

Susan crashed the phone down onto its cradle.

"He's crazy," she said to her empty bedroom.

Susan sat at the foot of the bed, thinking, absently fingering the lace spread. It was the oddest thing, how last night had ended. She had always been an organized person—the type that didn't relish the uncanny or the unexplained. Last night would have to be explained to her satisfaction, she understood, before she could let the matter go. What had happened? She hadn't a clue. At least, not yet.

She glanced at the slip of paper again. Astute. No message, just a phone number. She dialed.

"Yes?" He answered sleepily on the second ring.

"Mr. Teldaris?" she asked awkwardly. "Did I wake you?"

"No. I've been up awhile. Is this Susan?"

"Oh, yes. I'm . . . sorry I didn't identify myself."

"I'm glad you called."

"Yes, I assumed you wanted me to. What did you want?" She made an effort to sound casual.

"To talk about last night. You'll have to excuse me, I'm not really awake yet. I was up late, reading. Would you mind getting together with me later today?"

"I guess not. But I don't think I'm going to like it too much. Talking about last night, I mean," she amended.

"Could we meet for lunch?"

He sounded as if he was asking for a date. She should have resented it, but for some complex reason, the reverse was true.

"Where would you like to eat?" he asked.

"The Museum of Natural History."

"Where?"

She laughed, delighted to have taken him by surprise.

"The Museum of Natural History. It overlooks City Park and there's a good view of the mountains. We could spread a blanket and eat on the lawn. I'm not in the mood for a restaurant."

"I'm not either. Okay, we'll meet by the front doors."

"That's fine." She was relieved by his casual approach. Remembering their explosive encounter in the parking lot, she decided the light touch was best.

"What time? One?"

She could visualize him looking at a watch.

"See you there. You bring the blanket and I'll bring the food. One last thing, my name is Jason."

Three hours later, Susan parked her Renault in the museum's parking lot and walked to the main entrance. He was waiting there, dressed in jeans and striped pullover shirt. She wore practically the same outfit.

"Hi," Teldaris said sunnily. "You pick a spot."

"How about over there?" She pointed to a grassy knoll that afforded some privacy.

They claimed the knoll without further talk. He sat on the grass and opened a small wicker basket while she spread the blanket. The basket was smallish; however, he set out a long narrow loaf of French bread, a small salami, olives, raw scrubbed mushrooms, several cheeses, and brandied cherries.

"Fooled you, didn't it?" he said, opening a dark ale. "I'll bet you thought there wasn't enough food in that thing to feed a couple of healthy ants. Am I right?"

"Exactly. Hmmm, that looks good . . . my kind of food. How'd you know?"

"I didn't. I brought what I wanted." His easy manner set her at ease.

He sliced cheese and salami.

"I hope you don't mind if we tear the bread. I can't abide neat little slices of bread except for sandwiches," he said.

Susan leaned back and smiled. "I don't mind at all. You sound as though you have the makings of a gourmet."

Teldaris chuckled. "Nothing could be further from the truth," he said. "In my experience, a gourmet is someone who spends four hours preparing a meal, then gobbles it down in fifteen minutes. No, I'm not like that, but I wouldn't want to contemplate endless hamburgers and pizzas."

She nibbled a mushroom as he tore the bread.

"I'm afraid you'd be disappointed with me," she confessed. "Hamburgers are about all I can cook."

"So, whenever we eat together, I'll do the cooking."

"I'd appreciate it," she said absently, a clouded look coming over her features. Why should she feel so uneasy about enjoying this man's company?

He studied her, unsurprised by the look of discomfort on her face. "You're thinking about that scene in the parking lot," he stated rather than asked.

She reddened. A mushroom nearly stuck in her throat, and she coughed softly before answering. "I still can't believe I did that. I was never one for public spectacles."

"I don't know you well, Susan, but I suspect you're too intelligent to accept a role expected of you by others. Public or not."

"I've never cared a pee for the notions of others!"

"Untrue."

"Let's forget that day once and for all."

"Agreed." He had a look of genuine liking for her. "And . . . I never cared a piss either."

Jason observed embattled integrity on her face and guessed that she'd never stood with the crowd. That independence of spirit had marked Susan Tyler more than a physical deformity. It was there in her eyes. The mark of pain: bright, hard, cold.

"Sorry, I didn't intend to offend," she said, wishing to lessen his intensity. "I thought we were going to talk about last night."

"Perhaps we should." His face betrayed an unfathomably wry expression.

They finished the meal in silence, then Jason leaned back on his elbows contentedly. From the corner of her eye, Susan watched him gaze at the mountains for a time. Finally, he spoke.

"It's funny, I've seen mountains all over world, and no range doubles for any other. They only look alike in winter, when they're covered with snow. When the snows come, those west of town will somehow grow, turning grayer, taller, meaner. Then they'll look like the Andes. Then they'll look like the Alps. Then they'll be majestic."

He turned to her. "What do you think happened last night?"

"I was going to ask you the same question."

Janice checked the time as she mixed Vern a gin and

tonic. She realized that soon the kids would be home, and then, another hour or so later, her husband. She checked her blouse, secured a missed button.

Tyler's eyelids sagged, as he fought to stay awake.

"Got to go." She finished her drink.

He nodded, winked wearily.

"By the way, Kevin sends his regards. Says you better call him soon, or he'll get in contact with you." She laughed. "Says you owe him some matches."

"Who?" Vern frowned.

"You know, Debbie's man. My brother-in-law, remember?"

He shook his head blankly.

"Kevin. Adderson," Janice said with some impatience.

Tyler nearly spilled his drink.

They sat quietly for some moments. The mention of last night, Susan thought, had put them both into positions of convivial wariness—a feeling that would be experienced by duelists in the en garde position who also happened to be close friends. Neither would volitionally hurt the other, nor would he betray a weakness in defense. An impasse had been reached, unless one of them could skirt it. She decided on a different tack.

"You can't stand Vern, can you?" she asked.

"Am I that obvious?"

"On that point, yes. Tell me, why did you decide to join Third Eye?"

"That's easy," he answered promptly. "I'm working on a Gordian knot."

Susan tilted her head in curiosity.

"Remember the photo I showed you that day in the park?"

"Your wife." She nodded.

"I ask habitually. So I asked that brunette . . . uh . . .

Janice. She said that something was familiar about Gail. . . ." He paused, closed his eyes.

"That's her name?" Susan asked softly.

"Yes. Anyway, Janice said that her sister had a blouse exactly like the one in the picture. That was impossible. I'd bought that blouse for Gail. It was handmade, one-of-a-kind. I told that to Janice, but she insisted her sister had an identical one." He viciously pulled up blades of grass. "It's a lead."

"Tell me about Gail."

"Why?"

"Because I want to know."

"Why?"

"I don't know," she replied honestly.

He smiled. "What is there to tell? We were married for five years. We were content, busy, and all that. At least, I thought we were. Last March, I woke up and found a note on her pillow. She was gone. Her clothes were gone. I found out later that she had closed out her bank account. The note said: 'I'm leaving. It's been good. Don't look for me.' Plus her signature. That's all."

"Couldn't the police help?"

"No. The note prevented that. She'd left of her own choice. There was no crime involved."

"Private detectives?"

"Yeah. I spent a small fortune on them. She was traced to Denver. She used a credit card to pay a hotel bill. So, here I am. Satisfied?"

No, she thought, although she nodded. "Sorry if I pried," she apologized.

"It's okay. I wouldn't have told you if I hadn't wanted to."

Instinctively, Susan knew that he was a man who wouldn't do anything unless he wished to do it.

"Thanks," she said, "but something about your story doesn't ring true."

"What's that?" He had lain back, was watching clouds scudding through the sky.

She looked down at him and was unable to answer immediately. This was the most handsome man she'd ever met, she realized. Not pretty, but handsome, with the kind of looks molded by strength and intelligence. Somehow, she doubted that he was fully aware of his appearance. He turned to her.

"What's wrong?" he asked.

"Nothing. What was I saying? Oh, about your story not ringing true."

"That's right."

"Well, it's just that I don't see you joining Vern's group solely to ask about pictures."

"I didn't."

"Well then?"

"Intuition. A hunch. A feeling that definitions would come to me."

"Did they?"

"Not yet. Susan, what happened to you last night?"

"I don't know." She saw his expression and continued. "No, I'm not evading the issue. I simply don't understand what happened."

"Neither do I. I didn't expect you to understand any more than I." He sat up. "When Vern started to read that poem, something happened to me. It's difficult to describe. I felt those words in my gut, and I knew you felt them, too."

"Yes," she whispered.

"I felt that, impossible though it sounds, you and I were very close. That we'd known each other for a long, long time and that we owed each other . . . something."

Susan nodded. "Where do we go from here?" she asked.

"We find out the source of Vern's poem."

"And then?"

"Then what will happen, will happen."

* * *

Janice rubbed her eyes, trying to read tiny-lettered directions on an aerosol can. A loud rapping came from the patio door. She saw her sister pointing to the inside lock, and wondered why Debbie would visit at this time of day. She made a mental note to ask about the embroidered blouse.

"Deb, what's up? I thought you were at work."

"I called in sick today. Have you seen Kevin? Did he call?"

"Why, no, should he have?" Janice asked, puzzled. She noted her younger sister's disheveled appearance.

Deborah burst into tears. Janice coaxed her to the dinette, then put on a kettle. She seldom saw her sister, and couldn't remember Debbie ever being overly emotional. She tried in vain to recall pointers Vern had taught her concerning calm and crisis. She grabbed a plateful of ginger cookies by instinct, and pulled up a chair beside her sister. Gradually, the tears subsided.

Three cups of tea and four cookies later, Deborah completed her story. Kevin had left in the middle of the night and not returned. That was three days ago.

"Why did you keep it to yourself, Deb?" Janice scolded. "What do you think sisters are for?"

"I . . . kept thinking he'd phone or come back." Deborah lowered her eyes.

"What did the police say?" Janice pressed.

"Uh . . . you're the first person I've told."

"What! You didn't call the police? What about the car?"

"He didn't take anything. Not the Volvo, his wallet, or a change of clothes."

"This is crazy!"

"He's done it before, Jan."

Janice looked confused.

"But never more than a day," she added. "There's a lot you don't know about us."

Janice put a hand to her forehead.

"I couldn't call the police. Jan, even if he's gone a year."

"Why, for heaven's sake?"

"It's against our . . . religion."

"Deb, we were raised as agnostics. To be open-minded about—"

"I've adopted my husband's views on everything, Jan." Deborah made an effort at self-control.

Janice leaned back, feeling a cold chill, realizing her sister had developed into a stranger over the last several years. She felt bewildered and lonely. Had she lost all touch with her only living relative? She experienced a small stab of dread for her own children. Might they become strangers, too? Images of pillow fights and Christmas mornings crowded into her memory, but she forced them aside. The woman next to her was *now*.

"Why wouldn't Kevin want the police called? What's he done?" she questioned.

"Jan, don't be that way. Not today," Deborah pleaded. "I wasn't . . . just . . ." She paused. "Kev believes it's a private thing. We don't go to church, you know. We keep to ourselves. We've adopted an alternative . . . uh, life concept. . . ."

"I wasn't trying to pry, Deb, or to crowd you," Janice said, hurt. "Your husband's disappeared. I still think something should be done."

Deborah became morose, toyed with her cup.

"Deb, is it . . . another woman?" Janice berated herself for being so dense. "I've wondered about Kevin. He always seems miles away, thinking . . . who knows what?"

Deborah stood abruptly, knocking over her chair. "It's not another woman! It can't be! I've done everything he's asked. Damn it, no woman on earth would do what I've done! I could tell you things . . ." She stopped, putting both hands to her cheeks.

"Go on, Deb, tell me."

"No! Nothing's wrong, really. . . ." Deborah stammered like a child. She rushed for the patio door. "I've got to go. Call me if you hear anything."

Janice was dumbfounded. "What? Why are you going? I thought—"

"I can't stay any longer! Forget it."

High winds whipped the treetops, caused them to sway violently. Adderson closed his eyes, gasped for breath. There was an ear-ringing blow against his head. He was aware of derisive laughter, intermixed with calls of encouragement. Cool air gave scant relief. Pain surged through him, but the ropes prevented any movement. Nothing eased his ritual torment. Veins swelled ominously on both his legs. Hours of unbroken pressure had at last penetrated his drug haze. Cold water was thrown over him when his head sagged. He jerked upright.

Adderson ground his teeth, no longer thinking in words; images were his sole mental activity. The arms tied behind his back were no longer his. Chants and drumbeats came in syncopation with his heart. All desire melted into a sole longing; that distant moment when his worthiness would be acknowledged, when an old knife would cut the ropes, when he could fall to the ground. . . .

Another blow was inflicted. Adderson's dry lips pulled tight. Soon, very soon, the images promised, it would be over, and it would be good.

"Is it suitable, Mistress?" Joy asked.

Thea Markidian raised an eyebrow.

"My pleasure is not evident?"

Joy smiled with satisfaction.

"But Denver itself," Thea said, with mild distaste. "Why . . . here?" She stood by a front window, fingering the leaded glass. Vistas of a sleek, modern, polluted city held her attention.

"Who is to say?" Joy answered.

Thea moved gracefully across the parquetry flooring, toward the tiled entrance. She stopped to study the pattern.

"Have you seen him?" she asked unexpectedly.

"Yes." Joy pointed in the direction of the park. "There."

"Tell me."

Joy hesitated, then walked to a splendid rosewood etagere. "He is older."

Thea waited, cheeks indrawn. "As am I. Is he ready?"

Joy looked away. "No."

"Why?"

"I think it is this culture . . .," Joy began.

"What is wrong?"

"America is wrong, Mistress. Too many distractions, too many freeways, magazines. Television, noise, confusion."

"If this is so, we must compensate," Thea solemnly stated. "Must we not?"

Joy nodded.

Thea glanced to a platter of food. Joy moved to serve her, was waved away.

"What of nephew?"

Joy smiled.

> The dawn becomes desperate, dandelion
> As Deborah lies sleeping sleeping sleeping
> Tired of weeping weeping weeping
> Wondering what became of Kevin.

Adderson leaned close to his sleeping wife, whispering in her ear.

He shook her roughly.

Blond hair flying, eyes, black as night
Skin so red and white, fair and bright.

He issued a half snort, half yawn, and lay down beside
her startled figure. She cried out in delight, and flung herself against him. "Kev, where have you been?" she demanded.

He drew back and studied her with tired eyes. "You
love me, don't you?" he said, as if discovering it for the
first time.

"Oh, Kev," she cried, "I was so worried."

"You *do* care, don't you?" He pushed her arms from
his shoulders. She dried her eyes, and switched on the
bedside lamp.

"Where were you? What happened? Was it something
I . . ."

"Hush, hush." Adderson put his fingers across her lips.
"I've got to think." He stood suddenly, paced across the
room twice, then stopped.

She rose, found a robe and covered his back to warm
him.

"Did you tell anyone I was gone?" he asked harshly.

"No, no one, not even the cops."

"No one?"

"Kev, what happened? Work called. I told them you
were sick with the flu, but they didn't believe me,
and—"

"The hell with 'em. I won't be going back anyway."

"Kevin." Her voice acquired stridency. "I deserve an
answer. Who were you talking to in the closet?"

"Go fix me some food," he ordered. "I haven't eaten.
Then, I must sleep, I must refuel. . . ." He became lost
in thought.

"Kevin, you're burning up with fever!" She felt his
forehead, concerned. "You didn't eat for three days?"

"I'm too exhausted to talk anymore. Get me something

easy to digest, and just let me sleep. . . . '' He sank down again on the bed.

"Not till I get some answers."

"I did it, dandelion. I proved myself."

"What?" Comprehension seeped in slowly. She lowered herself beside him, knees nearly buckling.

"Initiation?"

"Initiation," he confirmed.

"But . . . how did you know? I mean, how did you know you were ready?"

Adderson smiled ruefully. "When it's time, you know. Believe me, they let you know."

"I long for thee," she whispered into the cool night air. "Willst thee not show thyself, but for a while?"

She stood before a red brick apartment building. It was three in the morning, and the streets were deserted, peaceful. Enswathed head to foot in raven-black silk, Thea moved amid the shadows. A shade darker than jet, she appeared as night within night.

In silence, she had made her way through the streets to him in this nightly ritual of passion.

A single light shone from the corner window of his apartment.

"What sinister force requires us to meet thusly, my love? Why are the paths woven with such distortion?"

Thea shrank back, hearing a car approach from the distance. She cast a baleful eye toward the coming noise, then a last longing look at the window, before vanishing into a side street.

Teldaris gazed through the shuttered windows of his study, uncomfortable with the certain sensation of being watched.

Janice knocked at the door. She viewed the rented house

with distaste. It was identical to thousands of others thrown up east of town during the military boom two decades ago. It resembled postwar tract houses, except that it was more shoddily constructed and on a smaller lot. Every house on the street was identical, but each was painted a different pastel. This one still showed a peeling residue of the original white. Kevin certainly wasn't a putter-around-the-house type.

She pressed the doorbell again, suspecting it didn't work. The furious barking of a dog inside the garage unnerved her. She shook a lock of brown hair away from her face, feeling more than a little foolish about making the long drive from Green Mountain without calling first.

She turned in time to see the door open a crack. The chain remained in place. In the narrow gap, she saw her sister's face.

"Deb! Hi! I thought you weren't home," she said with relief. She put one foot on the threshold. Deborah, however, did not move.

"Yes?"

"Yes, what? Let me in." She leaned toward the door, practically nose to nose with Debbie.

"I can't."

"You can't? Why not?"

"Kev's asleep."

"Kevin's what? You mean . . . he's back?"

"Yeah, I guess."

"You guess?"

"Yes, he's here. He's back."

"What the hell is wrong with you?" Janice snapped angrily. "Why didn't you call me? Bill and I were worried sick, we thought—"

"He's okay, just left on . . . business. Lost his job, though. Do you think Bill could get him one down at the plant?"

"Deb, let me in so we can discuss this."

"I can't. Kev's asleep. Bye." Deborah's face disappeared.

"But I drove all the way—" Janice's words were cut off by the solid slam of the door.

She stood stunned, then left in bewilderment.

Adderson touched the circles that had formed under his eyes.

"There's only room for the beast now," he whispered to his reflection. "Smile, snake-man, you ordered it, you eat it." He thrust a defiant fist at his image.

"Kev, you still in there?" his wife called from the bedroom.

He continued the inspection. Why hadn't Deb said anything? Hadn't she noticed the changes? His face seemed longer, eyelids stretched into wider planes, and his hair appeared darker. Had she noted the change of appetite, weight, or any of a hundred tiny departures from the old Kevin? Probably not.

She would notice the other changes, though. He smiled. Mrs. Adderson was about to travel in heady company.

"Did Mistress sleep well?" Joy served breakfast for the first time in the mansion.

Thea sat up straight in the mahogany bed. For a moment, she appeared disoriented. The moment passed and she regained composure, her face acquiring its usual serenity.

"I awakened unusually fey this morning, Joy."

Joy placed the tray upon her lap and lightly smoothed a silk coverlet with her free hand.

"Perhaps the strange surroundings . . ."

Thea considered this, shook her head. "I would discern something so obvious. No, I had a troubling dream."

"Bad memories?"

"Yes. Often, I wish that the past did not rule me so."

"Would you then be you?" Joy interrupted.

Thea studied her for a moment. Joy waited by the side of the bed patiently.

"You must be protected, Mistress," she volunteered.

"What threatens me?" Thea smiled.

"All." Joy's almond eyes gleamed.

"Are you content with your existence?" Thea asked, intrigued.

"You must be protected. That is my existence." Joy spoke without hesitation. "Contentment and purpose are one for me. Now, is there anything you wish?"

"Is my glass unpacked?" Thea touched her lips with a linen napkin. Fluidly, Joy lifted the trunk lid at the foot of the bed. She retrieved a golden-stemmed oval mirror and handed it to Thea.

Thea smoothed her hair, then placed the mirror on the coverlet, satisfied.

"You were the most beautiful in all antiquity," Joy said, with barely concealed pride.

"Save one."

"Nefertiti was but a consort. You were Pharaoh."

"Thank you, Joy."

Thea ate a pear slice thoughtfully. "Do you remember that song, the one about dagger's flowing ring of blood?"

" 'Were you there after the world wakened mad?' " Joy nodded.

"That keeps going through my mind."

"Perhaps the rhythm."

"Or perhaps it is a sign?"

"Remember your frescoed golden apartments?" Joy asked, hoping to divert her. "Would you like these to be the same?"

"It was mere gold leaf beaten onto shesham wood," Thea corrected. "No, I do not wish it to be the same. All things pass."

"How would Mistress desire it?"

"You adroitly refuse to permit gloom this morning." Thea laughed.

Joy nodded in satisfaction. Her device had been seen as such; but it had worked.

Food! From mothers to little boys to proud men to wrinkled grannies. Take them. All, all, life to me. Onward. Use them. Corrupt them. Raise them. Harvest them. Reap them. Sow them. Rape them. Mow them. Castrate them, blind them, hack them, burn them, reward them, promise them, fool them, terrorize them, spread them, multiply them, suck them, drain them, kill them, soothe them, prod them. Food. Pull them, feed them, multiply them. Food. Millions more. Billions more. Food. Multiply them. Power. Nudge them, drain them, save them.

Adderson rolled over in his sleep.

FOUR

Ba

LET THEM WHO SEEK TO DESTROY US
FALL BY THE CRUELTY OF THEIR OWN
KIND.

LET US BUILD A NEW CIVILIZATION
UPON THE ONE WHICH SHALL SOON
CRUMBLE BETWEEN OUR LEGS AND
OUR UN-BORN CHILDREN'S BODIES.

—Hymn to Hat-shepsut,
  from *Shadow of Khufu*,
  Cecil Rupert-Lewis, 1894

THERE, IN A HANDFUL OF PHENOMENALLY PAMPERED acres, the arid had been transformed into the lush. Joy walked, deep in reflection, unmindful of the people who gaped at her exotic appearance. Nor did she notice the whistles that came from the youths playing soccer. Her beauty was rare, exquisite, yet Joy was almost unaware of it, for she served a woman beyond compare.

Pipe smoke reached her nostrils, dogs barked and children squealed. Once, many years past, she had seen an American magazine cover by the illustrator Norman Rockwell. Its rose and amber hues had beguiled her for a moment into believing Rockwell's vision was subjective. Yet she'd known better than to believe in such maudlin perfection, even in childhood. Colorful accents had marked the painting. So it was now. The blues and greens of soccer uniforms accented the warm summer day. The bright clothing of strollers, the vivid oranges and reds, were poignant assertions of individuality. Window dressings. Underneath those bright exteriors lay still-suppressed souls who had lived and toiled as laborers, fishermen, scribes. There were artisans, maids, women of the bazaar. Here, in this very park, were those who'd bowed before Pharaoh. Perhaps that child had served Mistress herself. Maybe that sunbather, in fascination and fear, had once watched a gilded barge float by.

Joy tensed her jaw slightly, forebearingly, as a Frisbee flew in front of her. She glanced about for its launching source—and paused in stunned perplexity, Frisbee forgotten.

Jason Teldaris talked with a woman, older than he. They sat close together on a wooden bench. Joy narrowed her eyes as he touched the woman twice with animated gestures. His companion listened intently.

After several minutes, they rose and wandered in Joy's direction. Teldaris continued to speak as the woman walked closely beside him, nodding occasionally.

Joy followed, casually. Features set in a disciplined placidity, she realized that here was yet another specter, one that, unfailing, she must defeat.

Janice blocked her doorway, turning the tables on her sister.

"Jan, don't be mad. I'm sorry I didn't let you in the other day. I was half drugged . . . ," Deborah pleaded.

"He's got you on drugs?" Janice held the door wider.

"Drugs? Jan, you don't believe—I meant I hadn't had any sleep. You know me better than that."

"Debbie, I don't think I know you at all."

"Okay . . . I treated you like shit, and I'm sorry! Can I come in?"

"I suppose so, we *are* still sisters."

Obligatory questions about spouses, neighbors, and

other small talk took them through the first round of coffee. Janice had just poured a second when Deb's face took on a serious look.

"Jan, I love you," she said.

"Of course. We have our share of feuds, but we're still family." She was touched, for Deborah was seldom sentimental. She was distracted from her emotion, however, because for the last few minutes something had been nagging at her memory.

"Deb, now I remember! There's this guy at my TEE seminar. He keeps after me about some girl in a picture. She's wearing a peasant blouse exactly like yours."

"I don't have a peasant blouse."

"Sure you do, I've seen you wear it recently. It's the one you said Kevin bought after—"

"Who is this man? What did you tell him?" Debbie demanded, unable to control a rising fear.

"Deb, what's—" Janice leaned back in surprise.

"I might've known. No one can be trusted. Even you!" Deborah stood. "It wasn't our fault, Jan, it was an accident!"

"What are you talking about?"

"What do you think, we murdered her?" Deborah yelled.

"You'd better go," Janice said tightly, frightened by Deb's talk of murder.

"Don't expect to see me again," Deborah threatened. "Everything has its price, Jan, everything."

"Please leave."

Deborah paused. A moment passed. She stormed to the door, turned, and saw that her sister remained seated. She cried vehemently, "I won't be back."

The goad brought no response. Deb exited, hoping Janice would follow.

Something inside her, and not just the clear entreaty

she'd seen in her sister's eyes, told Janice to go after Debbie. But instead, she laid her head down on her arms. Deborah's behavior replayed itself within her mind.

Swiftly, she slid into deep, effortless sleep. Images came into focus—larger, more dimensional than life itself.

Camels. Caravans. Kevin.

She grunted with discomfort as she felt a hot dry gust of wind. She was bundled in dark rough clothes, and perspired over every inch of her body, except her eyes and bare feet. Janice stood among other women like herself—figures tiny against the great dromedaries. Swarthy traders argued noisily in the background, but she was fascinated by an upright form in a chariot. The vehicle was gold and blue. Its youthful passenger stood straight, proud. Something about him . . . it was her brother-in-law.

A trader approached, brushing flies away from his beard. She started in fear. His seamed face resembled a dried leather pouch, he spat frequently, and she saw he had no teeth. He reached toward her veil, but another trader stopped him. The sun beat down oppressively, though it was still early morning. She licked her lips, but her mouth was dry. Leather-face grabbed her roughly, forced a calloused hand inside her garments. The three women beside her moved from side to side nervously. One clutched her tighter, another issued a low clucking wail.

Another man—a stranger, bartered fiercely. Janice looked up to the figure in the chariot, tried to call for help, but no words formed. There was a rough prodding in her genital area. Although her garment was left intact, she had been violated. Now, she understood why the men argued. She was being traded, sold. The buyer had inspected the merchandise as his right. A cry more desolate than the desert wind burst forth from her lungs.

She looked up with tortured eyes, but the chariot was gone. A hoarse sob rattled in her throat.

"Help me . . . please. . . . " The sound of her own voice awakened her. Janice looked around. Avocado linoleum came into focus. She'd expected to see Kevin somewhere close by, but she was alone.

Her children noisily ran up the driveway. What were they doing home this early? She focused on her watch and saw that two and a half hours had passed since Debbie left.

" 'The veil becomes a facet of the face it hides. Until, at the end . . .' "

Teldaris turned the thin maroon book over, then flipped through to discover where the inscription continued. At length, he realized it did not. The deliveryman was long gone. He searched vainly for some clue on the brown wrapping, then through the book itself, but the sender's identity remained a mystery.

He sat back and perused the yellowed, finely printed pages. Some were dog-eared. Others were marked by spidery crimson asterisks. *"Shadow of Khufu,"* he read in a low voice.

He turned to the author's foreword.

No one, not even Akhenaten hundreds of years later, possessed the joy of life so strongly, with such vigour, as did Queen Hat-shepsut. Her incredible tale, and that of her favoured Sen-Mut, is one of history's finest love stories. Their tragedy is also one of the least known.

Teldaris closed the book, lost in thought. He pushed aside *Studies in Ancient Architecture* and two sloppy stacks of books, then pulled out a huge notebook.

"Why do you put up with me?"
"What?"
"Answer my question."

"What question?"

"You heard. Why do you put up with me?" Adderson threw himself to the floor and studied his wife with mild interest.

"Who else would?" Debbie shot back with an uneasy smile.

"I mean, at first, we fucked every night, and there was always tomorrow. These days . . ."

"I do everything myself." She pantomimed a nagging hausfrau.

Kevin smiled halfheartedly. "You're not stupid, Deb. It looks like I'm a washout. No job, no money. Only hope, always hope."

"At least that's free."

"Let me finish! What do you *want*, this instant?"

"To have weekends off."

"Forget that. I mean, what do you truly want?"

"No more split shifts. Just work days, part-time—"

"Skip it," he said in annoyance. He rose and kicked a pile of magazines out of his path. "You've atrophied."

Debbie turned back to her crossword. "So have you." She didn't look up.

"Don't you hunger for anything? Don't you crave!" he exploded. "You did, once."

"Of course I want things, but I see everybody else settling for what they've got. Maybe I'm tired of living in the future, dreaming the present away. I'm tired of waiting. The rest of the world just may have the sense to be content with what they've got. They could be right."

"I pity you. I'm not worried about *my* future. I was born to achieve things. I'll fulfill my wants, because I was meant to."

"Kev, is it worth it?"

He disregarded the question. Adderson drew himself up straight. "I was born to lead. I've known that since I was a child." He paced, speaking with agitation.

Deborah returned to her crossword and eyed the

78

dictionary across the room. She'd weathered countless variations on this theme throughout their marriage.

He stopped, saw the lapse in her attention toward him and leaped across the room in rage, snatching the paper from her hands and tearing it to shreds before she could react.

"Listen when I'm talking to you!" he shouted. Debbie sank back into the sofa. "Don't sit there looking at me like I'm insane. And don't pretend you're nothing but a good little wife. Blood is on your hands, too!"

Susan curled up on her couch with the latest novel by her favorite author. Her grandmother's satin comforter was unnecessary but cozy. A mug of hot cocoa was beside her hand. She studied the author's picture, then the inside flap of the jacket. For that price, she thought, it'd better be good.

Just as she tasted the first sip of cocoa, the doorbell rang. Susan held the liquid in her mouth and cast a hostile glare in the direction of her hallway.

A second, longer ring motivated her. She swallowed, threw on a robe, and went to the door muttering imprecations.

She looked through the fish-eye peephole, saw nothing. Someone was covering the lens on the other side.

"Who is it?" she crossly called out.

"What's locked in there? Gold bars?" Jason asked with a laugh.

She unlatched the locks and admitted him.

He gave the steel door a couple of hard raps with his knuckles. "They spent more on these doors than on the rest of the building."

"I live alone," she said defensively. "Sorry if I'm security-minded."

"Don't take it the wrong way. . . . I approve of lead doors. Even *I* can't see through them."

"Very funny." Susan glanced down at her robe, then at him. He was wearing a black leather pilot's jacket with a dark wool shirt, and looked very handsome. "You look decidedly rakish this evening," she said admiringly.

He smiled curiously. "People don't talk like that anymore."

"I do," she replied as she closed the door behind him. "Want some cold cocoa?"

"No. Get dressed and come down. I've got something to show you."

Susan looked askance, but at his insistence, obeyed.

Five minutes later, she reappeared in a lamb-suede shirt with matching slacks. Teldaris put down her new book.

"That's more like it. Snazzy." He whistled.

"People don't talk like that anymore," she imitated in a husky voice.

"I do." He chuckled.

"What's all this about? I was about to—"

Teldaris took her by the hand. "Don't bother finishing that book, you wasted your money. The president's double is really an old Nazi saboteur who works for the Russians."

"Jason!"

A few moments later, they stood in the tiny parking lot adjacent to the building.

Susan blinked her eyes. Jason grinned as he watched her reaction.

"Well, c'*mon*, tell me! Is it fantastic, or is it great?"

Susan put a hand to her lips. "It's beautiful, Jason, but . . ."

"But nothing on earth beats a shiny black sports car!" he pronounced.

"Jason, your car was a classic. Why did you have it painted black?"

"Because"—he considered it briefly—"I'm a Gemini."

"It's a Gemini thing to do," she agreed. "But, I thought

the selling point of a DeLorean was the stainless-steel finish. Weren't they all—''

"They were, so I had it customized. The hell with value, I'm concerned with style."

"It *does* look good, I'll admit that."

"Besides, now I can steal around after dark and no one will ever spot me."

"True enough." She laughed.

"Hop in!" He opened the doors.

"Where are we going?" she asked once they were on the freeway heading north.

"To Cheyenne."

"What?"

"It's only a few hours away."

"Why there, of all places?" Susan sat forward. She hadn't even brought a purse.

"An all-night truck stop there serves the best burgers this side of"—he laughed when he saw her expression—"Laramie."

Joy roamed through Teldaris's apartment. She studied and cataloged everything for possible later use, including the slim book on his desk. Mistress would demand to know all she saw. She went swiftly from room to room, unconcerned about his return. She had watched his apartment for three hours from her parked car and knew to the minute when he had left. He would not return soon, she knew, for his habits were thoroughly familiar to her. They should have been, for Joy had studied Teldaris closely for years. As always, Mistress had been right. The mysterious book sent to him had produced the proper response—he had left, presumably for a long drive. Evidently, he did much of his thinking while driving. Joy wondered briefly what was going through his mind at that moment, then shrugged as if her curiosity were irrelevant. She took the narcotic vial and the hypodermic from a pocket, checked them, and walked toward the kitchen.

Susan smiled. "I haven't done anything like this since I was a teenager. By the way, when can we stop for cigarettes?"

With a grin, Jason produced a pack of her brand from his jacket.

She thanked him with a look of pure delight.

"Since I came to Colorado, I've spent more time in this car than anywhere else. There is a certain luxury about long drives. I'll ride in any direction to get away from . . ." He frowned, clamped his mouth shut.

Susan turned to him.

"A couple of days ago I went to the Springs. Didn't see it, just pulled off once for gas, two Cokes, and a pit stop. I did recognize the Air Force Academy Chapel, though, on the way by."

"Get away from what?" she asked.

"Forget it." He pointed to a farmhouse bereft of trees or vegetation, illuminated by a solitary outdoor utility light. "A lot of desolate plains east of the foothills, I've noticed."

"Get away from what?" she repeated.

"Nice country, but I wish—"

"Jason!"

"Nothing. I'll tell you some other time. Let's just enjoy the night."

Joy entered, holding two snifters of brandy.

The paneled library had been Orientalized. Instead of endless rows of dusty volumes, the built-in bookcases contained vases, busts, and statuary. Some were museum replicas, many were originals. Flower petals floating in silver bowls sweetened the air. A deep blue Persian rug enhanced the inlaid oak floor. The room's one window was a massive bay that overlooked the park's edge. Large, tasseled pillows were scattered in its recess.

The few books evident were stacked on end, atop the bay's deck. They were bound in red hand-tooled leather. The one piece of furniture in the room was an antique cherrywood highboy, improbably set in the center of the floor. Within the many drawers were scores of scrolls, tightly bound and written in a dozen languages, some of which had not been read aloud for hundreds of years. The secrets, intrigues, and life's work of countless minds were locked within that tall wooden cabinet.

Nothing in the spacious study was superfluous. Foremost, there was beauty. Next, unassuming, came wisdom culled from the ancient world.

Bent over a colorful pack of Tarot cards in the cushioned womb of the bay window, sat Thea, bathed in candlelight.

She swept aside the worn cards and looked up at Joy. She accepted the drink gratefully, motioned Joy to sit beside her. Neither mentioned the task the latter had just completed. There was no need, for Joy would not be here without first having accomplished it.

Thea sipped silently for several moments, while Joy watched the silhouettes of a strolling couple against the distant lights from the park.

"Joy, do we have a deck of playing cards that have never been touched? Still sealed?"

Joy smiled, reached gracefully under a pillow, and produced the pack she had placed there days earlier.

Thea frowned. "Have I become that predictable?"

"No, I have become that efficient," Joy stated.

Thea smiled in appreciation.

She took the deck from Joy and broke the seal.

"I never get an accurate reading from the Tarot. I do keep trying, though." She began to place the cards in a fashion very similar to solitaire.

"What works for me is of my own devising. I have no luck throwing the sticks and consulting the *I Ching*, like you." She concentrated on maneuvering the cards.

"Your desire is unyielding before any impartial answers the *Book of Change* may offer," Joy spoke measuredly. "I have no better skill than others. I merely allow the hexagrams to suggest."

"You are saying that I try to influence the cards. That I read what I wish to read."

Joy took a leisurely drink of the brandy, savoring this infrequent evening spent in relaxation. "Don't you?" she responded at last.

"No, not when I can help it. Otherwise, what use is divination, as opposed to desire and wishful thinking?"

"Often they are intimate cousins. Wanting a certain future, and foretelling it, may bring about . . ."

Thea scattered the cards in disgust, then reshuffled the deck. "I tire of forever asking this one thing. I am bored with its elusiveness." She held out the cards. "Touch them with both hands. I shall read your fortune."

Joy complied, a smile coming to her lips.

Thea dealt the cards in sequences known only to her. She moved the cards in rhythmic precision, and kept her reactions stoical.

"Joy, tell me something truly. Are you ever lonely?" She did not raise her eyes from the cards.

"A void within a void is indiscernible."

"Cryptic, as usual," Thea whispered with humor.

Joy finished the last of her dram. "Except in your service, my lady, I have always been alone. Wanted by many, wanting none . . . I have never been lonely."

"Perchance loneliness takes another form."

"Everything, including loneliness, can be disguised. Yet, I have not known the terrible, silent ache that I witness each day. I am fortunate to have never found my love. Fortunate that I do not suffer a subsequent loss. It is better never to have loved at all." Joy studied the other's expression, then amended quietly, "It is, for me."

Thea set down the cards. "Remember the legends of the succubus? In a sense, desperate love can mirror that. Instead of the living dead, one imitates the reverse."

She quickly returned to the cards.

Susan swallowed against a belch.

She saw Jason puff his cheeks similarly. "I give that truck stop a one-star rating." She chuckled.

Teldaris laughed, handed her the antacid roll he'd bought on the way out.

"Make that a quarter-star rating," he said. "The chef had an off-night."

"I'm skeptical about cooks who come to the table to check if you've eaten anything."

"I'm skeptical about cooks named Louie."

The DeLorean sped through the night. Jason played a tape of soft modern jazz. They drove in silence for many minutes, absorbed in the music.

"I hope you don't mind," he said at last, "but I unwind by simply driving and listening."

Susan smiled. "I see what you mean. I haven't felt so relaxed in ages. The troubles of the world seem so far away this late at night."

"That's because the world sleeps this late at night."

Susan shifted in her seat, put one leg up under the other for comfort.

"Tell me about yourself," she asked casually.

He laughed and shook his head.

"Really. Please."

He shrugged. "There's nothing to tell."

"Uh-huh, sure." Susan reached for a cigarette. "A man with an automobile worth a small fortune, a traveler who doesn't work for a living . . ."

"Stop it, Susan." His voice was cold.

Concerned, she wondered what nerve she'd touched.

"I have this little quirk," he said in a softer voice. "I'm not being secretive, just . . . I like my privacy."

"Jason, please, I wasn't . . ." Susan apologized, astonished and not knowing what to say next.

"No, let me explain. It has nothing to do with you or tonight." He reached for her cigarette and took a long drag.

"I had an unusual childhood, a strict adolescence. I don't like talking about it. What's the use?"

Susan watched him finish the cigarette.

"Were you poor?" she asked in a low voice.

"Poor in everything except mind and money."

Susan tilted her head.

He explained. "I was brought up in boardinghouses, shunted about without explanation. My legal guardian was a bank in Switzerland. I had no long-lasting friendships, no real recreation, nothing reassuring. Only a series of tutors, rented quarters, and disciplines. I suspect the bank did it deliberately."

She hesitated. "Did you ever ask why?"

He snorted. "Ask? Who would I ask? You don't fully comprehend. My guardian wasn't someone *at* the bank. It *was* the bank."

"What!" Susan shook her head. "I don't understand."

"Neither do I. Now you see why I seldom talk about it. As a matter of fact, I've only talked about it once before."

Her thoughts darted to the girl in the picture.

"What about your parents?"

"My parents? I was handed some bullshit about a car accident, but . . ." He stopped, squinted. ". . . well, I suppose I'm the bastard son of someone who couldn't afford the publicity. Someone powerful or rich enough to force a major institution to become my overseer."

"But who raised you?"

"Nurses, governesses, all the old stereotypes. Then,

when I was eight, I was left in the keeping of . . . I'll call them drill instructors, for lack of a suitable description.''

"Didn't you try to find out more?"

"Of course! I spent a decade trying!"

She drew back.

He shook his head against the memories. "Sorry," he apologized.

"I can't fathom this." She scowled.

"My education was odd, too."

"How?"

"Well, it was different from the normal course of study. I was filled with little that was practical. I learned dead languages, arcane science, history, and ethics that were obsolete before Rome."

"Latin?"

"Nothing that useful," he replied. "Anything I know about surviving was learned after I was freed. Anything useful, like cooking, I taught myself."

"Freed?"

"On my eighteenth birthday I got a small trust fund, best wishes, and a monogrammed suitcase."

She reached for a cigarette.

He changed cassettes and said nothing more.

"Bill, wake up. I have something for you."

Hughes opened his eyes and focused on his wife. Janice stood beside the bed, looking anything but covered by a sheer black gown. Her short hair had been brushed into an attractive swirl, and she wore makeup. She attracted him more than she had in years.

"Come here, sexy girl," he growled, trying to remember the last time they'd made love in the morning.

She looked good today, and he approved. The makeup made her face seem more seductively molded. Her eyes were different, too. Or maybe the eyebrows . . .

He reached for her, but Janice twisted away, laughing.

"Not yet," she objected, waving a finger before his nose. "Not till you've had your breakfast."

"What did you have in mind?" he teased.

"Don't be coarse," she chided. "I spent an hour making eggs Benedict. If you're good, we can play around later."

"Do we really have to wait?" he protested.

Janice smiled and walked gracefully from the room, leaving a bewildered husband. He hurried to the bathroom, thankful it was Sunday. He took a couple of swipes at his underarms with a deodorant stick, then brushed his teeth and hastily threw on a terry robe.

He was surprised to meet her on the stairs, ascending with a food-laden tray.

"What are you doing out of bed?" she asked. "Get right back up there."

He practically sprinted back to the bedroom.

She followed and placed the tray on the bed.

"Thanks, hon." He picked up a slice of toast. "Why all the special service? Has something expensive caught your eye?"

"No, nothing like that. It's just that—well, I was thinking about Deb last night when I went to bed. I woke up this morning realizing what a lucky woman I am. So, I made a resolution that this would be a special day for us."

"Hmmm. What about the kids? Where do they fit into this wonderful day you have planned?" He began to eat quickly, like a child who must endure a Christmas breakfast before opening presents.

"Don't worry. I'll get rid of them."

"Good." He hesitated. "Jan, what have you done with yourself? You look great."

"Do you like it?" she asked, pleased. "Nothing much. I decided to kick out the old me and be somebody else. Any objections?"

"God, no. You look fantastic—ten years younger," he

lied. She did look great, he thought, but she would never look twenty-six again.

"Thank you, sir," she responded gaily. "And are you satisfied with your breakfast?"

"Very. I'm still hungry for something else, though."

"You can wait a few minutes. I'll take down these breakfast things and take care of the kids. Come down soon, I have a present for you."

"But, I thought . . . what about us?"

"Don't worry. We have plenty of time."

"Okay. I'll shave and be down in five minutes."

"Make it ten." She turned and left the room.

As he shaved, Bill thought he heard music. The melody had an unusual, displaced rhythm. Janice must have turned on the stereo. He went downstairs. The kitchen, dining, and living rooms were deserted. He walked to the large den at the back of the house and found Janice and the children. They were hanging upside down, ankles tied by coarse sisal rope from the oak beams he'd put up last year. Their arms were unbound, free to dangle toward the floor. Their throats were open, slashed deeply. Blood had run over their chins into mouths and nostrils and lay in pools on the green tile. Janice swayed and jerked feebly.

In helpless horror, Bill watched his wife die.

Susan entered the interrogation room, giving the cubicle a quick once-over. It contained three steel straight-backed chairs and a table with a four-inch partition down its middle. She restrained a smile when she first saw the officer. His face was deeply lined, the face of a man in his sixties, but atop it was fluffy red hair that would have better suited a teenager.

"Detective Muldrow?" she asked. "I'm Susan Tyler. My brother is waiting outside."

"Hello. Won't you sit down?" He glanced at his watch.

Susan did as he asked, lit a cigarette and studied the man.

"I suppose you know why I asked you here?" He began affably.

"I assume it has to do with Janice Hughes."

"Yes. What can you tell me about her?"

"Not a thing. I barely knew the woman."

Muldrow shuffled papers, pointedly giving her time to rethink her answer. She flicked an ash into an aluminum ashtray, waiting.

"Miss Tyler," he said, "I think that was a bit understated. Your brother runs the study group that Mrs. Hughes attended, isn't that right? I have some notes from the Consumer Complaint Depart . . ."

"Yes," she interrupted, "but actually, I'd only seen her two or three times."

"Truly?" Muldrow frowned.

"Truly," she echoed.

"Your brother is the leader of this cult, isn't he?"

Susan caught his eyes and held them. "We'd better get something straight, right off," she said. "Maligning my brother and his *study group* won't get me angry enough to betray anything I wouldn't tell you anyway. Frankly, I joined his group in order to keep an eye on him, that's the only reason."

"Would you explain yourself?"

"All right. I don't trust him; it's that simple. I was afraid he was setting himself up in order to con a bunch of ignorant people."

"What makes you think he's that kind of man?"

"He's my brother," she replied. "I've known him a long time."

"It says here that you're in business with him." He searched through additional papers.

"No, he works for me. I let Vern call himself a partner. It's a harmless enough pretense, soothes his ego."

"Has he ever broken the law?"

"I'm not sure."

"You don't come to his defense readily, do you?"

"No, and I don't have any reason to do so."

"And if you're so concerned about his ego, why did you horn in on his territory?"

Susan flushed. Muldrow had uncovered a sensitive area. She cleared her throat before answering.

"That's a good question," she replied. "In one way or another, I've tried to answer it for years. A minor reason would be that I don't want any scandal attached to me or my business through him, but I think that's evasion. . . . I suppose I *am* protective toward Vern, no matter how much I dislike the idea."

"You don't seem the type."

"Thank you. I take that as a compliment." She paused. "I feel a sense of responsibility toward him. Secondly, I want to prevent him from hurting too many people."

"How are you involved with Third Eye Enterprises?" he asked. "Are you a silent partner?"

"*No*. I told you that I joined to keep an eye on my brother."

"I thought, since you were in business together, you might have decided to branch out."

Susan's eyes narrowed. "I've already told you *twice* about my relationship to that group."

"What about your relationship with Janice Hughes? Did you know her very well? Did you ever see her privately?"

"No."

"What did you think about her?"

"Nothing. She wasn't an active participant in the group, at least not the few times I was on hand to notice. She seemed . . . colorless."

"So, you didn't like her? Why not?"

"You said that, not I. I didn't like or dislike her. She was a stranger who didn't interest me in the least."

"I should think that anyone who dies like that would be an object of some interest."

"How could I know how she would die?"

"What do you think happened?"

"The papers said her husband probably went berserk and killed her and the children." Susan shuddered, thinking of the children during their final minutes.

"Why do you think he did it?"

"I don't know."

"What would you say if I told you the papers didn't know everything?"

Susan studied him, puzzled by the statement. "Why should you tell me anything?" she asked.

"To see your reaction," he replied. Muldrow rubbed his forehead tiredly, but decided to tell her the rest since he'd already gone this far.

"Well?" She waited, with raised eyebrows. He appeared to have forgotten her.

"Just this; premeditated murder."

"Of course it was!" she cried.

"No. That's not what I meant. Someone other than Mr. Hughes."

"What . . . do you mean?" she whispered.

"I'll tell you something—something the newspapers didn't mention. The Hughes' next-door neighbor saw a strange car leaving their driveway in a hurry that morning."

"My god!"

"So now you know why I'm pestering you with these questions."

She felt nauseated. "Do you want me for anything else?"

"No, you can go. For now."

"Hello, hound."

"I don't—"

"Heel, dog!" Joy ordered harshly.

Adderson instinctively fumbled for his blindfold, but a stinging blow stopped him.

"Why do you do this?" he protested.

"Because it pleases me, pup."

He felt for a wall, leaned against it for support.

She shoved him. His head bumped the wall.

A defiant surge erupted. "I don't have to put up with this!"

Something struck his cheek.

He raised his hands again, as if to remove the mask, but he bit his tongue and forced himself to stillness.

Joy smiled.

She ran a smooth fingertip against his lips. He pulled away, then slowly relaxed.

"Why?" he whispered in bewilderment.

"It's part of our game, as are my late-night phone calls to you. Do you grow weary of it?"

"Why me? Why did you pick me?"

"You're a good breed, from a good bloodline."

Her fingernails applied pressure to his lips. A trickle of blood appeared.

Adderson fought to control a flinch. He thought back to their first meeting, then their second. The times he'd been called late at night and ordered to this or that motel. The first time he'd obeyed out of curiosity, afterward out of greed. He tried to recall some details of the room they were in now, but couldn't. As always, she'd been behind the door, waiting to blindfold him before he caught more than a glimpse. And her? He'd give anything to know what she looked like. If her looks were anything like her voice . . .

"Is he a good boy?"

Kevin raised his head suddenly. Her voice was next to his ear.

"Yes," Joy purred, "he's a good dog."

Her hand slowly moved down his neck, causing him to break out in gooseflesh.

"I like my hounds well-heeled. You know that by now, don't you?"

He nodded.

"You'll play and you'll fetch because you like my game, don't you?"

He nodded again.

Her hand trailed over his arm. She felt the tension build up in his muscles.

Adderson swallowed.

One hand moved to his waist. Her other rubbed against the nape of his neck.

"He'll be a good boy, or he'll be punished."

Her hand moved lower.

"But I think he's trained now."

Adderson didn't move.

"If he obeys, he'll become rich with his reward. It is pure, white, and beautiful. . . ."

A small package was thrust at his stomach. He seized it with both hands and held on for dear life.

"Yet, money isn't everything," she whispered. "A good dog likes his treats, doesn't he?"

Adderson's lips parted. The game was worth it.

She rang the bell seven times, but there was no answer.

Jason noted her expression in the dim light on the stoop of Vern's duplex.

"Are you wondering why you called me?" he asked.

She looked up. "How'd you know that?"

"A guess."

"You guess too damned well," she said. "Well then, why *did* I call you?"

He shrugged, turned to the door.

"That makes two of us," she whispered. She felt as if she'd depended on him for years, and she was grateful. She needed Jason to help her face Vern. He had agreed, once he'd heard about the police interrogation.

The door flew open. Tyler leaned against the doorsill, backdropped by darkness. Every light inside was off.

"Whadya want?" he growled. His face was like a store mannequin's, vacuous and dull, with a hint of bad temper underneath.

"Drunk," Teldaris muttered under his breath. Susan heard, nodded slightly.

"Fine, just fine," Tyler slurred. "Everybody wants to talk to old Vern these days. I ought to charge by the hour."

He turned and stumbled into the living room. Susan switched on lights. Tyler slumped in his favorite chair, a half-empty bottle of vodka on the table beside him. There was no sign of a glass.

"Vern," she demanded, "how much have you drunk?"

"Never touch the stuff."

"This is a hell of a way to start," Teldaris commented.

"What are *you* doing here?"

"What did Muldrow tell you?" Susan asked.

"Nothing. That bastard didn't tell me a thing." Tyler belched. "I did all the telling."

"What did he ask you?" Teldaris prodded impatiently.

"He asked me everything. Everything."

"Like what?" Susan pressed. "Vern, *please* tell us. It's important."

He looked at them suspiciously.

"What are you talking about? What's so important?"

"Listen," Susan said. "That detective told me that Janice's husband might be innocent. Do you understand me? Somebody else could be the killer."

Tyler dropped the bottle. It fell to the floor; liquor splashed his pants. The bottle rolled along the carpet until it collided with the leg of a coffee table.

"Did you hear me?" Susan asked.

"Yeah."

"Did Muldrow tell you anything about it?"

"No . . . he just asked a lot of questions."

"Like what?" Jason asked.

"Did I know Janice well? Intimately? He asked about my group, too. He wanted to know if I believed what I taught."

"What did you tell him?"

"I said of course I believed . . . or else I wouldn't be teaching my friends. Then, he asked how much I was charging for my friendly instruction. He was a bastard, a real . . ." He trailed off.

"Then," he continued in a monotone, "he said you didn't trust me. You're a bitch for saying so. That did me a world of good. Why in hell did you do it? Susan, what have I ever done to you?"

She lowered her head, unable to reply.

"Thanks a lot," Tyler snarled. "I always could count on you, couldn't I?"

"If it makes any difference," she said quietly, "I said those things before I knew you could get into trouble. I'm sorry."

"Doesn't help, does it?" He seemed determined to rub it in.

"You don't act surprised that someone else might be the killer," Teldaris observed.

"Then why is there a puddle of vodka on the rug? Of course I'm—surprised. But what does the killer have to do with me?" Tyler answered brusquely.

"Christ, you're a callous bastard," Teldaris said.

Susan spoke before Vern could reply.

"Vern, I think you're a suspect," she said.

"I . . . thought that might be the case."

"I'm sure of it. The way Muldrow talked, he couldn't have meant anything else."

"That's ridiculous! Why would I want to kill Janice and her brats? There's no reason in the world! Why should I? She was the one I wanted . . . I mean, one of the easiest . . ." Tyler halted before he said too much, but their faces indicated he already had.

"I believe you," Susan said flatly, "but Muldrow seems to be after you, anyway."

"Why? It doesn't make any sense."

"It does to him," Jason said. "He may think that there was more between you and Janice than a teacher-pupil relationship. Anyone who's been to more than one or two of your meetings could have suspected as much. I wonder who told him? But, I guess that's irrelevant. The main thing is this—you're a prime suspect."

Their westbound car was crawling with hundreds of others in rush-hour traffic. Deborah sat sulking over her husband's enigmatic attitude.

"*Why* won't you tell me where we're going?"

"It would spoil the surprise."

"Why are you wearing a suit? Did you get a job?"

"Of course not!"

"We need the money, Kevin."

"Do we?"

She turned on the radio in annoyance. An unpleasant thought occurred to her.

"Please, Kev, I couldn't stand to go to Jan's house yet. We're not going to Green Mountain, are we?"

"No," he said flatly. "Thanks for thinking so highly of me."

She fiddled with the door handle.

"Why do they call it that?" he said, trying to spark conversation. "It's never green."

She didn't respond.

Thirty silent minutes later, they cruised by the plush residences of Lookout Mountain. Deborah found herself caught in daydreams, wondering how it would be to live like this. They turned onto Skyline Drive, which crested at a cliff's edge and overlooked the city. At the very end of the road stood a small futuristic house, surrounded by transplanted aspens and well-tended firs.

"What do you think of your new home, Mrs. Adder-son?"

"Huh?"

"Do you like it?" He watched for her reaction.

"W—what?" she stammered in disbelief. This neighborhood was populated by wealthy professionals and other upper-middle-class types. She said as much.

"Money isn't the only medium of exchange." He rubbed the back of her neck playfully. "Besides, I've made a bit lately."

"Please don't kid me, Kevin, not about something like this." Her mouth remained open. The lines of the structure nestled naturally against the slope of the land. She saw huge windows, soaring cedar beams, and balconies. The fiery circle of the setting sun reflected off the glass front door. An arbor stretched toward a curving driveway.

"I'm not joking. Not now, dandelion."

She was captivated by the place. Dusk was upon them, a sudden darkening in the mountains. In the distance, the smog haze over the city evaporated into night. Lights throughout Denver popped on magically, creating a sprawling, twinkling aureole. At that moment, the Queen City of the Plains lived up to her name.

"It looks like . . ." She couldn't finish.

"We'll see this every night from our front yard." Kevin put an arm around her waist.

"I don't . . . I can't believe it! How is it possible?"

"Reptiles take," he said wryly, "and this is the perfect place."

"Perfect place? Reptiles?"

"To entertain our friends, eat our enemies, and start over again." He threw his head back and laughed. It was an odd, harsh sound.

Deborah watched him, puzzled.

"Atmosphere, dandelion, atmosphere."

"Who got you all this?" she asked.

"*I* did. Snap go my fingers . . ." The staccato sound

punctuated the air. "Everything falls into place. Snap. Just like that."

"Kev, how?" she repeated.

"I told you it would happen. Will this change your attitude about never giving up?"

"I can't believe it."

"Believe it, dandelion," he murmured. "It cost a lot."

Night swept upon them as they overlooked the city.

Joy had accomplished her task with elegant efficiency. She had zeroed in on a bowl of fruit, selecting an orange. The drug would have instantly discolored an apple or pear, and the discolored flesh may well have been discarded. But the narcotic blended well with the juices of citrus fruit, and its bitter taste would be disguised by the orange tang.

When Teldaris bit into the first slice, he noticed nothing unusual, nor did he realize that he had taken the most eventful bite of his life.

That night, the dreams began.

"How long before he knows, Mistress?"

"The narcotic acts differently in every instance. No longer than two months. No shorter than one."

FIVE

Set

I AM PHARAOH.
LET US ADVANCE IN NUMBERS
AND LOGIC,
THE SCIENCES, MEDICINE, LAW,
PEACEFUL USE OF OUR GODS,
AND THE USE OF A NEW SPOKEN WORD
AND WRITTEN LANGUAGE.

THEN, LET US STOP AT A GIVEN POINT
AND LET OUR MINDS AND MANNER
CATCH UP WITH OUR SOCIAL AND
MATERIAL PROGRESS.

FOR, TO USE A SWORD
THAT HAS BEEN TAKEN
OUT OF THE FIRE
AND IS FINISHED,
BEFORE WE SWADDLE OUR HAND
OR WAIT FOR THE METAL TO COOL,
SHALL RESULT IN BURNING OF THE FLESH,
AND PUNISH THE OWNER—THE CREATOR—
FAR, FAR SOONER THAN
IT WILL HIS ADVERSARY
OR THE USE TO WHICH HE
INTENDS TO PUT IT.

—Hymn to Hat-shepsut,
  from *Shadow of Khufu*,
  Cecil Rupert-Lewis, 1894

TIME PASSED, IMPARTIAL ABOUT THE VERY EXISTENCE of humankind. August came and ended, the hottest and driest in Denver's history. September began, determined to imitate its predecessor, but in its last week the weather cooled and promised a beautiful autumn.

Detective Muldrow spent the weeks in frustration, but doggedly continued the investigation into the Hughes murders.

Vern Tyler doubled his schedule of study sessions. Several newspaper interviews had brought him a surfeit of publicity, and new members, fancying themselves a daring lot, basked in the notoriety attached to the nebulous Third Eye Enterprises. Only Betty, Susan, and Jason remained from the previous group. Janice was often in their thoughts, but rarely in their conversation.

Susan attended her brother's meetings, but always wished she was elsewhere.

Teldaris patiently waited for something to happen. A change had come over him lately, but it was too elusive for anyone save Susan to notice.

One Sunday morning in early October, Tyler took a group on a nature walk outside the city. He chose a spot above Evergreen, secluded enough so they could meet in privacy. A little stream rushed through the small mountain canyon. Pines, firs, and spruces grew right down to the fast-running water, but the visual impact of the evergreens was diminished by the colors of the turning aspens farther up the slopes. After a short time, Vern herded everyone to an open area by the stream.

Teldaris was entranced by the vivid yellows and golds. A breeze stirred the leaves, caused him to think of a stadium crowded with people, each waving a bright yellow pennant. His reverie was interrupted by a grating voice.

"My name is Gary," a new member introduced himself. "I'm twenty-eight and own a Skin-Kare franchise."

Jason concentrated harder on the shimmering leaves.

"I've always been fascinated with the supernatural and its manifestations," Gary announced to his audience.

"Since I was a child," he continued, "I've held the belief that this world is a passing thing, a stage. The real happenings occur elsewhere. It's been said this is all illusion. I know that to be true. . . ."

"How?" Susan asked. She sat on a nearby log, by the stream. Her face was a mask betraying vague boredom.

"What?"

"How?" she repeated. A small scowl pulled at the corners of her mouth.

"What are you talking about?" he asked.

"You said this was a world of illusion, and sounded so definite about it that I wondered what proof you possessed." She didn't raise her eyes from the rushing water. "In other words, how can you be so positive?"

"Let's put that on hold for a little while," Tyler interrupted, seething. He attempted to placate. "Gary, did you have anything else to say?"

"No." The man ran his fingers through his hair, then looked away.

Tyler hurriedly broached a new subject to cover the awkward moment. "Consider this, group: everything that exists has a spirit of its own."

"Then, why haven't more people noticed that, and talked and written about it?" Susan asked.

"I don't know, Susan," her brother replied through clenched teeth, "so many things have been repressed for one reason or another." It took great effort from him to be civil to her.

"Are you saying that most of the ancient world's knowledge has been lost?" she questioned.

"Sometimes I think it has."

Betty sat on the edge of a gray boulder, raptly listening to every word. "Why would anyone suppress that sort of knowledge?" she asked, perplexed.

"Suppression of any kind is wrong," Tyler said. "But it happens. *All* the power-holders of history have at least partially maintained their power by suppressing knowledge. They fear the effect certain information will have on those they oppress; the knowledgeable person is usually one who demands freedom as a right, thus endangering those who would rule him. But, I digress. I'll repeat what I said, it's important: everything, absolutely everything, has spirit."

Betty patted the stone beneath her. "Like this rock?" she asked jokingly.

"Yes. If it didn't have spirit, it wouldn't exist."

"I don't understand that," Susan said. Jason smiled and closed his eyes.

"Take any two things, like that boulder and, uh, the water here. Okay, you know there are one hundred and some-odd elements, right? They're the building blocks of the universe. So, really, only a hundred-plus things should make up the entire cosmos. But something else noses in. That something is spirit, or will, or purpose. Without will, that water would be hydrogen and oxygen. The elements that compose that stone would be separate, too.''

''Are you saying that all things are alike, with spirit?'' someone asked.

''No. Just the opposite. No spirit is like any other. There are groups that share common basics, like man, for instance. Even then, we're hardly identical. You're not like Betty, or me, or anyone else. Yet, you're much more similar to us than a stone, an inanimate thing. Any object that's so alien to us that we don't consider it being alive, is *truly* difficult to imagine having spirit.'' Tyler spread his arms. ''However, everything has it.''

''Then I don't imagine that rock likes an ass pressed against it,'' Susan muttered to herself. She saw Jason smirk, and wondered if he had overheard her.

Tyler sank into the sofa and reveled in its softness. He skimmed through the morning mail, then stopped to admire his acquisitions. Every stick of furniture in the living room was new. The sofa-and-two-chair ensemble were giant pillows held in hardwood frames. They were luxurious and even comfortable, if a person didn't mind sitting a bit lower than usual.

Things were going well of late with TEE and he had indulged in a small spending spree. Soon, he hoped, he'd be able to break loose from Susan. For good.

He returned to the mail, pleased to find no bills. Then, something on the dining table caught his eye. It was a small, beige envelope of very heavy paper, perfectly blank. How had it gotten there? He tore it open. Inside was one small sheet of matching paper. Tiny handprinted letters filled both sides.

Sixteen years ago, you stole something from a thief. That the thief was an institution is of no consequence.

What you took belongs rightfully to no single individual, particularly not one who is ignorant of its value or history. The institution acquired the item through another thief, who, fearing certain aftermaths, attempted to shirk responsibility for what he had done.

Neither thief escaped.

You may begin to understand the gravity of your situation, but you do not fully appreciate it yet.

Remember the demise of the woman Janice Hughes.

Tomorrow you will hear of another.

Take tomorrow as a guarantee that what you stole will not remain in your keeping.

Tyler read the letter four times. Each reading chilled him more.

"Are you the lady who phoned about the Hughes killings? Something about William Hughes being innocent?"

"Well, I didn't say that!" Betty chuckled in spite of herself.

"Sorry. I must have the wrong address." The reporter started to walk away.

"I wanted to agree with Janice's last words," she called to the figure halfway down the corridor. "It was uncanny . . . she was my best friend." The man stopped, considered, made an about-face.

She ushered him into her kitchen, where two cups of hot tea and a plate of pastries were set out.

"My name is Betty Carmon. I'm a widow." She perched atop the closest stool. "My Julius died twelve years ago," she said. "I'm, uh, fifty-eight years old. I don't have a profession. When I was younger, I was a homemaker. Shouldn't you be writing this down?''

He went through the motions of taking notes.

Betty now regretted having called the newspaper, but she felt that she had reason. She did *not* want Janice's death to be forgotten. She wanted to create attention, to do something to keep the air stirred up. Mr. Tyler was no help. He wouldn't talk about it. There had been the neighbors at first, but lately things had calmed down. . . .

"You were saying?" The reporter mumbled through a mouthful of pastry.

"Oh, yes. . . . I thank my lucky stars that Julius left me financially comfortable. Since he passed over, I've had time for self-improvement. That's where I met poor Jan, at one of my seminars.''

He saw she waited, and pretended dutifully to jot down her words.

"I became interested in the psychic sciences while I was still a young woman. In my early twenties, I had a most unusual experience. I dreamed my mother was dying. She spoke to me. . . . ''

Betty paused, eyes unfocusing as the memory hit her hard for the first time in years.

She was again twenty-two years old, asleep with her husband, whom she still thought of as a stranger. Abruptly, she heard a voice.

It was her mother, who called to her as she had done every day of her childhood.

"Yes, Mother, I'll be down in a minute,'' she whispered drowsily. She opened her eyes. Moonlight still shone through an open window. She looked around, convinced she was dreaming.

In the corner, by the window, her mother stood, wearing a pale nightdress. She appeared older, much older, than Betty remembered.

Betty lay quietly in bed, not daring to move.

"Don't do it, Betty,'' the figure whispered. "Don't do

it. If you don't love him, if you're not happy, then leave. You may not have another chance. If you don't love him, leave him. Do you hear me, Betty?''

"Mrs. Carmon?" A hand touched her.

Betty started, and stared blankly into the young reporter's face.

"Are you okay?" he asked, moderately concerned.

She blinked once.

"Oh, yes, I'm fine," she replied. She took a deep breath, recovered. "I'm so sorry. I suppose I was daydreaming." She saw he was preparing to leave.

"Don't go yet. I'll tell you something the police are trying to cover up. Something horrible. It'll put a whole new light on Jan's. . . ."

Jason tossed restlessly back and forth in his bed, experiencing yet another of the vivid dreams that hounded him of late. He woke briefly and sat up, thinking that he could no longer put off the inevitable. He must seek professional help soon. The dreams were beginning to dominate even his waking hours, forcing changes upon him. He felt as though he was slowly merging with his ''dream-self''; that the final metamorphosis would be someone new, neither dream nor waking-self, but someone stronger, sterner . . . yet mostly, someone still desperately, fatally in love with . . . whom? With what? His exhausted mind refused to go past that point. He lay back, and as his head hit the pillow, the dream continued. . . .

The building would soon be finished. From his pavilion set on a hill overlooking the site, Sen-Mut gazed down on his vision in stone. No breeze broke the heat shimmering upward from the royal valley. Below, slaves were adding the last pieces of marble overlay to the structure. The blazing white of the temple under the high sun was almost painful to view. But he studied it nonetheless, looking for flaws and, finding none, was satisfied. Pharaoh would arrive tomorrow to appraise his work; Sen-Mut hoped that she would be pleased.

Joy interrupted her yoga exercises, emerged from the Lotus position, listened. She switched off the cassette player; sounds of flute and harp halted. She wrapped a dark skirt around her ivory tights, loosened her long hair from its braid.

The sounds below her room were almost beyond detection, but there. She quickly descended the back stairwell.

Thea was quietly working in the kitchen, preparing food.

Joy limbered her muscles with a long, slow stretch. "I thought I heard prowlers."

"Only I," said Thea, preoccupied with an assortment of chilled fruits.

Joy corrected her posture, then shook her head to release an errant strand of hair. She nibbled on a wafer-thin slice of melon.

"I was going to make—" Joy began.

"I know. I was . . . restless." Thea stirred a thick mixture that simmered in a tiny copper pot.

"It smells like the kitchens of a sultan," Joy said, voicing her approval. Thea smiled.

"It should." She laughed softly. "I was taught to cook in such a place."

Joy took in the rich aromas as she looked around at the amount of food, then at the number of bowls, pots, and other utensils assembled.

"Mistress, there is enough food here for—"

"A banquet," the other completed. She set down a tray of canapés. "I was in the mood to prepare a feast," she said briskly. "And I have."

"Only . . . there is no one to eat it," Joy said sadly.

"There is you and there is I," Thea answered, defensive.

Joy noticed she had set on the counter the makings of service for three.

"May I help with anything? Shall I set the table?"

"No. I wish to do it all myself. Go. Finish your yoga. I'll give ample warning." She paused. "Of course, we will dress formally tonight."

Joy raised an eyebrow.

"All this food . . . ," she questioned.

"What is left, we will throw out. Leave me. Can you not see I wish to be alone?"

Joy paused, observing her closely.

Thea looked up, strangely moody. "Joy, do you ever wonder . . ."

Thea stopped, eyes narrowed, and gazed out an oval kitchen window. Her features softened.

"Mistress?"

"What would it be like to have friends?"

Joy tilted her head in curiosity.

"Do you often think about what we miss in being so insular?" Thea turned. "I demand too much, I suppose. What sort of people could *I* entertain?" Her glance returned to the napkins and silverware.

Joy had no response.

"Only a madwoman would set a place for someone who will not appear," Thea finally admitted.

"Yes, Mistress, only a madwoman would," Joy assented.

Thea's lips paled. She walked to the counter and returned the third set of china, with silverware, to the dining buffet.

Joy moved a step closer, but Thea moved away.

"Leave me," she said. "We dine at eight."

If you want the truth, meet me tonight.
This is your last chance.

Don't ignore this note as you did the others.
You owe it to Janice Hughes.

Betty nervously ran a manicured nail along the border of the typed message. This was the third note placed inside her apartment. No one believed her: the police thought her a crank, Mr. Tyler hadn't returned her calls, her neighbors were politely dubious.

Betty felt small, isolated, and alone. Who had gotten inside her apartment? *Why?* Nothing was missing, not even disturbed.

"Why me?" she asked aloud. "Go to the police, leave me alone!" Betty looked again at a newly framed picture of Janice and Bill on her dresser and decided to comply with the note's directions.

He saw himself as an expanse of plain. There stretched a muscular chest, a flat, navel-jeweled stomach, a white loincloth, and slender legs, receding far into the distance.

Adderson closed his eyes, content. He was Pharaoh, he was power, he was all.

The wind noisily flapped the hunting tent. He nodded, acknowledged that the wind, also, was Pharaoh. It shook all, beating remorselessly, day and night, moon wax upon moon wane.

The attending girls whispered among themselves. They thought he slept, but he was awake even in deepest slumber. Perhaps, in their gibberish, they wondered about his latest favorite, or if their feathered costumes smelt, or if the cosmetics painted on their breasts would please him. Or did they talk about a dagger placed between Pharaoh's ribs at the height of his pleasure with them? Perhaps the garrote, while he ate? The poisonous drop from a hidden vial that would touch his lips? One royal death to set their homelands free, until the next Pharaoh.

He was content, and rested at peace. The mute ones

guarding his every moment saw to his safety. They saw all but reported nothing, for the tongueless cannot say.

He motioned to the first girl, as his eyes opened a bit. Was she fearful? His pleasure could mean her freedom, perhaps an emerald. Displeasure would mean the loss of a hand.

He rose, satisfied with his handiwork. She lay still, quieted now, and uttered no more than an occasional whimper. He grinned as he viewed her. Her head, propped against the brick wall of a garage, caught the light from a streetlamp. Her nose was broken, bleeding from his first blow. Her lip had been split by the second. Her dress was torn open, revealing her breasts. Her skirt bunched around her waist. The pantyhose were gathered around her ankles. She looked like a discarded doll.

She'd been easy. He had followed her for four blocks, then pounced. She'd put up a struggle. Stupid, stupid slut.

She stirred and groaned.

"Shut up, bitch, or I'll do it again," he snarled.

Terror widened her eyes and she began to cry thinly. He walked away, sauntered unhurriedly down the sidewalk. Nobody would come to help her, not until it was too late.

Susan sat upright in bed, awakened by pounding. Her bedside clock showed seven-fifteen. She threw on a robe and hurried to the door.

"Who is it?" she called out.

"Vern! Let me in!"

She unlocked the door, alarmed by the urgency in his voice. Tyler burst in, shut the door, carefully replaced the chains. Without a word, he walked to her kitchen and poured himself a drink. Susan followed.

"What . . . what's wrong?"

Tyler returned to the living room and sat down heavily.

He didn't answer, instead he downed the liquor in one gulp. Susan crossed the room and stood before him, arms at her side.

"Tell me about it," she urged.

"Susan, I'm in trouble," he said. "Terrible trouble."

The panic in her brother invaded her. She sat, gripped the arms of her chair, and took deep breaths.

"Tell me about it," she repeated. She braced her back against the wood, prepared for bad news.

"Betty's been found dead. I just heard—"

"Betty? Your Betty?"

"I couldn't sleep, so I took a drive. On my way home, I heard on the radio that the police had found Betty dead in some garage. They didn't give any details, only that she'd been beaten and raped."

Susan was silent.

"There's more," he continued. Vern pulled a crumpled paper out of a shirt pocket and handed it to her. It was the note he had found on his dining table, the one that accused him of theft. She skimmed it, then reread it slowly.

"Now you see what's upset me," he said, growing uncomfortable at her muteness. "Sue, what am I gonna do? Muldrow already suspects me of killing Janice. It's been some time since she was murdered, and I was just beginning to be able to get some sleep nights. Now this! First there's this note, threatening me—then today, Betty . . ." Tyler covered his face with both hands.

Susan watched him for a long moment before she turned away.

"What did you steal?"

At the question, his head jerked upright.

"I didn't steal anything!"

"Vern, tell me the truth, or I'll kick you out and go back to bed."

He shook his head. "*Nobody* could know about it! I'd nearly forgotten the incident. I hocked it years ago."

Susan sat up straight.

Tyler felt like a man before a firing squad. "When I was in college, I stole something. I didn't think it was valuable."

"Why did you steal it?" she asked emotionlessly.

"To get back at the school, I guess. I thought it might . . ." He didn't finish.

"What did the school do to you?"

"Nothing. I can't explain it. I had a compulsion. I was just a kid."

"What?"

"For god's sake, I was only twenty!"

"For the last time, what did you steal?"

"A stone. A damned scarab."

"A what?"

"A scarab. You know, a beetle. An Egyptian beetle. They made a million imitations a few years ago, and even sold some authentic ones. I tried to pawn the damned thing and got hardly anything for it. Hundreds like it, probably. That's when I came home and went to work. I'd nearly forgotten about it."

Susan opened her mouth and shut it again. She'd sometimes wondered why he'd left school so suddenly, but this . . .

He saw her confusion and nodded, hoping she would believe his half-truths.

"That's all, Susan, I swear! A goddamned scarab!"

"Was it valuable? Was it cut from a gem or something?"

"No. It's . . . was . . . carved from a stone."

"Then, what's all the furor about?"

"It was part of some Pharaoh's collection. On loan, I think, from an Egyptian museum."

"None of this makes sense."

"I know . . . that's why I came here."

"What do you mean?"

"Because you're the strong one." His tone implied just

how hard it was for him to admit this. "You've gotten me out of scrapes before."

"You're a damned fool! If that letter is to be believed, then Betty, Janice, and three children have died because you once had an urge to steal something. There's more to this than you're telling me!"

He lowered his head.

"Are you going to help me?"

"Yes, damn you, but this is the last time. If I get you out of this, you're going to have to pay me for it."

"How?"

"You'll promise to leave Denver."

"Why?"

"So I'll never have to see you again."

"But—"

"That's the deal. If I get you through this thing, you'll disappear from my life. Completely."

"But . . . I can't, Sue. You're my sister."

"Then get out now and take your chances."

"I can't do that!" Tyler wrung his hands, looked around the room in desperation. "Okay . . . anything you say." He relented at last.

"Is there any reason why you can't go to the police?" She reached for a cigarette.

"I told you, it's Muldrow. He's probably got them out looking for me already."

An image of Jason formed in Susan's mind. If anyone would be sympathetic about this mess, he would. She could think of no one else who would even listen. She walked to the phone, dialed. His phone was busy.

"At least he's home," she said.

"Who?" Tyler asked.

"Jason."

"No! Don't call him!" he protested. "What can he do?"

"I don't know, but he's got a good mind and might come up with something."

"I don't trust him, he's . . ." Tyler thought back to their confrontation in the bar. Could this be part—

"You sure as hell can't stay here," she said, interrupting his thoughts. "Or at your place. Running from the cops is going to make you look guilty as hell. You know that, don't you? I don't suppose you would reconsider?"

He shook his head in negation.

"Give me five minutes to get dressed, and we'll go to Jason's apartment."

"You know where he lives?"

"Yes, somewhere on Capitol Hill. I have the address somewhere." She hurried to the bedroom.

When she was gone, Tyler reached inside his coat pocket, paused a moment, then slowly pulled out a small carved object. Delicate, green flecked with gold, the beetle's back seemed to emote a shimmery radiance. He raised and lowered it over his palm, feeling an attraction, like two magnets played against each other. He gently rubbed its belly, wondered again about the hieroglyphics; he'd never deciphered them. He closed his fist over the scarab. "Mine," he whispered. "I'm sorry. I have to do it. I've got to leave you for a little while."

He glanced around, made a quick decision, and went to the dining table, where he swiftly removed oynx fruit from a silver bowl. He placed the scarab at the bottom of the bowl and carefully covered it with the fruit.

Susan's sudden reentry made him jerk upright. She tried to phone again, tugged at her earlobe nervously. "Still busy. Let's go. By the way, if you haven't guessed already, I'll make this simple. You're fired."

Half an hour later, Susan parked in front of a dark brick apartment building that appeared to be at least fifty years old. She and Vern entered the lobby and found Teldaris's name on a mailbox; number five, third floor. A narrow stairway terminated in a paneled teak door that displayed the number above an antique brass knocker. She was reaching for the knocker when the door swung open.

Teldaris stood there wearing a brown robe. He didn't seem too surprised by their appearance.

"I'm sorry to bother you, Jason." Susan hurried an apology. "I need your help."

"I know. I heard about Betty on the early news. I've been trying to call you. Come in." He ushered them inside. "Make yourselves comfortable while I put on some clothes." With that, he disappeared down a hall.

Susan and Vern stood in a long, wide room that must have taken up at least half of the building's upper floor. There were two large skylights. The walls and ceiling were paneled in teak that precisely matched the front door.

Brother and sister examined the room with keen eyes. He evaluated, she appreciated. This was the most luxurious room Susan had ever seen in a private dwelling. A coffee-brown carpet covered the floor. There was no evident decorating style, for modern and antique were mixed, producing an extraordinary effect. Everywhere she looked, something caught and held her attention. A Regency table stood in an alcove. On it was a brass candelabra holding at least twenty scarlet candles. Side tables along one wall were of matched fruitwood. A brown sectional sofa stood before an immense marble fireplace. Scattered about were objects which Teldaris obviously considered beautiful or interesting. As did she. Sculpture, rock crystals, and shells were in evidence from every angle, though not a single painting interrupted the eye as it traversed the lines of the paneling.

Their inspection was cut short by Jason's reappearance. Tyler, who had temporarily forgotten his troubles upon seeing the place, said, "Nice. It must have cost a fortune." He did not note the daggered look Susan shot at him when she heard the comment.

"Not at all." Teldaris smiled politely. "I did most of

the work myself. Matter of fact, I did every last bit of it, from the paneling to the carpet."

"Still . . . ," Vern persisted.

"Get your mind off my money. This is my *home*. And, if I wanted to, I could sell at a profit anytime." He saw Susan's perplexed look. "No, I'm no great businessman, though I *do* know value. The subject is closed. Now, precisely what kind of help do you need?"

He led them to leather wingbacked chairs. Susan thought it unusual that three would be grouped together. A shadow of a cloud dimmed the light from the skylight above.

Teldaris listened while she explained the situation, then reread the note several times. He appeared neither shocked nor surprised by the tale. Even Betty's death did not seem to move him—but of course, as he'd told them on their arrival, he had already had that news.

Tyler had remained woodenly silent throughout Susan's narration, spending the time watching Teldaris closely for some sort of reaction and getting none. Frustrated, he nevertheless felt he might yet have some control of the situation if he revealed as little as possible about anything.

Jason's eyes passed over him lightly before returning to Susan.

"Why did you come to me?" he asked her gently.

Her eyes widened. For a moment she was afraid he would turn them away. "I . . . I don't know. Honestly, I don't. When Vern showed up this morning, you popped into my mind. I suppose some instinct . . ." She reddened, deeply embarrassed. Till this instant, she'd considered herself to be rational and logical, above the dictates of instinct.

Jason's sudden smile set her at ease. "One more question then," he said. "Can you think of any reason *why* I should help you?"

"No."

"I thought not. Then Vern hasn't told you everything."

Tyler shifted uncomfortably when her eyes suddenly flicked to him.

"I'm going to tell you some things, Susan," Teldaris continued, "but first I want to assure you that I *will* help you. No matter what happens."

"Let me ask you your own question. *Why* should you help?"

"I'll answer fully when we have time. First, something you probably didn't think about. The police may have followed you here."

"What?" she exclaimed, and was echoed closely by her brother.

"What car did you come in?" Teldaris asked.

"Mine," she answered.

"Good. That might buy us some time. I assume Vern left his car at your place."

"Yes. Why?"

"Think, Susan! That detective—Muldrow? Yes, that's his name. We can assume that he's looking for Vern. There's probably an all points bulletin out on his car."

"Oh, damn," she cursed, as the realization struck.

"That's right. Muldrow will come calling at your place when he can't find Vern. And, Vern's car will implicate you. If there's already a warrant out on him, they can get you for aiding and abetting. You're in trouble."

"But . . . can't anything be done?" She began to tremble slightly as she forced herself to accept his words.

"Maybe, but we'll have to move quickly." Teldaris stood, in complete charge of the situation. Susan had not realized it yet, but a few moments before, she had placed her entire trust in this man.

"First you, Vern. Where are your car keys?"

"Here," Tyler said as he handed them over.

"Good. Come with me. I have a storage room where you can hide for a while."

"Why can't I just stay here?" Tyler protested.

"If they get suspicious and decided to track you down, the police might knock at any minute," Jason snapped.

"But *why* should they be after me?" Tyler remained obstinate. "I didn't do anything!"

"Pure as the driven snow, huh? Don't you understand that you're the primary link, maybe the *only* one between Janice and Betty? The police won't overlook that. We don't have time to argue. Come on, both of you."

He led them down to the basement, opened the storage-room door and ushered Tyler into it.

"This is it. There's an old couch in here somewhere. Make yourself as comfortable as possible. If we're not back by evening, you're on your own." He shut the door just in time to cut off Vern's protests, then led Susan outside.

"What are you going to do?" she asked.

"There's a bus stop about a block away. I'll get a bus to your place and look around for a while. If it looks safe, I'll take Vern's car and ditch it somewhere."

"But—"

"No time for questions. Answers come later. Go back to my apartment and wait. I'll be back as soon as I can. If the police show up, tell them you spent the night with me and that I'll be back soon."

She laughed lightly. "You *do* think fast, don't you?"

"Yeah. I do." He smiled, turned and was gone. Susan thought of the Cheshire cat, for his smile seemed to linger even after he was out of sight.

"Something is wrong."

"Mistress?"

"Something goes amiss. . . ." Thea lowered her head, studied the ground absently.

"I sense it," she completed at length.

Joy moved beside her.

"The scarab?"

"Yes." Thea touched a slim bracelet on her wrist. "The power holds someone, I feel it. They won't let go, or . . . ," she paused, "it won't let them go."

Joy frowned.

"What if I do the wrong thing?" Thea asked, as if the thought had never before occurred to her.

"All of life is a what if."

"All of life is a one-line philosophy?"

Joy did not respond.

"I am . . . forgive me." Thea stood, moving away from Joy.

"There is nothing to forgive."

"A malignancy exists somewhere," Thea decided. "I trust it lies not with us."

"The scarab itself?" Joy asked, concerned.

"Perhaps, perhaps not." Thea walked to a bush of yellow roses. It barely clung onto life in the carefully tended garden. She touched its wilting petals.

"Something is wrong," she repeated. "If the beetle becomes restless, then all who come into contact with it may be affected."

She gently brushed a rose with a fingertip. It disintegrated; a rain of separated petals floated to her feet. She studied the shattered flower for a long moment.

"Why must everything I touch surrender?"

Susan looked up when Teldaris entered the front door, followed closely by Vern, whom he had released. Her eyes were full of urgent questions.

"Everything's all right," Teldaris said. "I had no trouble at all."

"I was getting worried. You were gone so long."

"Sorry. It took a while for me to be certain no one was watching Vern's car." He turned toward Tyler. "Here are your keys. Your car is in the thirty-day parking lot at Stapleton. It should be safe there."

"Thanks."

"You think I'm out of trouble?" Susan asked.

"Not yet. Muldrow may come around asking questions. Just tell him you don't know anything."

"But—"

"No more questions. I don't know about you two, but I'm starving. There's cold cuts in the kitchen. Come on, let's make some sandwiches and open a bottle of wine."

Some minutes later, they were sitting around a large oak breakfast table. Susan ate slowly, more engrossed in watching the two men than in her sandwich. Vern was sullenly quiet. He probably resented having been cooped in a dark storage room for most of the day. Jason adroitly avoided answering all questions from Susan, but told her with a glance that she would soon hear more than enough.

Half an hour later, they reentered the living room, coffee cups in hand. Teldaris started a fire in the marble fireplace as though he did it daily. He sat on the floor and stared into the flames for several minutes, leisurely sipping coffee. Finally, he turned to her.

"Susan, I've said that there are three reasons why I should help you," he began. "One of them you know about. My wife."

She frowned, but found nothing to say.

"Gail was, I believe, associated in some way with Vern." He turned toward Tyler and explained, "I'm looking for my wife. You may have known or seen her sometime in the last year. I'll give you a photograph in a while. I haven't shown it to you before because, frankly, I didn't trust you to tell me the truth. She was last seen in Denver and she's the reason I'm here. I hope you will help me."

"Certainly," Tyler responded. "I'll do anything I can." He felt totally perplexed and more than a little frightened.

"Good. By the way, I left my cigarettes on the kitchen counter, I think. Would you mind getting them for me? I'm just too damned comfortable to get up right now."

Though puzzled, Tyler rose in compliance and left the room.

Teldaris turned back to Susan. "The second reason is you."

"What do you mean?" She flushed, despite an effort to stop it.

"The group session at Vern's. We both experienced something strange that night."

"Yes. We've talked about it."

"The experience binds me to you in some way. And you to me, whether you admit it or not. Since then, the feeling has grown, at least on my part. Incidentally, did you ever ask Vern about the source of that poem?"

"No," she answered uneasily. Susan had felt a reluctance about pursuing the subject. She had been afraid that she was being pulled toward something she would not be able to control.

Tyler returned and handed over the cigarettes.

"No matter," Teldaris said, still talking to Susan. "I've found it on my own. It's an obscure bit of literature out of ancient Egypt. I told you about my education, didn't I? All the history, and other subjects. The research took some time, but I found it. The poem is considered a mourning ode for a lost culture or kingdom. It's generally attributed to Pharaoh Hat-shepsut, who, as I'm sure you both know, was a woman."

"What in blazing hell does that have to do with anything?" Tyler demanded, losing patience entirely.

"I don't know. Yet." Teldaris stared back into the crackling flames of the fire. He seemed to have forgotten their presence.

"Jason." Susan spoke after some minutes of waiting. "You said there were three reasons." Complexities and coincidences were compounding; one tangling with another, becoming incomprehensible. An Egyptian scarab. A fragment of a Pharaonic poem. Two members of her brother's group murdered. A young wife missing, recognized by one of the dead. Above all, this dark-haired man who stared unblinking into the flames. She *had* to know all. She must!

"Something over one point five million dollars," Teldaris responded.

"What?"

"The scarab. Its value. Somewhere between one and a half and two million dollars." He spoke mechanically, with no inflection whatever. His eyes did not leave the fire.

Susan looked toward her brother, who appeared astounded, then back toward Teldaris as he resumed speaking.

"Because of my education in the antiquarian, I've something of a minor reputation as an expert. I'm not attached to any one institution or university. You could say I free lance, on a commission basis." He sighed once, then continued. "I find things that are missing or stolen. One could say that I'm sort of detective, I suppose. I've had some luck. I came to Denver because of Gail. Just before I arrived, I was contacted by the Cairo Museum and told about the scarab. It's been missing for years. I agreed to try and recover it. After settling in here, I did some investigating. The necklace was stolen from a university where it was on loan. I went through the school's records and found that one Vern Tyler left school unexpectedly just three days after the scarab was stolen. So, I joined Vern's TEE."

She did not feel betrayed by this admission.

"I don't trust you, Teldaris." Tyler interrupted her thoughts.

"I don't trust you at all. You're lying. About the scarab. About everything. Why should we believe this story? You could have been the one who sent that note and killed Betty and the others. Why should we believe you?" he repeated.

Teldaris turned from the fire to Tyler, eyes implacable. "Because I approached you openly about the scarab. I offered you a great deal of money for it that day in the bar. And, I recorded the conversation. Would you like to hear it again?''

"No."

"I would," Susan said.

Teldaris quickly rose and put a tape into a cassette player. The voices were tinny but recognizable.

"My methods don't include murder," he said when the conversation was finished. "Stop trying to evade responsibility, Tyler. You stole the scarab and, because you refused to give it up, have indirectly caused the deaths of five people."

"No . . . that's not true! I didn't know what would happen."

"Of course not. You're an innocent. You just steal jewelry worth millions, but you never hurt anybody, do you? Where is the scarab, Vern?" Jason demanded.

"I—I don't have it! I sold it years ago. I had no idea it was so valuable!"

"Then, *why* did you steal it?"

"Please—"

"Don't beg. I told Susan I would help. But I'm not through with you. Not by a long shot." Teldaris walked to his desk, then came back with a photo. He handed it to Tyler.

"Vern," he said, "if you tell me about this woman, I'll provide you with a place to stay. Where neither the police nor anyone else can find you."

Tyler started when he saw the picture. "Yes. I remember her," he said. "She attended a few of my classes last year, but I don't remember much else. She seemed to be friends with another student. They both quit the group at the same time. I forget their names. . . . "

"Gail. Hamilton, if she used her maiden name."

"Yes . . . I seem to . . . yes, that's right. Her friend's name was Deborah something."

"You may have just saved your life," Jason said. "Janice's sister is named Deborah Adderson. That's all I need. Come with me and I'll show you your new home.''

When Tyler entered the dark room, the first thing he did was bump his head on a low-hanging water pipe.

"Christ, what is this? A cage for midgets?" He cursed, rubbing his forehead.

"Now you see why it wasn't rented until today."

The apartment was no more than seven feet wide, but ran the length of the basement. Everything was built into one wall. An army cot was judiciously placed at the very end, under a naked light bulb that dangled from the ceiling.

"This must've been built by a sadist," Susan said.

"You expect me to stay here?" Vern whined.

"Better than other places you might be," Jason replied. "I could put you back in that storage room across the hall, but you may have noticed that among the old sewing machines and rusted-out bicycles and gardening tools is not one pot to piss in. Your best other alternative is a jail cell."

"This place does have a john?"

"Is that it, next to the stove?" Susan ventured.

Tyler blanched.

"This was for the furnace tender, when they used coal at the turn of the century. They figured an immigrant would accept such quarters. The coal shute is next to the boiler, through that metal door. It's rusted shut, I think."

"So much for that gentler, simpler time." Susan leaned against a table. "Can I light up, or will we explode?"

"Try." Jason smiled. "We'll find out."

"It's easy for you two to laugh," Vern complained, "you won't be stuck down here!"

"Go astral traveling anytime you're bored," Teldaris suggested.

"You're doing this deliberately—"

"Enough," the younger man said sharply.

Susan began to perspire from the radiated heat of the pipes.

"The windows don't open," Vern muttered as he brushed cobwebs off the oilcloth window shades.

"Of course not. Burglars." Teldaris watched Tyler roam the efficiency and noted that he could not stand upright without brushing the radiator pipes.

"Jason, I think Vern has a point." Susan looked at the chipped brick walls and felt a slight twinge of guilt.

Teldaris took her by the arm, cutting off further protest.

"Vern needs to be alone. Coming to terms with oneself is difficult with an audience." He avoided the low pipe, and led Susan through the door. They walked back up the steep stairs to ground level.

Thea hesitated. The impulse went against her inclinations. Yet, she yearned. Perhaps at this time of day . . .

She emerged from the Bentley dressed in a long black gown. Her instructions to the hired driver were concise. At this one hour, of this one day of the week, people would be scarcest. Workers were homeward bound. Businessmen imbibed at their favorite cocktail lounge. The busloads of children had disappeared with late afternoon.

She looked up at the gray modernistic building that was the Denver Art Museum. It resembled a twentieth-century interpretation of the Bastille. She tilted her head to one side. The forbidding structure appeared designed to imprison beauty, rather than shelter it.

She entered with a casual manner, head high, and passed the registration desk. A guard, then a receptionist, looked up—fascination showing on their faces. Good, evil, wisdom, and folly all worship at the altar of beauty, and Thea Markidian was beauty's very archetype.

She stepped off the elevator at the correct level, discovered to her satisfaction that she was alone on the floor.

She did not permit herself a smile at the familiar objects. Instead, she closed her eyes and swept the years away. Once, her slender hand reached out and touched a cold Plexiglas case that protected the relics. Under it was a small alabaster unguent jar, the type given to ladies of the royal court.

She ignored a sarcophagus, ghoulishly displayed upright. Instead, she walked toward a small ebony-and-silver chair after assuring herself that there was no guard in the immediate vicinity to interrupt her. Thea unhooked the velvet restraining rope, let it drop to the floor. She sat down on the dais beside it, feet placed on the second step, and tightly clutched the tiny throne.

"Daughter, I will avenge thee."

Soon she rose and walked out, neck stiff, staring ahead with eyes like flint. She entered the waiting limousine, which instantly moved into the cloudy night.

"What have you brought this time?" Tyler asked sourly. A day's growth of beard made him look seedy.

Teldaris dumped the tray on the table. Silverware clattered.

Vern advanced toward the tray, hiding all anticipation of food. He threw the napkin aside in disgust.

"Sandwiches again?"

Jason remained nonchalant. "Pretend you're a martyr. The diversion should amuse you."

"Maybe I'll sneak out after dark and get some real food," Vern grumbled.

"Tyler, if you weren't Susan's brother, I'd knock your head off to see how far it would roll."

"I've had enough of this treatment—"

"You'll have to raise your tolerance level, because you're in for more." Teldaris leaned against a hissing radiator. It was hot, but not enough to make him move. "I brought you some magazines."

"The light's burnt out."

"You'll live."

"What makes you so goddamned high and mighty?" Teldaris didn't respond.

Vern had begun to doubt the wisdom of hiding out. He sorely missed a radio, television, and other comforts.

"You're up to something, Teldaris," he said.

"Astute."

"So, what's your share of the take, eh?" Vern took a bite into the ham sandwich.

"Is that *all* you've devoted your life to?" Jason moved, put one leg across a broken-down rocker.

"I look after myself." Tyler searched on the tray. "No mayo?" He frowned.

"Not on rye. There's the mustard. Quit complaining. It's all free to you, which should make it more palatable."

"Needs will out," Vern mumbled through another mouthful. "You've never needed anything. This building, that apartment upstairs. You don't know what it's like to go hungry, or be without."

"And you do?"

"No, but I've learned that if you don't take what you want, somebody else will."

"Spare me your justifications. They got you into this mess."

"This beer is warm."

"Pretend you're in Liverpool," Jason whispered to himself. He watched Tyler wolf down the meal.

"Someday, when this is sorted out, I'll—"

"Find a good woman and settle down?"

"You enjoy being a prick, don't you?"

"At least I don't go around promising spiritual enlightenment while unbuttoning somebody's blouse."

Tyler nearly choked on his sandwich. "You bastard, how could you—"

"I've seen you give your female members the eye. I noted your act, but it was none of my business. Besides,

I felt it might be good for leverage someday. Today's the day."

"When Susan saw people quit your sessions, she assumed they were tired of being screwed financially. I knew they were tired of being screwed, period. Only, Janice was different, wasn't she? You two were having an affair, weren't you?"

"What do you want from me?" Tyler trembled.

"What do you have that I could possibly want?" Teldaris turned to go. "Nothing, except one very special scarab. Think about it."

"Sphinx is a sphinx is a sphinx," Jason muttered. He splashed cold water on his face, then checked his watch; it was late, but not late enough. He let the water dribble down his face onto the black turtlenecked sweater.

He walked to the living room, glanced out the corner window and switched off his desk lamp. He waited in the darkness. Tonight, he would watch. Tonight, he would possibly see.

Other forces now come into play, he thought, and settled back comfortably on a large pillow. Could he be any more ignorant? He chuckled in self-derision. All his actions had been based on a trail of crumbs. Cunningly placed crumbs, though, starting with Gail's last letter. His eyes narrowed further, and he silently swore as a thought struck him: How could he be sure it was his wife who'd written it? He'd accepted that on faith, not even taking the time to meticulously compare handwriting.

"A sphinx is an . . ." He stopped himself, leaned forward, squinted. A shadow passed below. He grabbed the binoculars, trained them, saw a dog sniffing near the curb. He drew back, fiddled with the glasses impatiently.

He closed his eyes, fought for self-discipline.

Teldaris rose, walked to his desk, and carefully removed

a silver knife from a hardwood case. He returned to the shutters, waiting, hoping that the watcher in black would appear tonight.

SIX

Ḳerḥ

WE SHALL PUT
AN END
TO THIS CLAMOR AND UNREST.
AND TO THOSE WHO HAVE NO FAITH,
LET THEM HAVE FAITH IN THEIR
FAITHLESSNESS.

—Hymn to Hat-shepsut,
   from *Shadow of Khufu*,
   Cecil Rupert-Lewis, 1894

TELDARIS CREPT DOWN THE BACK STAIRS, DETER-
mined. Tonight there would be two watchers in black.
He'd fastened the knife under the left sleeve of his leather
jacket. The shrubs against the brick alleyway divider pro-
vided perfect camouflage and an unobstructed view. The
stranger was overdue. He worried, for it was after three.

"Only thieves, murderers, and whores should be out at
this hour," he thought, huddled against the cold brick. He
shivered. The temperature had plunged.

He stilled his breathing as a shadow paused on the periphery of his vision. It seemed to glide directly ahead,
yet there was no discernible motion.

The figure became illuminated by a streetlamp's faint
light. Jason inhaled sharply. It was a woman. Grace in
black, he thought. She stood silhouetted, looked upward
to his apartment balcony, swaying in a patterned motion.

Teldaris experienced a tingle of recognition that he could not quite define.

"Women can be assassins, too," he told himself. He moved for a better view. The exposed stiletto edge scraped against the wall and caused the woman to start. She whirled away into the darkness.

Teldaris shot out from cover, forced himself not to call out. His only hope now lay in tracking. Once discovered, she might never return. His eyes caught a glimpse of cloth flying in the wind from the next alleyway. He headed toward it, but lost sight of her as he crossed the street.

Intuition caused him to turn around. Somehow the woman in black had maneuvered in a circle around him. She leapt toward a third alleyway. He followed, feeling an adrenal surge. Somewhere, a car motor started.

Scrambling across an abandoned dumpster, he saw a heavy-set woman in a nurse's uniform behind the wheel of a car. He looked around desperately, gasping in the thin air. Despite stamina built up from running, he had been outdistanced by his quarry.

Cursing, he went toward the car. The nurse saw his approach and drove off in fright.

Then, Teldaris saw the figure he sought. Reflections from the car's headlights had betrayed her. She was disappearing into the park several blocks ahead.

He bolted, and soon gained the extra speed he needed. He cut across the park on a seldom-used hiking trail, in time to see the figure vanish into a playground.

Against this eerie predawn backdrop, they were the only creatures that moved.

He took up position, crouched behind a slide.

She was several yards away. Tall, with a slender profile, she strolled evenly, unhurriedly, as if crossing a crowded room. He sprang soundlessly in her direction. She stopped, waiting.

Teldaris slowed down several feet from her, disconcerted by her sudden calm. She turned at his approach, and all his thoughts of violence evaporated. Her features were completely obscured by a thin veil, the kind worn by Middle Eastern women; he felt a surging shock of . . . recognition?

They regarded each other for long seconds.

As he was about to speak, she said softly, "No, not like this."

She tilted her head slightly and walked away.

He followed at a distance, and soon watched her enter a mansion off Sixth Avenue. He stood for some time, bewitched, feeling a heavy pressure against his chest and knowing with an absolute surety that meeting that strange black-draped woman had irrevocably changed his life. He worshipped her, though he hadn't seen her face.

Jason ignored the bell button and knocked firmly.

When no one answered, he pounded. In the half-light, he noted that willow blinds covered each window of the mansion.

Several moments later, the tiny call box opened.

"Go. It is not appropriate for you to be here," a voice warned in a clearly discernible whisper.

"I'm sorry if—"

"Leave. You are not ready."

"Now, listen . . ." He leaned closer, caught an aroma of jasmine and a glimpse of well-formed lips.

"Please go." The call box latched shut.

Jason unleashed another battery of knocks.

The door flew open, revealing a striking Oriental woman dressed in a fawn-colored robe.

"It is small of you to persist at this hour." The voice was now another's, a woman's, issuing from farther within.

He waited, arms folded.

The woman nodded slightly as she turned back to him.

"Enter. I am at your service, as before."

* * *

Teldaris stepped across the threshold onto a green Persian rug. The woman beckoned to him. The tranquil expression on her high-cheekboned features bore no trace of her initial disquietude, but her manner definitely did not invite familiarity. He followed her quietly and allowed himself to be seated in a huge room off the entrance.

Exotic scents teased his nose. Some seemed to stir deep and emotional, yet undefined, responses within him. His nostrils guessed, while his eyes explored the room. Works of art, apparently authentic, stood or hung everywhere. En masse, they expressed no single theme save one—beauty.

"I am Joy." The woman interrupted his perusal.

"Do I know you?" he asked, though the question was ridiculous. Anyone would remember such a woman.

"Perchance you do."

When he got no more by way of a reply, Teldaris decided on a different approach. "Was it you I followed here?" he asked, in spite of his certainty that she was not. "Why did you run away?"

Joy's facade of calm broke when she smiled, revealing not only mirth but warmth as well.

"I do not run, Master," she said. "I pursue. You followed my lady."

"Why do you call me that?" he demanded.

"Master? That is what you are to me, though you know it not."

"I've never seen you before in my life!"

"Literally, you speak the truth. Qualitatively, however, you know me well. I am there, in your soul."

"You act as if you had been expecting me," he said, nonplussed as much by her attitude as by her words.

"We have." She bowed slightly from the waist, then straightened. "I shall return shortly."

He watched her go. An inner voice urged him to leave

quickly, to run away from this place before he was inextricably caught, netted like a fish. But, he knew he would not go, indeed, could not. Not yet. He rose and walked around, studying the room and its contents. The sculpture and paintings were fine enough to distract him. He noticed still lifes and landscapes but no portraiture, until he discovered a recess, a shallow alcove set into the wall.

There, framed by an arch, was the portrait of a standing woman. Black hair about bare shoulders, she was dressed in folds of eggshell-colored material. Olive eyes gazed out and caught him. Jason's senses reeled at her loveliness, and at something else. He felt he *knew* her. He shuddered, a sudden fear passing through him. He returned to his seat.

Joy reappeared soon and offered him a small round cup in which ice tinkled.

"Who is she? The woman in the painting?" he demanded.

"She is Mistress. You will meet her tomorrow, when you return. Here, drink this. It will help you regain your . . . self." There was just the slightest twinkling in her eyes.

"What's in it?" He regarded the cup suspiciously.

"There are no English names for some of the ingredients. Drink quickly. You must leave."

Teldaris sipped the drugged beverage compliantly.

Jason fought to keep heavy eyelids open. *Shadow of Khufu* fell from his hand. Groggily, he retrieved it.

> Thut-mose III was quite young at the death of his father. His throne was usurped by his powerful aunt and stepmother, the remarkable Hat-shepsut, who believed her claim to rule was stronger.
> The struggle for the rule of Egypt culminated in an intense rivalry between Hat-shepsut and her

nephew. The young man was held isolated, in total eclipse for the first two decades of his life, until his abrupt emergence. Hat-shepsut earned her nephew's undying hatred by her scorn of him.

Hat-shepsut delivered internal glories to Egypt, not external conquest. The beautiful Deir el-Bahri temple was built at her command. It is highly significant that her favourite, Sen-Mut, was Minister of Public Works and Architect.

Her end came suddenly, unexpectedly, after seventeen years as the first woman to successfully rule over Egypt. Precisely what happened is unknown. The coup d'état seized power, it is suspected, with the aid of the fickle priesthood of Amon. Evidence of the vindictive fury of her nephew, how-ever, is clear. His followers stormed into the Deir el-Bahri temple, toppled the statues of Hat-shepsut, and sent them tumbling into a near-by quarry. Her monument inscriptions were chiselled away by her wrathful successor. Sen-Mut, the architect, vanished from history. The disappearance of the party of peace was abrupt and violent.

The book fell into his lap, and Teldaris slipped into deep sleep.

And the dream ran on. It rolled out before him, instructing him, cajoling him, hurting him, and changing him. The woman Joy appeared out of a misty embankment and told him of the drug she had twice administered— once, some days ago in an orange, and again in the herbal tea he had quaffed. Teldaris nodded, having suspected as much, and dismissed her with a gentle wave. He was otherwise occupied, did not have time for her confession. The dream rolled on before him, waiting for him to enter, at any point he chose. Would he choose the delightful beginning, the bountiful middle years, or the frightful end?

"Nay, my love. Think not so. Choose what thou wilt,

but know this. There is no end. Thou seest but a mote in the eternal circle. Look beyond thy pain. See? The tale continues.''

The voice faded slowly away, like an exorcised aural spirit. He grasped for it, but it was gone. As always, her voice eluded him.

Meanwhile, the dream waited patiently. It flowed streamlike past him. He entered. And immediately became more alert. More vital. More awake.

Olive eyes stared at him from beneath lush black lashes. He sat across the short table from her and drank ruby redness from his silver wine cup. She followed suit, emptying a gold-chased goblet. She laughed, and the tinkling, merry sound filled the room, echoed through stone corridors, and passed out into the dusty streets. Her laughter could have filled and made joyous the entire world.

He left the dream there, with the sound of her gaiety dancing in his ears. It was as if, in a waking memory, one could say, "Stop. There. This is the perfect ending. Go no further.''

Thusly, he controlled the dream as he departed and reentered it, making it into a series of lyric vignettes. Like jewels on a chain, they touched at certain points, fusing parts into a whole. Yet, each vignette retained its identity.

In one randomly chosen jewel-story, he found himself frustrated. His daughter played before him. The ball she tossed to a nurse was vividly green. She laughed, missed the return catch and scrambled after it with the charmed lack of grace possessed only by five-year-olds.

But she pointedly refused to look at him, understanding with infallible infantile slyness that her evasion would wound him deeply. He sighed, looked between his bare knees at the paving stones of the courtyard. Idly, he thought they were becoming worn, should be repolished or replaced.

A cool hand was laid on his shoulder. "Give her time,

my love. She is too young to understand the depth of responsibility placed upon you, and upon me.''

He nodded in agreement, but the pain of his frustration did not lessen.

So, the dreams rolled on. He had tasted, had lived, and remembered them all. Though her voice had admonished him for thinking of endings, of climaxes, it still seemed to him that the coldness and stiffness of death, after all, did have a certain finality.

Briefly, he wondered when he would be strong enough to carry these dreamscapes back with him into the waking world.

Sixteen hours later, Teldaris awoke.

An eye gazed out at his face. The brass call box slammed shut and Joy opened the front door.

"You should have returned yesterday."

Her scolding tone worsened his already dark mood; he still felt a slow burn over having slept the day away.

"That was hardly my fault, now, was it? Perhaps you should be more careful about the drugs you administer in your tea."

A quick start of surprise passed over her features, then she nodded once and beckoned to him. Teldaris followed her inside warily. The instant he had stepped onto the mansion grounds, he had experienced the certainty of being watched. The sensation would not leave him, but it could not compel him to depart this place. Not until he met the woman in the painting. Not until he heard from her own lips *why* she watched him at night. He felt with instinctual surety that here he would find answers to many questions. It was against his nature to turn away the opportunity.

"Thanks for the book you sent," he said, deciding to go on the offensive early. "*Shadow of Khufu.* It was you who sent it, I assume. How did you know I enjoy histories?''

Joy smiled. ''Play no games with me—I was never a cloistered mama-san, Master, never naive, regardless of how I appear.''

''Don't call me that. I don't know what you mean by it, but I don't like it.''

''It would be improper to address you otherwise.''

''Then you will be improper or I will leave. Now.'' He hoped the bluff would work, for he had no such intention.

Her face flushed. Teldaris guessed that embarrassment was not often experienced by this woman. Joy's next words confirmed his suspicion.

''I will tell you something,'' she said. ''There is but one other who walks this earth with the ability to so casually disconcert me. I should have expected this, but in truth, I did not. Please go easily until I have adjusted, Ma—''

''My name is Jason Teldaris—'' he began.

''Born on June thirteenth, to be precise, at St. Thomas, on the Virgin Islands, during a violent electrical storm.''

''How do you know that?'' he demanded.

''I know more about you than *you* know.''

''How?''

She searched his eyes before replying.

''The answers lie within, next to the questions.''

Sunlight threw filtered shadows across the foyer. It was late afternoon, almost dusk. There stirred in him a strong urge to relax, but he submerged the desire.

Joy walked to a serving table and returned with an already poured glass of iced tea. He shook his head, refusing the drink.

''You were expecting me?'' he asked.

''For a long, long time.'' A woman appeared beside him, the woman in the portrait. Jason had succeeded in convincing himself that his memory had failed him, that her beauty as painted had not been so superlative. The living reality of her destroyed the pretense.

"Come." She held out a hand.

He stepped forward to greet her, then stopped himself. The effect was a lurching halt.

"My love, the waiting is over. There can be no breach of formality between us. Be comforted. Come to me." Her perfectly formed hand waited.

"Who are you?" he asked huskily, unable to meet her eyes.

She lowered her hand gradually. A slight frown shadowed her mouth. "You are changed."

"Are you the watcher in black? The one who waits, who watches my home late at night? Every night?" he asked, still unwilling to drink in her beauty in its fullness, understanding that if he did, he might lose control, might . . .

He further averted his gaze.

"Ah, that." Relief swept over her features. "It was shyness over my affection. Do not be embarrassed. It is . . . that I missed you so. A glimpse of you, a sight my soul demanded . . ."

Teldaris faced her now, eyes blazing. For a moment, her physical faultlessness caught him unawares. She was passion personified. A pale gown draped over her figure made her almost too magnetic. Her long black hair flashed in the dying sunlight.

"After so long an interval, his reaction to you is . . ." Joy attempted to save the awkward moment. Till now, she had remained quiet, thinking silence served better than interruption.

"He has a tongue." Thea smiled. "Why do you use yours in commentary?"

Joy's gaze fell. She stepped back.

Anger raced through Teldaris. "Who *are* you? Why were you watching me? What do you want?"

"Does not your heart know its own rhythm? I am Thea,

once a queen, as you are Jason, once my husband. Know this: a man, whether nameless or much-named, is yet a man. And, to every man born of this earth, there is a woman. Striving, they become one. As one, they are whole. Though they be separated for millennia, they will meet again, will know the other as part of that whole. Are your legs not my legs, are your arms not my limbs, does your soul not answer mine?"

He retreated one step, then paused, held by her eyes; made breathless as though by some great exertion. She was evidently, patently insane. And irresistible. He could not leave her until she wished him to.

They were seated in a great room, serene with soft water sounds.

"Perhaps I, too, practice self-deception," she said candidly. "There are no boundaries on foolishness."

Teldaris nodded, not drinking any of the rose-colored liquid poured by Joy. No quick or easy answers would come from this woman. So, he bided his time, patiently waiting for her story to unfold.

"I was born in my father's house just outside . . . you call it Istanbul. I was named Thea Markidian."

"You don't look Turkish," he offered, deliberately inane.

She laughed lightly. "My mother was Greek, my father Armenian. My name means shining."

"Jason means—"

"Healer," she completed. "Of old wounds."

"How did you know that?" he questioned.

"I know you," she said simply.

"I don't believe that. Granted, you and she"—he nodded toward where Joy stood waiting—"seem to know a great deal about me. I'm beginning to understand that you *think* you know the depths of my soul, so I'll ask this question. How? Are you a mind reader? A clairvoyant?"

"American men pride themselves on brusqueness, do they not?"

"I consider candidness a virtue."

"Subtlety has its own merit." Thea smiled.

"I'm not here to learn your prejudices," he snapped.

Thea took this graciously. "Very well then. I was born with a caul. . . . The midwives took it to be of great significance."

"So I've read. Are you a telepath?"

"Not so much so as . . . as one with total prenatal recall. But, how curious that we sit here conversing as strangers! Of all the improbabilities that fate casts up, this is one I did not foresee. Do you truly not recognize me?"

"Prenatal recall," he sidetracked. "Are you saying you can remember past lifetimes?"

She looked at him with forbearance. "Yes," she replied softly.

"What did your father do?"

"Concerning what?"

"For a living, I mean. What was his profession?"

"Why should this interest you?" She shrugged. "He exported opium."

Jason's drink sloshed over the cup's side.

"The poppy, you know. His business was one of the world's largest."

He glanced around at the opulent furnishings. "So that's how . . ."

"Does the trivial intrigue you so?"

"Tell me—" he began.

"What is there to tell?"

"Why do you so often speak through rhetorical questions?"

"It is my manner," Thea answered.

"You indicated that you know . . . about my life?"

"Always, I knew there was you. No childish notions . . . conviction. Understand, I was born an old woman. I was never a babe, never a girl. I had no childhood. The body, yes. It was normal, it grew. But, never the soul, never the mind—they had never shrunk. I terrified my mother and the governessess. They believed me possessed. By the time I was four, my mother thought me a witch. How else could one so young know so much? But always, from birth, I remembered you. And, I knew where you would be born. That knowledge was certain."

"When others spoke of loneliness or doubt, I smiled. I knew you waited—for me."

Simultaneously embarrassed, electrified, and fearful, Teldaris tapped a cadence with his fingers. "This is impossible," he mumbled, unable to say anything else.

"Each morning I wakened knowing I was one day closer to meeting you. Years passed, and I hoped that by chance we would meet. How I studied every stranger's face! The deceptions did naught but mock me. When it is time, it will be time, I told myself." Thea looked away. "What a long journey the soul must make."

"Why did you—"

"Devotion imprisons us all."

"Is the sentence worthwhile?"

"This prisoner has not been left with that doubt. The one comfort of her certain waiting has been doubtlessness that the waiting would end in fulfillment. The only question is when."

"How . . . can you know that I'm the one you seek?" Teldaris asked.

"I . . . know."

"Are you certain?"

"I am unfamiliar with the undercurrents of your thoughts. Your manner is curious. Yet, you are you."

"What I'm saying is: could you have deluded yourself into believing—"

"Delusion! *You* speak of delusion? Are you not here, in front of me now?"

She fell silent, and sat for a moment in concentration.

"A chasm separates us that must be spanned. For me not to have considered this . . ." Her words trailed off.

"*Am* I the one?" he demanded loudly.

A quick look of impatience crossed her face. "Answer for yourself. Am I not the one whom you have always sought?"

He was stung by the backlash of his own question.

"Was it not I whom you dreamt of in the gray hours before dawn? Am I not familiar to you?"

He could not reply, for the only truthful answer was incredible. Teldaris stood, pushing the cane chair slowly back with his legs.

"When you gazed at the heavens of an evening and felt . . . somewhere, at that very moment I, too, stared, seeing the same moon—did not that knowledge overpower the night chill?"

"No," he lied, remembering many such nights. "No, it never did."

"Leave me. Leave this house," she ordered. "Your words are hurtful. Yet, I say this truly: you shall return to me. You shall return to me and you shall love me."

Joy stood by the opened front door. As he left, she whispered in his ear:

"The book. Study *Shadow of Khufu*. It is the story of your life and hers. Avoid the careless heart, Master. My lady has endured much. Do not now cause her pain, nor debase yourself. Heed your soul, for it speaks wisely. Your heritage is in your countenance. Mask it no longer."

Her words followed him down the walkway.

SEVEN

Ḥeḥ

AND TO THOSE OF US WHO KNOW,
OUR AMBASSADORS
—THE AMBASSADORS OF OUR KIND—
SHALL TRAVEL TO DISTANT LANDS
AND PEOPLES OF DIFFERENCE
WITH SILVERY SPEED
AND SHALL BE KNOWN BY THEIR
GOLDEN ONENESS.

—Hymn to Hat-shepsut, from
  Shadow of Khufu,
  Cecil Rupert-Lewis, 1894

"WHY?"

"He is uncertain."

"That is not sufficient."

Joy hesitated under the intense scrutiny.

"There . . . appears to be another."

"Do you no longer wish to serve me?"

Joy looked up. "With all my fiber."

"Then why do you deceive me?"

"I shall always protect my lady."

"And cause more pain through the culmination of that protection?"

Thea's stare was unnerving, but Joy met it calmly.

"There *is* another."

Thea brushed her fingers against walnut wainscot. "Remember the corridor of figured marble? How it was done with such care?"

"Yes, Mistress."

"Fathers who began their carving would die, to have their places taken by their sons, then their sons' sons."

"It was built to last for all of time."

"Then why mold in sand?"

Joy paused a moment, then said, "He is a man. Waiting hurts too much."

"No."

Joy thought again.

"Fear of being is what frightens him," Thea whispered distantly.

"That is the most fantastic story I ever heard!" Susan drained the last of her wine. "Ever!" she added.

Jason smiled cynically. He signaled the passing waitress for their tab. The noise from the lunch crowd annoyed him.

"My treat." Susan snatched the ticket off the plastic tray. "It's not every day I get to hear stories about ancient Egyptian queens reincarnated into modern-day Istanbul."

"But—"

"The story was worth it." She smiled wickedly.

Jason wrinkled his forehead, unable to share her humor, unsure about why he had told Susan so quickly, so trustingly.

Flames erratically flickered from torches, despite sufficient pitch. Thea opened her ceremonial robe, revealing herself, and gazed upward. A large alabaster Isis rested on a draped altar. The faint play of light caused the statue's face to appear serene one moment, glowering the next.

Thea's voice echoed within the brick-lined chamber:

Death will come and take her swiftly now.
May the jackals rend her soft white throat.

May the eagles claw callous eyes from bloody sock-
ets.
Death will come and take her swiftly now.
May the lions smother a gasping mouth.
May the wolves shred apart splayed limbs.
May the hyenas feast upon stilled flesh.
Death will come and take her swiftly *now*!''

Thea closed her eyes, concentrated.

Susan drifted past the mountain lake. Dense fog swirled
off the shoreline. Shrouded peaks loomed nearby. Within
that fog, a blurred image agitated, an apparition that
frightened her. A spectral female thrashed several inches
above the waterline—haunted, demented, vengeful.
Alarmed, Susan tried to depart. She turned, but couldn't
move. She looked down and screamed. Her legs and feet
seemed rooted fast to the ground. The specter whirled
closer, she moaned for mercy. . . .

She woke from the nightmare and fumbled for the light
switch in agony. A terrible burning raged in her side. The
bedside clock read just past three. She tried to stand,
swayed against her nightstand, and knocked bottles,
brushes, and perfumes to the floor. A sweet aromatic mixture rose that sickened her further. She battled nausea.
Through the pain, one thought persevered: call Jason. A
foot into the hallway, she stumbled, fell to the floor.

Susan dragged herself toward the phone, elbows used
as crutches, while time itself seemed to still. Her long
negligee ensnared her numbed feet.

In the dining room, she collapsed entirely as her elbows
splayed. A soft hiss escaped from her lips. White and blue
bands of light streaked across her vision, punctuated by
scarlet. Susan knew that she must either stand up and walk,
or die. As through a haze, she stared in horror at her hands
as they bent before her into inflexible claws. Wildly, she

clutched at the closest chair. It tumbled over after she was partially raised. She grabbed a low corner of the tablecloth and tugged desperately, bringing china and pewter crashing to the floor. Onyx ornaments tumbled in all directions.

Her right hand unflexed of its own volition, crawled spiderlike to a small greenish object fallen among the cracked stone. She felt a warm pulsation shoot into her fingers, through her hand, past the wrist, up her arm. Her pain steadily diminished, displaced by a sense of lightness, of well-being. Abruptly, she lost all consciousness.

The torch blew out. Thea fingered a gold-handled knife and scowled. Seconds passed as she waited.

A roar thundered throughout the house, shaking the mansion with an earthquake's fury. Sounds of breaking glass and groaning wood came from the floors above. A frigid gust of wind howled upward from the basement. Thick plaster dust cascaded like volcanic ash.

Thea sat down, an island of calm amid the chaos.

Joy flew toward her, down the steps.

"Mistress!"

"I am thwarted," Thea said without emphasis.

"How is that possible?" Joy stared in horror: a thin trickle of blood ran from Thea's right ear.

"The scarab is dormant no longer," she replied slowly. "It is used against me."

Deborah was up to her elbows in soapy water, unwilling to trust the dishwasher with Janice's imported crystal. Tears over the memory of her sister still came easily and without warning. Evidence glared everywhere around her, silently accusing, of how she and Kevin had profited from the tragedy. The TV, stereo, Jan's furniture. It made her uncomfortable. They'd argued violently, but in the end, Kevin had won. Poor Bill, his mind given way, was in the state hospital down in Pueblo. None of this stuff was of any use to him.

Debbie gasped in surprise as Kevin hugged her from behind. A lusty growl purred from his throat.

"Kev, you're squeezing too tight!"

"Good morning to you, too." His hands fell away from her.

"Why . . . up so early?" she mumbled.

"Gotta make my second pickup today," he said on his way into the living room. He walked to the stereo, where he switched stations in disgust, and turned the volume higher.

"Great sound. That's one thing about Jan. She bought a good system."

His wife turned on him savagely. "Don't keep on about it!"

He looked surprised, then angry.

"Please, Kev, it still hurts."

Adderson shrugged coldly. "Look what it got you."

"What's that supposed to—"

"Nothing. Drop it, dandelion. What's to eat?"

"Kevin, stop playing with me! We need to talk, seriously, this morning." She stood in his path.

"Sure. Just fix me some breakfast first." He sideswiped her, sat in a director's chair, propped his feet on the table.

"Where did you get the money to buy this house? Are you some kind of courier?"

"You might say that." He laughed. "Go on."

"Go on?"

"Say it. Say what you're thinking."

She grimaced, then shuffled about the kitchen through cartons, straw, and shredded newspapers.

"Why don't you do something about this mess?" he said, goading her.

"Kevin, I left work at one in the morning, got five hours sleep, and was up again working. What more do you want?"

"Breakfast."

"When can I quit that job?"

"When I give the word."

"And when will that be?"

"Whenever."

"If you make enough money, doing whatever it is you're doing . . ."

"What I'm doing," he spat out, "is dealing." He slammed a fist on the table.

"In drugs?"

"No, I'm selling encyclopedias door-to-door."

"Kev, that's dangerous."

"Shitting can be dangerous."

"How did you—"

"That's my business! I'm into something a little higher up than hash."

"Why—"

"I've got plans that require money."

"Then why can't I stop bringing home all that—"

"Because our friends might not like it."

"Our friends?" she repeated.

"We never wanted you to get that job for the money," he snarled, "or have you forgotten?"

He walked back to the chair.

"Will I have to keep stealing that stuff forever?"

"No." He smiled blandly. "Just till we don't need you anymore."

Shafts of daylight played across Susan's face. Her eyelids fluttered. A dull throb reminded her of the life-and-death struggle. She felt ravenously hungry. She forced herself up. Her muscles ached mercilessly. She made her way slowly and stiffly to the kitchen, reminded of her one disastrous athletic attempt. Enrolling on the women's track team in college, she had quit after three days of hobbling to class.

Susan plugged in the percolator, surveyed the broken china and cracked onyx.

A thought struck her. Both hands trembled, as she remembered. On her hands and knees in the next room, she searched for what might only be a memory. Unable to locate the missing clue, she scratched the base of her neck in puzzlement and emitted a startled cry, pawed at the thing around her throat. But it wouldn't release its grasp.

She forced reluctant legs to run to the bedroom mirror, ignoring the broken glass that cut her feet. She gazed at her reflection in fear and wonder. A beautiful necklace hung around her neck. A green scarab flecked with gold was centered prominently against her collarbone. Barely inhaling, she fiddled with the intricate clasp behind her neck. Long minutes of persistence passed before the ornament would be unfastened.

Tyler shoved his weight against the rounded coal door. A loud metallic creak told him that the rusted hinges were about to give. He rubbed his shoulder, in pain. He glanced at his watch. A half hour before noon, which meant that he'd been working on the door just over two hours. Yet, he'd come this far . . .

He rammed against the boiler-room door again.

Oktoberfest tourists noticed nothing distinguishing about the seedy-looking man who hurried down the sidewalk. It was the elaborate festival that seemed out of place, just several blocks away from the gathering place of winos, street punks, and runaways. The man looked as if he belonged there.

The matronly bookshop owner immediately recognized him.

"You're the last person I expected to see," she said with open hostility.

"Am I welcome?" Tyler ventured.

"Is this some joke? Why are you here!"

"Maybe to do a little business. . . . " He paused, disconcerted by her attitude. "Like old times."

"A time before you decided to discredit the Denver metaphysical community?"

"What the devil are you talking about?"

"Precisely, Mr. Tyler."

"What, I don't . . . ," Vern mumbled.

The store owner recognized his bewilderment and lowered her voice.

"Don't you bother to read the papers?"

"I've been . . . on retreat. Meditative retreat," he faltered.

She disappeared behind a curtain of beads. Soon she returned, bearing a crumpled newspaper that she handed to him without comment. He steadied his hands and began to read the circled article.

"It's . . . it's about Betty," he stuttered. "And me!" He flipped the paper over, checked the date. He recalled the morning of Betty's death. During the battle to save his own neck, he hadn't given her much thought. "I've been away, out of touch . . . ," he said lamely.

"Why didn't you demand an immediate retraction? Your silence only served to substantiate this story. How could you destroy in a day what's taken us years to build up?"

"But, listen to this," he moaned, "it's crazy."

"No, I've had enough of it." She watered plants with a copper teapot.

"The article says that she gave the interview just days before her death, that the reporter didn't take it seriously until she was killed. How could she have said these things!"

Tyler leaned against a wicker basket crammed with used paperbacks, reading. "Devil worship, black magic, Oriental mystics buying up half the city. This is nonsense!" he protested. "Who would believe it?"

"The pulpit, the press, and the politicians." She went past him, en route for more water.

"I never said any of this! Not a damned word, I swear!"

"She was a member of your study group. You were at least partly responsible for what she said. By not speaking up, you gave her interview credence." Her eyes bulged indignantly.

Tyler gulped, set the paper down on the counter slowly. Her look shamed him.

"This was the busiest alternative bookstore in the city." She pointed to a cluster of empty chairs grouped around a Franklin fireplace. "Not any longer. A lot of people are leery about coming in. This could force some of us out of business."

"Do any of my old friends—"

"You don't have a single friend left in this community," she snapped. "You're an outcast now."

"Why, for god's sake! Because of one damned article?" She looked at him in disgust.

"There is something . . ."

"No one will even listen to you," she stated darkly, and leaned forward.

"One last thing—" Tyler mumbled as he rose wearily.

"I will listen this once, because I've known you many years."

"I need money. . . . "

"Please leave," the store owner said tightly, "before I forget myself."

"Please! Could you loan me a couple hundred bucks? Just enough to get—"

"Get out of my sight!" She came toward him with a rheumatic gait. He fled from the store, ducked into an alleyway, and ran.

Susan was picking fragments of glass from her instep when she paused, an uneasy feeling having overcome her.

She thought of Jason, put aside the tweezers, and hopped to her bedroom on one slippered foot.

She dialed his number, but there was no answer.

Twenty minutes later, she rushed down her apartment stairs to the Renault parked on the street below. Her right hand was clenched into a fist.

Tyler walked swiftly through the maze of back alleys and parking lots off East Colfax Avenue. He cut across the yard of an old brownstone being demolished, stumbled over a pile of bricks and lumber, and paused to rest on what was left of a back porch.

His breathing stilled when he sensed a movement. A moment later he heard soft footsteps. A shadow appeared.

Tyler turned with a jerk, panic flashing across his face. Directly above him, swinging a benailed lumber stud, was a man he had never wanted to see again.

"Hello, Vernon," Kevin Adderson said politely.

Tyler gagged as a muscled hand grabbed the nape of his neck and dragged him backward into the rubble. Before he could cry out, a leg swung across his chest and he was straddled.

"How about a little game of sorry?"

"I'm . . . sorry . . ." Tyler managed to choke out.

"No, that's not how it's played." His hands tightened their grip. Where a signet ring was reversed on Adderson's right forefinger, the *A* pressed into Vern's chin.

Tyler blinked, schemed, sought a quick way out. "What do you mean?"

"You know damn well!" Adderson exploded.

Tyler heaved himself upward in a desperate attempt to dislodge the younger man. A hard thrust by Adderson into his abdomen stilled the resistance. Tyler's eyes watered.

"Get off me!" he rasped.

Kevin complied, convinced Tyler wouldn't try to run.

Adderson leaned against a surviving porch pillar and looked down at him.

"Why the hell—"

Adderson responded with a sharp kick to the ankle. Tyler winced and attempted to rise, but changed his mind. Kevin grinned.

"We don't like to be ignored, Tyler."

"What?"

"I thought once or twice would be enough. Didn't Betty's little sexual rendezvous seem more than coincidence to you?"

"You *can't* be behind all this. I saw you acting like a scared rabbit down at police headquarters after Janice—"

"You're right. I *was* acting. Didn't you get my note? I left it in plain view right there on the table."

Tyler blinked in surprise.

"How . . . did . . ."

Adderson leaned toward the still-prone man.

"It can't be . . . that would mean—" Tyler wiped sweat from his lower lip, whispering, "No. You wouldn't kill your own sister-in-law."

Tyler closed his eyes. His mind reeled. Could he get the police to believe him? Could he explain . . .

"Why kill my cat?" he protested.

A blow to his mouth silenced him.

"Shut up, fool!" Adderson hissed. Tyler touched his bleeding lip. A facial muscle twitched.

"No," Kevin surmised, "don't hope a chat with the Denver Police Department will do you any good." Vern spat blood, but said nothing. "We both know. The whole town's crying for someone to pin five murders on, and you're ripe for nomination. Will they believe you? Make them believe I killed your cat, executed my nephew, niece, my own wife's sister, plus a harmless old broad. What was my motive?"

Tyler's hope sank.

Kevin lowered his voice. "No, it wouldn't be to your advantage."

Tyler attempted to rise. Adderson leaped upon him. He pulled a revolver from a corduroy coat pocket and placed it directly against Tyler's left temple. Tyler's head jerked in reaction to the steely coldness.

"I could kill you on the spot and never be caught."

Seeing the look on Adderson's face, Tyler recognized the expression of a seasoned killer.

"You listen, I talk. I propose, you agree. It saves time. I have an appointment elsewhere." Adderson glanced at the sinking sun.

Tyler nodded dumbly.

"Give me the scarab. I'll get you out of town safely. Simple?"

"How much . . . ," Tyler whispered.

"Not a damned cent. Your life is your payment."

"I don't trust you. I won't do it."

"I never said you had to." Kevin bent forward, gripped the gun tighter. "Good-bye, Vernon."

"Stop!" Tyler issued a high-pitched cry.

Adderson waited.

"Where will I go? What guarantee do I have?"

"No guarantees, except my word."

"I . . . I'm—" Tyler's voice wavered.

"The scarab?"

"It's yours." He sighed in resignation.

Adderson stood, removing the gun from beside Tyler's head. He waved it to indicate that Vern could rise.

"By midnight." Adderson brushed himself off.

"Where?"

"Your place," Adderson said coldly. He wound his way through the rubble. "Don't renege, or you'll regret it," he warned.

"It's yours, I said."

Adderson disappeared down an alleyway without a

backward glance. Tyler growled between clenched teeth, "Like hell it's yours."

Susan knocked at Jason's door twice. When there was no response, she bit her lip. Then, the sound of a man's laughter penetrated past the wood. She recognized the voice.

She felt foolish and decided to leave. But before she could retrace her steps down the stairs, the door swung open.

"Sorry for the delay . . ." Teldaris began casually; he broke off when he saw the look on her face.

"I didn't . . ." Susan was at a loss for words.

"Caught me, didn't you?" he said with wry amusement.

For an instant, she stared dumbly at his bare chest.

"Mean to intrude," she completed.

"You didn't." He opened the door wider.

Susan entered, taking rueful note of her rumpled appearance as she passed a hallway mirror.

"Isn't it a little cold to be wandering around without a coat?" Jason pulled a velour sweatshirt over his head. His last words were muffled.

Susan shrugged, dismissing the subject. Now that she was here, she felt very foolish. Jason was obviously all right—her feelings of unease concerning him had been proved patently false. He was just fine. Oh, god, she thought, am I becoming an hysterical old broad? The sound of another laugh interrupted her thoughts.

"Sorry . . . I'm an addict. Those guys break me up." Black and white images of two slapstick comedians flickered from a small screen. He clicked off the set and shut the cupboard that hid the television from view.

"A little diversion," he mumbled as he kicked some exercise equipment aside.

Vaudeville comedy? Susan wrinkled her forehead at this

other facet of the man, uncertain if she was disappointed or relieved.

"Susan, are you all right?"

"Why . . . uh . . . yes." She indicated two wet towels on the carpeting. "But what about you?"

Jason patted his waistline. "Nothing a little less gluttony wouldn't fix." He saw her shiver. "Come sit down. I'll get us some coffee and start a fire." He drew her toward a radiator, then enroute to the kitchen, pulled a pair of jeans over his shorts.

"Don't go to any bother," she whispered.

"Too late, I've already bothered," he said. Soon he handed her a steaming earthenware mug. He watched her relish the warmth of the coffee. "Hungry?"

She shook her head.

"Too bad. I am, so you'll just have to watch me eat." He smiled.

"What about that waistline?" she chided.

"Did I mention I was also a glutton for punishment?" he called.

"I wonder about exercise fanatics."

"I'm fanatic for one thing only—a good life," he reassured her, returning with a tray laden with food.

Susan saw there was enough for two.

He crumpled newspapers with one hand, reached for kindling with the other.

The fire crackled. A wave of heat pulled her toward the flames. She held her fingers close to the fire.

Jason took her hands in his. "Here, let me warm them up." She pulled back in reflex, but his grip was too strong.

"They're ice cold," he said softly, and rubbed his hands over hers.

There's magic in those fingers, she thought.

"You should have been a pianist."

He appeared to be puzzled.

"The spread of your hand. The length of your fingers."

She examined his palms, then his fingertips. "There, see? Not stubby, like a workman's."

Jason stood. "Well, you can see I was never a laborer. Or anything else, for that matter."

Susan felt she'd pinched a nerve again.

"Dish up. I'll get more flames going."

Susan did so, bemused by the undercurrents-within-crosscurrents of their relationship.

"You look a million miles away," she offered at length.

Jason rose distractedly. "I forgot the napkins. Sorry."

He returned shortly, frowning. "I'll have to fire the maid. Look at this place." He tossed several large cushions from the brown sectional beside the marble hearth.

"Who's your maid? Not you, I hope." Susan smiled as he nodded. "You should see Vern's place—Vern!" She dropped a cracker. "My god, I forgot about Vern."

"So did I." He opened a cheese crock, then settled comfortably atop a large cushion. "By the way, did I tell you he's disappeared?"

"What!" She rose quickly, crossed to an antique secretary, set the tray down in agitation.

"Don't worry, he's probably on the prowl."

Susan looked askance. "What do you mean?"

"Nothing . . . simply that—"

"Jason, what did you mean by that?"

"Vern's probably getting some fresh air. After all, he's been cooped up for nearly a week. It's almost dark, so he should be okay."

"What if something happened to him?"

"You should be so lucky."

"You're glib today."

"Practice."

"We should have locked him in." She fidgeted.

"I did. He got out anyway." Jason propped himself up on the pillows.

"How?"

"Quit worrying about him. Help me over here. This is

uncomfortable as hell.'' He squirmed, scattering pillows about.

She arranged a bolster behind his back, then settled down next to him.

Jason turned his head upward, and squinted. The skylight reflected dull gray.

"Are those snow clouds coming up?" he asked.

She didn't bother to look. "In October in Denver, all clouds can be snow clouds."

"And we never went back to see the aspen turn," he said with a touch of sadness.

"Don't say it like that!"

He seemed surprised at her harsh tone.

"Like what?"

"With such . . . finality. There's always next year, and the next. They change quickly, but always come back. Always." She ended forcefully.

"Right. There's always tomorrow."

"Don't be so callous. Cynicism should be reserved for the old."

"Lately, I've given little consideration about tomorrows. Yesterdays have filled my time."

"Will you be here next year to see the aspen?" she asked slowly, hating herself for the question.

He looked at her openly. "No."

"I probably won't he here either," she lied.

He watched her solemnly. She moved back, leaned against the side of a leather wingback. "Who am I kidding? I'll probably be found dead in that farty little apartment, killed by varicose veins or senility or—"

"You know what I thought?" he asked.

"You know what I hate?" she interrupted. "It's the thought of dying alone, and not being found for eight or nine days, until the smell prompts the landlord to . . ." She shuddered at the private phantom.

"I thought you might be more comfortable on the beach this winter."

"What?" She looked confused.

"I've never told you, but I have a little beach house on St. Croix. I think you'd like it."

"That . . . sounds . . . like a pro—" She broke off before finishing.

"Don't get carried away, it's not." The sharpness of the words was diminished by the gentleness of his tone.

She stiffened. "I don't like games like this."

"No games. I'm sincere. There's nothing in this world like Thanksgiving Day dinner on the beach."

"What?" She laughed in spite of herself. "Cook a turkey on an open spit? No thanks."

"Who's talking turkey?" He laughed. "Pun intended. I'm talking about warm champagne, cold hot dogs, and sandy French fries. Plus laughing at all the suckers spinning in the snow on the way to grandma's."

She fought a chuckle. "You're incredible."

"Of course I am," he jibed. "C'mon, how about it? This mess should be cleared up by then. I'll even spring for the bubbles and paper straws."

She smiled at the image.

"Therapeutic, eh?"

Susan reached for a slice of roast beef.

"What about it?" he pressed.

"Okay, Jason." She smiled thinly. "You've made your point. Drop it, don't spoil it."

"Spoil it?" He frowned. She avoided his eyes.

"You've done your part not to make me feel like the inevitable spinster. It was sweet and considerate. Now, what about Vern? . . ."

Jason took her wrist, held it firmly. The skin was smooth. "I meant it."

She waited for some moments. "Yes," she said finally, "I really think you do."

"Come stay with me on the beach. Please."

"I wasn't brought up that way." She glanced away.

"I know you weren't. That's all the more reason you should do it: because you want to."

She struggled out of his grasp.

"You know better than to wriggle out that way. It won't work."

"No." She gave him a determined stare.

"What harm could there be when you toast with Mickey Mouse straws?"

He pulled her down to the cushions with both arms.

"Quit fighting me, Susan."

"Jason, I hardly know you."

"So?"

"Jason, I'm different—"

"Ah, I know," he said, "you don't know how to swim, do you?"

"What's that got to do with anything?"

"You're embarrassed that I can body surf and you can't. Don't worry, I'll buy a life jacket and drag you along."

She smiled. "Jason, I may not look the same to you on a beach as I do here."

"Then I'll rent a kayak, tie you down, and steer you into the westward waves. You'll end up in Galveston just in time for Splash Day."

"Jason—"

"I mean it."

"Why now?"

He thought. "Because I didn't think of it before."

"That's the trouble," Susan said, rising. "I did."

"Then you should have started surfing lessons." He smiled, and pulled her down again.

"What are you doing?"

"Taking off my pants." He loosened the top button of his jeans.

"What do you think's going to happen when you do?" she demanded.

He planted a soft kiss on her lips. "Let's find out."

EIGHT

Mảu

WE SHALL EXPLORE
THOSE POSSIBILITIES
HERETOFORE UNKNOWN TO MAN
AND SEARCH AREAS WHERE
DARKNESS IS BOTH THE DAY AND THE
NIGHT.

—Hymn to Hat-shepsut,
  from *Shadow of Khufu*,
  Cecil Rupert-Lewis, 1894

TYLER FRANTICALLY SEARCHED THROUGH HIS SISTER'S apartment, but the scarab was gone.

Rage spurred by terror produced in him an alloy of viciousness. He pulled out drawers, thrashed through closets, upended anything which might conceal the necklace. He smashed china to bits, broke book spines, and shredded clothing with a long carving knife.

"You stealing bitch, where *is* it?" he yelled as he slashed a long jagged cut on a prized tabletop.

Soon, his energy was spent and he sank to the floor in despair, feeling that his life was slipping through his fingers. Drowsiness soon overtook him. He leaned his head against an overturned bookcase. If Susan entered, he'd make her talk, she'd see . . .

Tyler nodded off, failing to notice the faint odor of gasoline that slowly entered the room.

* * *

Dusk settled hazily on the city—a dismal, polluted contrast to the morning's autumn crispness.

Joy's drab coverall blended well, matching the grayness of the hour. She worked quietly, expertly. Critical areas were thoroughly dowsed. The building's fire alarm sounded minutes after she lit the first match. A second spark produced a racing stream of flame, making an L-shaped run for the ceiling. The first residents wandered out in annoyance, then panicked. She left the building without undue haste, past a jostle of excited people, a billow of smoke enabling her to disappear easily.

Assuming the fire department was up to form, all residents would be safe, except for the occupant of one apartment. For that one, there would be no avenue of escape, Joy had made sure of that.

Several minutes later, Tyler roused reluctantly. Bells and commotion ricocheted from sleep's edge. His eyes opened, and he instantly smelled smoke; a thin layer drifted through the apartment. He jumped to his feet, now fully alert, and rushed for the door.

Muffled shouts and cries echoed from the corridor. Through the peephole, he saw only a smokey orange tint. He struggled to open the door, but discovered it was sealed shut. He knelt and ran his fingers against the sill, and felt a caulk-like adhesive that had seeped around the edges of the door. Evidently, it had been applied from outside— from the hallway—some time before, for it was now rock hard. He straightened, backed up, then rammed forcefully against the reinforced metal door. He thudded against it uselessly. Tyler ran to the bath, soaked a hand towel in cold water, put it against his face. There was only one entrance to these apartments, he remembered in panic, and the narrow, chest-high windows ran horizontally along the walls, with no ledge or balcony.

He cast a last frantic glance around the room for the scarab, but screams and hoarse yells of other tenants jolted his mind back to his predicament. The apartment was filling rapidly with smoke. Somewhere, he heard a window shatter.

He yanked Susan's multi-colored afghan off the wall, snatched up a small braided rug, then pulled down her drapes. He looked at the narrow windowpanes, then, in dismay, at his wide hips.

He fashioned the items into the strongest knots possible. How strange, he reflected, winding the liferope around his waist—if Sue had been caught in here, she would've perished sooner than abuse her property as he was doing. He smashed the largest window with a brass floor lamp. Smoke stung his eyes, he coughed and wheezed at each breath. Any thought of finding the scarab was abandoned. He concentrated on squeezing his frame through the window. Halfway through, he stuck on a long sliver of glass, but couldn't release his grasp to dislodge it. Tyler closed his eyes and pushed, moaning in agony as the glass cut into his side. The moment he cleared the window, the lifeline tore under his weight.

She awakened with a smile. She paused only a moment, for the sensation's betterment. Her left hand crossed her right over a bare breast. The hand was still asleep, so she flexed it slowly, in wonder, then allowed it to fall limply upon the silk covers while she softly laughed. She arose, as if emerging from a golden lagoon. She walked as though she belonged to summer.

> She, cool possessor of uncompromised beauty,
> Server of nurture and delight,
> Teasing seducer,

Comforter,
She, bearer of promise,
She, emancipator, conqueror, lover, goddess,
She, soul-sharer . . . was Beauty.

Jason opened his eyes. A slow moment passed before a look of deep sadness settled into them.

Beside him lay Susan, nestled in his arms.

He turned his head to one side, as Beauty's song grew stronger.

"Forgive my weakness," he whispered to the sleeping figure.

The Bentley sped along a narrow street. The car went through red lights, made illegal turns, and rapidly executed a series of lane maneuvers. Eventually the car slowed, then idled. The headlights had been extinguished a block earlier. Joy emerged, wiping her hands against one another unconsciously.

He was there, at the prearranged place. She saw him walk toward her.

"Do not look at me!" she warned in a harsh voice.

"I wondered if you were—"

"Get behind that tree, your back toward me!"

"I meant no harm." He peered into the darkness, tried to distinguish some detail about her or the automobile.

"Do not attempt to pacify me—it will not be tolerated. Now, turn. Walk."

He did as bidden, then slowed, several paces ahead of her. The solitary elm stood as his mockery and his reward.

"I thought you might not come." He stopped, listened for her answer.

"You know the procedure."

He stood on one side of the huge tree. She leaned against the other, completely hidden from his sight.

"You doubted my arrival?"

"No, no . . . of course not." He seemed less subservient than in the past.

"Have you forgotten how to heel?"

He gulped.

"No, it's that—"

"I have no time for lies."

There was a pause as each maintained silence.

He sniffed the air, puzzled. Along with the usual scent of jasmine, there was another odor. A familiar one.

"Did you—"

"It is next to your left leg."

He glanced down in surprise. Somehow she had placed the package there without his detection.

"When do you . . . require payment?" he murmured, feeling the size of the parcel.

"When I present the bill."

"It's heavy."

"It is the finest yet."

"When . . . can we meet inside again?"

"Good-bye."

"One more thing . . ." He trailed off, realizing he spoke to himself. His head darted around the tree trunk in time to see a shadow climb into a darker shadow. The car pulled away in reverse, without headlights.

"Mistress, it is done." Joy resembled a tigress delivering flesh to her young.

Thea stretched with the lazy grace of a feline. She felt rested, refreshed. Joy related details as she listened in fascination.

"Now he is yours, with no distractions."

"This is wonderful." Thea rubbed the fingers of her left hand over the palm of her right. "Obvious, a trifle dramatic . . . but wonderful."

Joy smiled. "That which is weak, dies." She leaned

forward to pour a cup of minted tea. "I learned that from you long ago."

"What is to prevent him from selecting another?" Thea sipped the tea.

"He will not," Joy said reassuringly. "He has seen you."

Thea nodded absently.

"Is Mistress not pleased?"

"I fear he will not come to me of his own accord. Still, he must. I need him."

"He shall, Mistress. He shall be ready soon." Joy pondered. "Though he may recoil at the . . . tragedy . . . for a short while."

"I am troubled." Thea motioned for Joy to remove the tray.

"Mistress?"

"It perplexes me that you succeeded where I failed."

"My lady, I approached differently. A direct method that produced an immediate and . . . ," Joy colored, " . . . obvious effect."

"No, I understand my own complexities." Thea looked past Joy. "If the scarab protected her, then why did it not rebound similarly against you? Why did it maintain neutrality?"

"True . . . ," Joy considered.

"Unless it was not she whom you enflamed."

"This squabbling is undignified, without purpose," the leader said crossly.

"I challenge." Adderson calmly sat down, confidence bolstered by his meeting with Joy just hours ago.

"Your arrogant tricks won't work. I practiced them before you were born. I conversed with evil while you drooled at your mother's breast. I saw the Great Master while he was still alive."

"You're old, tired, and complacent. I have the hunger, plus the energy, to lead us."

The Circle observed Adderson with renewed interest. Glee lurked behind their impartial facades. Deborah feared the worst; she worried that Kevin had been too bold. She lingered over platters of sandwiches, eavesdropping from the kitchen.

"You speak through your loins." The leader dismissed him with contempt.

"Your mate hasn't even been tested," said a renowned physician.

"Today, I have means." Adderson addressed the mostly male gathering.

"We're not interested." The heir to a cattle empire swept his arms outward. "You were accepted when you were penniless. Your value wasn't measured in currency then, nor does talk impress us now."

Kevin surveyed the room. Wealth meant nothing here. A man whose great-grandfather built the first distillery in the state, a real estate impresario, and a Boulder city councilman were unlikely to be impressed.

"I speak of a thing greater than money. Something that I alone can obtain."

The doctor snickered, but said nothing.

"Why are we weak?" Adderson posed.

"Who says we are?" a portly woman demanded.

"We all know it."

"Answer yourself," the councilman ordered.

"Not enough power," Kevin replied.

"All things seek power," the leader said.

"All seek, seldom finding—"

"Because of the inherent dangers."

"Curse the dangers!" Kevin shouted.

Several of the younger members leaned forward, interested.

"Remember the case of the first Hermetic Lodge in Hampstead?" the woman asked, reminding them.

"Pandemonium broke out because they could not control the beast they created. They were afraid of their own power! Blind malice was their immediate end. Lack of foresight destroyed them, not the elemental they summoned."

"So what would you have done, had you been Algernon Blackwood?" The councilman had contempt in his voice.

"I would have protected my initiates with a power equal to that summoned."

Startled glances were exchanged at this.

"You need a lesson in humility, a good reminder against disrespect." One member stood, advanced slowly toward Kevin. Punishment within this group was immediate.

Deborah shrank in fear on the other side of the kitchen-counter shutters. She had seen several scars that spoke of older squabbles. She didn't dare enter the living room, not even for Kevin's sake.

"Our practices are diluted and weak, they are fit only for the old," Adderson goaded.

"You have gone too far. You will be punished," the leader pronounced. The atmosphere suddenly became electrically tense.

"Can you protect us with a power stronger than mine?"

"What power is yours, blasphemous child?" he snorted.

"The most powerful talisman of all."

"You have obtained it . . . where we failed?"

"Amon's Scarab."

Most were visibly affected. One man could not suppress an audible gasp.

The leader only flinched slightly. "Do not taunt us."

"I have seen it," Kevin bluffed.

"No. You lie." The tall member advanced another step.

"I shall produce the token by tomorrow's sunset. We will then perform works of discord and disharmony which have never been dreamt, protected by the scarab. We'll have the city at our feet, be feared and respected by those who've . . ." He paused significantly and sat back, af-

178

fecting a cool confidence lest his dry throat betray his nervousness.

Looks of doubt were exchanged.

"Only once can an initiate call a conclave. That you have done."

"A Supreme may convene us at any hour, any day. I do so tomorrow, at sunset."

The older ones looked at the wizened leader, who felt the pressure behind their stares. He *had* to accept the challenge, however much he resented this abrasive young upstart. On the other hand, if he wasn't lying . . . Years of scorn and derision would be reversed. A lusting beguiled its way into his thoughts. Their power would be checked.

"I challenge." Adderson forcefully interrupted his thoughts.

"I accept the challenge, Initiate. Be forewarned, however; deceit or failure is punished severely."

The tall one echoed, "Severely."

"And permanently if necessary," the old man added.

The others stared at Kevin for some minutes in silence, seeking to discover whether he was bluffing or not.

Adderson displayed a thin, mocking smile. Other "new ones" had not lived up to the expectations of the group. They had simply vanished. Their knowledge of the Circle had disappeared with them.

Jason stood before the ornate front door of the mansion. He continued to pound. In vain.

He *knew* Thea was in there. They were both inside. He could feel them watching him.

Teldaris thought of Susan. Was she still asleep, curled among floor pillows in exhausted slumber? He lowered his head. What would she think, if she saw him now? What *could* she think?

He cried. "Answer me!"

At last, when he could knock no longer, Teldaris turned

away and began the walk home. He stopped at the corner and saw the lights shining from the second-floor windows.

Joy glanced out the window. "Mistress, it seems so . . ."

"Cruel?" Thea's cheeks were indrawn.

Joy returned to watch. "He is gone," she said at length.

Thea relaxed, as though a powerful tranquilizer had taken effect. Her facial muscles performed a turnabout. Hardness vanished, and a cold goddess transformed into a serene beauty.

"Mistress, how will you know . . ."

" . . . if I don't see him?" Thea completed.

Joy nodded sadly.

"I will know when he is ready."

"More importantly, he will know himself when he is ready. Above all, he must *know* himself." Her lips parted slightly. "Love reclaimed in triumph. Then, and only then, will I take him into my arms. He will soon return to honor our pact: timeless love, merciless vengeance."

Joy picked up a brush and began to comb through Thea's hair.

"He will bring to my hands the scarab." Thea smiled grimly. "At that moment, he will remember all."

Joy drew back in consternation. "Mistress! You never indicated *that* condition!" Her hands shook.

"No, I never did." Thea held out a hand mirror and regarded herself.

"But . . . my lady, what of its power?"

Thea stared into the mirror pitilessly. "What of it?"

"Is he aware that he must battle the desire for it? It affects all men thusly."

"If not, he will understand before long."

* * *

Teldaris tried the wrought-iron back gate. It was secure. The spikes left no room for anyone to squeeze through.

He jammed a foot into one small gap in the scrollwork and hoisted himself onto the top of the garden wall. He rested on his stomach for several seconds before he crawled to the roof of the terrace.

A terrace lantern gave way under his weight and fell to the ground, crashing loudly. He stilled, expecting the Oriental to emerge at any moment, but even after several minutes, no one came to investigate.

Jason debated with himself, then chose the second-floor window that seemed most accessible. Next to it was a small balcony, with waist-high stone borders. He jumped, grabbed the balcony's balustrade, gritted his teeth with effort and pulled himself up. With one leg over the railing, he stopped and gasped for air. His ripped jacket and skinned knuckles went unnoticed.

He tried the balcony door first. It was unlocked. Unlatching the French doors a crack, he waited to hear the sound of an alarm. Nothing but silence. He could detect no movement inside.

He peered into the room, then stole in, but left one door ajar. An anteroom of some sort, it was dark, covered on all four sides by heavy tapestries. The patterns were indistinguishable, except for a woven lion's mane along the edge of the wall hanging directly ahead. There appeared to be no other furnishings. A fifth carpet hung from the ceiling, hammock-style, giving the room an impression of an Arabian tent.

He walked forward, felt for an opening in the tapestry. Flickering light penetrated through a thin parting in the curtains.

Teldaris pulled it back slightly, and froze.

There, in a large bedroom beyond, was Thea. She sat at an ornate dressing table, motionless, her back toward him.

He swept back the cloth and entered. A single oil lamp

gave insufficient light for the large chamber, but enough for him to see his own reflection next to hers in the glass. She did not move. She continued to stare into the mirror, seemed unaware of his presence.

He glanced around the room. An uneasy sensation passed through him when he realized that it contained no trace of the twentieth century. A large armoire, canopied bed, and several smaller tables were all carved from dark, heavy wood. In the flickering reflection of the mirror, the furniture appeared purplish-black. Deep-scarlet rugs, curtains, and bedcovers were embroidered with golden designs. Polished brass glistened. Parted blinds made him wonder if the lamp had been purposely set beside the window.

"You," he said.

She turned, slowly. Her entire figure seemed to rotate effortlessly, as though moved by will alone. She looked at him without surprise.

Her demeanor was unsettling.

"You lured me here, didn't you?"

Still, she kept silence. She was clad in a robe of deep green, her hair swept back, long past her shoulders. A single gem—either an emerald or aquamarine, he couldn't tell which—hung low, between her breasts. It was the largest jewel he'd ever seen.

He forced his gaze upward.

Her eyes were half closed, accenting the prominence of her cheekbones.

"You don't act surprised to see me."

"No." Her voice was flat.

"Why?"

"I said you would return to me." She looked at him directly for the first time. "And you have."

"I had no choice."

"I know."

"Have you laid some kind of spell upon me?" he asked hesitantly, unwilling to admit her power to do so.

"If love is a spell to you, then I have."

He walked toward her, halted.

"Aren't you apprehensive? I broke into your bedroom, I carry this . . ." He produced the stiletto.

"Does the sun consider each shadow it casts?"

She pointed to a figure on the floor, near to where he stood. He looked down, leapt aside in reflex, raised the knife to throw.

A five-foot-long Egyptian cobra was poised, head reared, hood spread wide in warning, inches from his foot. Jason squinted, and saw that it was nothing but a carved wooden replica. He exhaled slowly. He glanced back to her, angered, as his initial fear passed.

"Did you enjoy the humor?"

"There was nothing amusing in what I witnessed."

"You ungodly bi—"

"No one," she said sharply, "not even you, my love, may raise a voice to me."

Jason felt a cold wind race through his soul.

"Pick it up," she ordered.

"What?"

She indicated the carved snake.

He grasped the tail, then gasped involuntarily as the wooden reptile swung to-and-fro with a lifelike motion. Sections of the tail were fastened together cleverly, their hinges concealed. The liquid movement of the dark wood, aided by the subtle detail of the carving, almost convinced him that he held a living thing. He imagined a venomous hiss at the edge of his hearing.

"Stroke it," she directed.

He obeyed reluctantly, rubbed the back of its hood.

The wood felt very worn, warm, and he realized it was very, very old. A current somehow ran through it, as if it contained life. He turned the reptile around, to see its face. When he did, he jumped. Accurately melded into the cobra's features, framed by the regal hood, was a likeness of the woman before him. A snake with the face of Beauty.

Distantly, on the perimeter of conscious sound, her haunting song returned. It grew in strength, becoming more firm, more powerful, more resonant than ever before.

"It's *you*, after all. You want the scarab," he said quietly, almost to himself. A multitude of revelations began to attack his sanity. Revelations evolved into answers, then into consequences.

She watched him closely, allowed him to struggle uninterrupted.

"It was you, this whole time, who dropped clues, forged letters, tricked me into searching for the scarab."

"Yes."

"Why?"

"It is mine."

"How can you think so?"

"You gave it to me once," she replied. "You must do so again."

"You are out of your—"

"I warned you once about that tone. Others have found it detrimental to themselves to anger me."

"Why this scarab? Other than historical value—"

"I need it," she interrupted, "and you must obtain it for me."

"Once you have it, what will you do?"

"That is entirely my prerogative."

"Using such logic, you might march into Cairo and seize control of the country."

"Perhaps I shall, if it pleases me." She did not smile.

He regarded her for a long while. "As would a thousand other souls who think they're a Cleopatra or a Ramses."

"No." She spoke as if pronouncing judgment. She rose, then walked toward him. "No, you are not ready."

"For what?"

"For me," she whispered. "You are not yet a man."

Enraged, he seized her and kissed her brutally. She did not resist, nor did she yield.

After a minute, Teldaris released her and retreated a step. She did not move.

"If I am your long lost lover, then why don't you react?"

She smiled cruelly. "I do not kiss boys."

"I am a man," he spoke tightly.

"When you return with the scarab, then you may be. And I shall greet you as such. Then . . ." Her eyes held his as, almost imperceptibly, she inclined her head toward the bed.

"What if I decide not to wait?" he threatened.

"I would be cursed," she replied without pause. "I would be forced to take the knife from your hand and kill you."

"What?" He backed another pace.

"Do you think I am so weak as to be charmed by an aging youth? Or one unproven, untried? I have waited over three thousand years and will wait longer if I must. What is right, shall be. No one, nor any power, will stop us from being united. Be assured, architect, I can endure another thousand years if necessary."

She advanced a step.

"I can outwait anyone on earth."

"I detest you and your callousness—"

"You love me, no matter what means I use to secure our life together. You love me as your lungs love the air you breathe. You can love no other."

"There is another woman—"

"As there was once before."

Jason flinched. "What do you mean!"

"Anyone can be dealt with. Bought, sold, traded. Anyone."

"What do you know about Gail?" he stammered.

"I know nothing except that I alone have loved you."

"Prove it." He fought for self-control.

Thea did not respond.

"How do you know about her? Why did she come here . . . ?" he broke off in anguish.

"I only know the jingle of a few coins will make most women listen more attentively—"

"What did you do to her?"

"As it will lure most men."

"What do you want from me?"

"Only a woman would know."

"And only a man could understand why I won't submit."

"Leave me!" she said harshly. "I am not to be treated in this manner. I caution you against a quick tongue. When you hand the Scarab of Amon to me, then you will understand. You shall know your own strength, and that of your love for me. You shall forever free yourself of fear—"

"No! I shall free myself of you!" he vowed. Teldaris crossed into the next chamber, then out and over the balcony. She heard him scrabble across the terrace roof, down the brick wall.

"You would curse yourself, architect," she answered at last.

She retrieved the wooden cobra from where he'd dropped it to the floor. She stroked it gently, absently.

Joy entered unobtrusively from a corridor, knowing that he was gone.

"Mistress?"

Thea turned away as Joy approached.

"Mistress, are you . . ." Joy saw her impatiently brush away a tear, then two.

"Much love was lost today."

When Jason returned home, Susan's back was the first thing he saw. She tossed a cigarette butt into the fire's dying embers and turned to face him.

"Do you always disappear after sex?"

"Not always," he answered softly.

"I suppose you were checking on Vern?" Her voice was controlled and cold.

"No." A neutral look fixed itself on his face.

"Ah, right . . . pizza! You had a craving for pizza, so you decided to surprise me with one of those big gooey jobs from Angelo's. Correct?"

Jason removed his jacket. He walked to his desk where he scattered stacks of papers to locate a small hinged rosewood box. He set it atop the hearth, then built up the fire again.

Soon the flames were steady enough to ignore, and he turned toward her. Her face bore a trace of nonchalance. Teldaris approved, understanding what strength that trace implied.

"Susan, we need to talk."

"And I thought you had no sense of the absurd."

"Never write an elegy for a troll. All things get absurd at times, Susan."

"Once you tell me if Vern's been located, I'll leave, so as not to bore you further."

Jason took a small pipe from the rosewood box.

"Susan, I need your help," he said casually, as he stuffed leaves into the pipe's bowl. He crunched them methodically between his fingers.

"The pot will help you?"

"Yes."

Susan raised an eyebrow but remained silent.

Teldaris lit several matches before the pipe would smoke. He drew deeply.

"Helps to relax. No real high, but soothing . . . ," he trailed off.

"Where is Vern?"

Jason looked at her directly for the first time since they made love.

"You haven't gone through life for nearly forty years untouched."

Susan's eyes widened.

"You're no blushing virgin, or a shrinking violet. If you possessed that little intelligence, I'd never have been interested in you."

Susan waited.

"That's why I'll tell you something now, and you'll understand this is no sham."

"My brother?" she repeated.

Jason inhaled for a moment, then closed his eyes.

"You fell asleep, you must have been so exhausted. . . ."

Susan resolved to say nothing of her struggle the day before. She sat back.

"I'll tell you where I went because you'll remain to hear why. An ordinary woman would walk out of my life during the next two minutes."

A sneer distorted her mouth. "You're smooth, I'll give you that. You're good. . . . " She rose. "But a line is still a line, and I won't stay for the line that's coming."

He set the pipe aside. "The first thing I did after we screwed was go to Thea."

It produced the desired effect. She froze.

"Only . . . she wouldn't see me, so I had to break into her bedroom."

"How am I supposed to react to someone like you!" she exclaimed. "Why are you telling me this?"

"Why are you listening?"

"I'm not." She walked toward the door.

"Susan, I'm . . . I need help." She slowed, uncertain. The plea gave her gooseflesh.

"Why the hell do you think I was drawn to her tonight of all nights?" Jason stood suddenly. "I am obsessed."

An image of the scarab whizzed through her mind as her hand reached for the doorknob.

"If you leave now, you'll wonder for the rest of your life."

"No, I won't." She remembered her car keys, walked

quickly to the secretary. "I'll simply recall a few unreasonable situations, and one half-decent lay."

"Susan, I can't help myself."

"I can't, either. Tell my brother good-bye, if you ever see him again. I wash my hands of the both of you." She turned to go.

He followed her, grabbed her arm.

"Isn't this how we began?" Susan tossed back her hair, a gesture years younger than she felt.

"Let go of me!"

He firmly pulled her to the couch. She resisted at first, then gave up.

"Let's leave Denver tonight."

"You're high."

"*Look* at us, you're not blind to reality. We're both second-timers."

"What are you implying?"

"That we can save each other."

"I detest that word. Pardon my bluntness, but I don't think there's anything wrong with me."

"No? Why are you so protective as you are toward your brother, when he keeps going out of his way to prove he doesn't deserve it? Don't you have something better to do with your life?"

Susan's eyes lit up in fury.

"No, Ms. Tyler, I don't think you do," Jason said accusingly.

"You bastard!"

"Susan," he whispered loudly, urgently, "take me away from her."

She tried to pull back, but her hands were locked within his.

"Don't you see? If I go to that woman, she will consume me. I'll be eaten alive. I'm asking you to share my life. *She* is that haunting nightsong I've always heard. I'm drawn to her like a moth is to a flame. Pull me out. Come with me now, to the airport. No time to think, no baggage, no looks back.''

Susan wrenched herself free of him. She made for the door, then stopped for an abrupt about-face.

"Why did you set me up for this?"

"Susan—"

"How could I do this to myself?" She stood utterly still.

He spoke softly, "I never saw myself . . . really . . . until tonight." He paused. "If you'd seen me, a beggar pounding on a great wooden door . . ." He looked up. Susan frowned at his expression. "Then you would ask no more questions. You would either help me or you would leave. . . .''

She walked to his desk. She picked up a piece of paper, held it toward him, then let it flutter to the floor.

"Account closed. Insufficient funds. Why didn't you tell me that part of the story? Is she your fountain of wealth? All this subterfuge . . . you don't like the idea of suddenly being broke. Isn't that it? And to secure your future, you decided to make it with *this* old broad!'' She picked up the crumpled rejection from Cairo and allowed it to fall from her fingers as well.

"Thanks for going through my desk,'' he muttered.

"I thought you might've had the decency to leave a note. I'm not a snoop.''

"I don't owe you any explanations concerning my motives or finances. I did owe you an apology, with explanation. And that I delivered.''

"To think I was almost conned into believing you.''

"You're too . . . too logical . . . to be taken in by a scheme as brutish as you've described. How can you think I'm after your money? I doubt you have that much.''

"*She* obviously has plenty. Why don't you go back to her? You will eventually, anyway!''

"Because I think she had my wife abducted,'' he said in a rage.

"What?"

"Gail. Thea Markidian had something to do with her disappearance. And, she wants the scarab."

Susan sat slowly on the couch.

He moved closer beside her. "I was tricked. I was plied with offers purportedly from the Cairo Museum. *She* sent them. She's heavily involved in *all* of this. And, Susan, she's dangerous. Another point: I once told you that, though I'm no businessman, I do know value. I've saved quite a bit for some years and have a healthy nest egg or two put away. That should destroy your theory. I don't want your money."

"Thea told me that she followed me here. From Istanbul." He stared blankly across the room.

"Why are you telling me this now?"

"I . . . care for you. I don't want to see you hurt."

"You should have thought of that before."

"Hell, I'm not talking about confused feelings. I don't want to see you killed, or disappear without a trace, like Gail."

Susan started.

"I was attracted to you before I met Thea, remember? That should mean something."

"How does all this connect?"

"Don't you see!" he exploded. "She's insane. And for some reason, insanely jealous."

"You said obsessed."

"I said *I* was obsessed."

"Lovely," Susan muttered. "You're obsessed and she's insane. What am I?"

Teldaris ignored her remarks. "I believe she had my . . . wife . . . disposed of. So she could have me to herself."

"And?"

"And since she knows about you, might do the same."

"How would she know about me?"

"I told her."

"Told her what?" Susan asked hesitantly.

"Told her there was another woman in my life."

She said nothing.

He turned suddenly toward the front windows. "Do you hear anything?"

Susan listened. "Just sirens."

"Somehow, Vern, and Gail, and Thea—maybe others—are connected with the scarab." He tapped his index finger against the bridge of his nose. "But what does the scarab connect with?" he wondered aloud.

"I wish . . . you'd been more honest with me from the start."

"What good would it have done?"

"I don't know. . . . " She fought off exhaustion. Jason went to put his arms around her, but she shrugged him off. "I want to be alone for a minute."

"I understand," he said. Jason walked to a front window. "Want a drink?"

She shook her head tiredly.

He looked to the street below, as another ambulance raced past.

Tyler was in pain. He'd lain unnoticed for some time. He remembered falling, and flaming debris landing on either side of him, blacking out, coming to, crawling out of danger, hiding behind a thick planting of juniper bushes. Then, nothing but brief glimpses of fire engines, water gushing, people running.

Little was left of the building. He forced himself up, stumbled down the sidewalk. He didn't notice the blood drying on his clothes, barely felt cracked ribs and a sprained ankle.

The long meeting in Adderson's home continued. The chants died away. A joining of hands followed as the Circle united in the business of raising power. Beads of sweat broke out on their faces. Intense mental energy was aimed at a single target.

Adderson no longer felt agitated. He took his cue willingly, aided by those more experienced.

A tray of glasses was overturned by unseen hands. Not one of the group released his grip. Deborah's favorite picture crashed to the floor. Still, nothing interrupted their concentration. The lights on Lookout Mountain flickered, then dimmed before there was a difference in the atmosphere. Like minute flashes of lightning, streaks of red and orange whizzed marginally, just on the edge of vision.

At last, electricity failed completely on the mountain. A collection of sighs and wheezes burst forth from their exhausted lips. Power was restored within minutes, but the group in Adderson's living room was satisfied.

Deborah, summoned just long enough to serve wine, watched her husband nervously. She felt abused, treated like a serving wench, but knew better than to look to him for support in the presence of these people. She served quickly and retreated to the kitchen where she would remain until the meeting was over.

"Would you tell me one thing?" Susan cleared her throat.

Jason turned from the window. "If I can."

"You've never used the word 'love' in relation to me. . . ."

A moment quietly passed before he realized it was a question.

"No, I haven't." He walked toward her.

Susan nodded, as if in confirmation to herself.

"Shall I make some coffee?" he asked.

"Shouldn't it be mentioned in passing?" She reached for a cigarette, then remembered her last pack was in her car.

"Did you love your wife?" she asked softly.

"We were comfortable together, we each needed companionship."

Susan nodded again, remembering Gail's picture. When she looked up at him, her eyes were cold.

He walked into the kitchen without another word.

Susan listened to his movements for several minutes, then wandered to the kitchen doorway.

"I don't know how to be casual about my relationships," she said.

"What the hell made you think *I* was casual?" He banged two mugs onto the counter.

"That's not what I meant!"

"What, then?"

"You're a secretive man. On the run. Maybe on the run from yourself."

"Enough," he snapped with weariness, "enough. I can't battle obsessions, phantoms, and *you* at the same time." He rubbed his forehead.

She noticed a bottle of aspirin, almost empty, next to the sink. "What can I do?" she asked awkwardly.

"Maybe I'd just like to be alone for a little while," he mumbled. "Why don't you go downstairs to see if Vern's back?"

"Jason—"

"By the time you return, I'll have coffee waiting."

She accepted the nudge and slipped away without another word.

A moment passed. "If I could get away from it, if I could ever be free . . . ," he whispered, "I would be someone different."

To be free, fast, you dry those pretty tears
    'cause love cain't last,
And give your heart and soul to no one else,
    jest be,
Whoa-man, woman be free, woo-man be free.

"Oh, yeah, woman be free, woman be free," Deborah sang softly to herself. The country and western hit ended. She looked up, disappointed. She was sitting in the living room. After the meeting had broken up earlier, Kevin had gone off somewhere, leaving her alone.

She switched on the record again, this time setting it up for automatic replay, and wondered if Kevin had ever noticed that she played it often.

Deborah glanced upward at the sunlit cathedral-style ceiling, buttressed by cedar beams. Even the members of Kevin's group, on arriving earlier tonight, had been well-enough impressed by the home she'd made. They hadn't said so; they hadn't complimented one single thing. It wasn't their way. "Supercilious, dandelion, supercilious," Kevin would have said.

She smiled bitterly. Deborah *knew* she would never be initiated into the Circle. The others knew it, too. Only Kevin talked of it as a future event. Maybe he realized as well, and was just pretending otherwise.

Deborah felt too isolated from the rest of the world. She remembered how good she had felt talking with her new neighbor, a lawyer named Rick. He'd laughed a lot and talked mostly about his horses stabled in the valley. He seemed to be a decent guy who regarded her as another human being, not someone to insult, bully, or command. They'd talked for nearly an hour, until the night chill had forced her home.

Banished to the kitchen while the Circle performed their rituals, Debbie had at last understood that she feared her husband more than she loved or trusted him.

She put both hands to her temples to drive away the dangerous thoughts that rushed through her mind. She must check this surge of rebellion.

The stereo clicked automatically. Soon she was lost within the music.

"Woo-man be free," she murmured in lip sync, "don't take no more of those handsome, heartless ways. . . . "

* * *

Susan glanced down the street. Her attention was caught by a staggering drunk further down the block. He stumbled, then rose again. She hurried to her car, snatched the cigarettes, then hesitated. Against her intent, her right hand went to the door of the glove compartment. It lingered for a moment, uncertain. Then she opened the compartment and retrieved a small bundled scarf. Within the beige silk wrapping, a heavy weight generated warmth, sending a tingle into her palm. She looked around suspiciously, but no one was near. She locked the car and hurried back to the building.

On the second step up the stoop, a picture of warm breezes, bluish-gray waves, and endless white surfside flashed into her mind. She shut her eyes, held the image for a moment longer. Susan opened them in time to see a figure lurching toward her. The drunk. In defensive reflex, she hastily negotiated the remaining steps.

"Where . . . is . . . it!" His hoarse, guttural voice slurred the words.

In shock, she recognized her brother.

"Where . . . is it!"

Before Susan could speak, a look of unbelieving pain entered his eyes and he collapsed at her feet.

Tyler lifted his head feebly. He got an impression of Susan and Teldaris. He was simultaneously aware of alternating cold and hot pain, experienced the sensation of being lifted, then a burst of hotter pain.

He was unconscious, he knew, and yet alert. Tyler understood that he had been carried downstairs. He sensed the lumpy cot, concerned voices, a network of pipes, the sting of antiseptic.

"Where is it?" his mind asked.

"Where is what?" it answered.

Teldaris and Susan continued to apply bandages.

Tyler felt himself lifting, rising higher. In fascination, he watched their ridiculously slow motions from a position just above their heads.

He floated effortlessly, no longer absorbed with the bulk on the cot. He was engrossed by little things, unnoticed before. Like Jason's well-hidden cowlick.

He was content to glide without will, to study a dust mote descending toward Susan's upturned, slightly wrinkled collar.

Gradually, unwillingly, Tyler slipped into a deeper state of unconsciousness. The borders of time became indistinct . . . and . . .

Trained monkeys lugged ebony trays, torchlight glowed against high white walls. Noise could be heard from adjacent kitchens. Seven dining couches were placed in a semicircle.

He dimly comprehended that he was trapped somewhere, or somewhen, else.

He studied the elaborate furnishings, golden utensils, and colorful frescoes in fascination. Without doubt, this was old Egypt. A night meal of fowl, fish, and fruit was spread on serving tables. He heard strains of soft tinkling music, a waterfall celebrated by harp. Yet he could smell no aroma from the steaming food. Snow from faraway mountains had been carried by countless runners to serve as an extravagant chiller of wine. Time lingered as he witnessed the slow melt of the packed ice. He studied the movements and gestures of the roomful of diners. Then, the action accelerated. He stirred when he saw what the scene began to unfold.

Tyler recognized himself on one of the couches. He seemed different. The body type was foreign, but he recognized his persona. His head and eyebrows were recently shaved, as were his short fleshy legs. A paunch was hidden by folds of his priest's robe. He reclined on his right side, the sole diner who was left-handed. He chewed large handfuls of food with an open mouth. A small-breasted girl sat at his knees and fondled him without interest. He shouted a joke to the others, hiccoughed twice, then downed wine until it sloshed down his chin. The border of his robe was lined with white and gold, the status of a high official.

On one of the couches nearby was Kevin Adderson. In a different body, as was himself, but unmistakably Adderson. Older, postured as vastly superior, he wore royal military attire. Enstrapped with tightly buckled leather and goldplate, he returned Tyler's glance. A smile of pleasure appeared on his wide lips. Others deferred to him. Some of the priests exhibited nervousness. One or two poked at their food anxiously. Adderson did not eat, instead sat stiffly, and observed the room closely.

Tyler shuddered. The dream would not release him. He tried to bring his hand to his stomach, but it wouldn't move. He fought the images, struggled to return to Denver, but could not escape Egypt.

Without great surprise, he saw himself begin to choke. He quaffed more wine as blood rushed down a nostril. The others stopped eating as he began to vomit.

Another became ill, then a third.

Cries of ''Poisoner!'' ''Betrayer!'' ''Defiler!'' filled the air. The tongue sounded phonetically alien, but he understood perfectly.

A young priest rushed for Adderson, dagger in hand. Adderson did not even draw his sword. Instead, he laughed as the attacker grimaced in pain and fell into convulsions.

The young girl ran from the temple. Guards at the main archway stopped her, but Adderson signaled them to release her. They did so, and she fled into the night.

Tyler swore curses at him, clutched his belly in agony. Adderson stood and unsheathed his sword. In three broad strides he crossed to the priest. As Tyler began a forlorn cry, the blade plunged into his neck.

He tumbled through a series of black shadows, encircled with flaming red.

Tyler awoke in a sweat, gasped for breath and fingered the mattress for reassurance. He trembled as he tried to sort the images. Pain from the burns and sprains penetrated his recollections. He saw Teldaris standing a few feet away.

"I had . . . a psychic . . . a vision," Tyler croaked.

"I know. I heard you."

NINE

Āba

WE ARE ALL PHARAOHS.
WE ALL ARE ONE
AND IN OUR UNIFICATION
WE SHALL DIVERSIFY
AND MAKE GOOD.
WE SHALL ENDURE MUCH
SUFFERING AND HARDSHIP
AS WE ARE JOSTLED AND TRAMPLED.
THE IGNORANCE WHICH FILLS OUR SOULS
SHALL BE BLED FROM OUR BODIES.

—Hymn to Hat-shepsut,
from *Shadow of Khufu*,
Cecil Rupert-Lewis, 1894

SUSAN PEERED THROUGH THE SHUTTERS, ALERT FOR any sign of Jason. The amber glow from the corner street-light gave the cascading snowflakes a golden tint.

Afraid he would return any moment, Susan's search ended with the opened secretary.

"Mine." She studied the beautiful necklace lovingly. A faint smile crossed her lips.

She placed the bundle in the small space behind the lowest drawer. The stone seemed to leave her hand with reluctance.

"Mine," she whispered to soothe herself, "tomorrow I'll find a better hiding place."

Teldaris sat on the edge of the cot where Tyler lay. Vern tried to move away, but pain from a rib made him wince and caused him to stop struggling.

"I'm not going to strangle you," Teldaris said flatly. "Stay still. We can't take you to a hospital, you know."

"Where is it?" Tyler demanded.

"I ask you."

Vern looked away.

Teldaris rose and began to pace the narrow, dingy apartment. Momentarily, he forgot the prone man and the seedy room. Tyler had talked during his dream, and his words had catalyzed Jason. It did not much surprise him that Tyler, too, evidently had a link with an Egyptian past. Indeed, very little would have surprised him now, for the change had begun in him, the metamorphosis that Thea Markidian had sought. He felt someone awaken within him, someone who was, and at the same time was not, himself. Painfully, inexorably the two selves began to merge. The process was inevitable. Memories of the dreams came to him, whole, but dim. He knew that with time, they would become as clear as yesterday. His body continued to pace as his two selves, which shared a single soul, knit together and strove toward oneness. His thoughts became flashingly, blindingly accelerated and focused on one object—the scarab.

He paused by the cot and looked down. The scarab. *It* was the pivot, the hinge upon which all these events turned. Tyler, the mysterious person or persons who had threatened and killed to obtain it, even Thea. Even himself. All were drawn toward the nexus of the scarab. Whoever obtained the necklace would likely become irresistible. Tyler, he might be able to deal with, and the others who sought it could not be speculated upon without more knowledge. But, one thing he knew as a surety. If Thea Markidian came into possession of the talisman, he would be lost forever. He would slavishly, helplessly love her until he died. A part of his twin-self smiled at this, for the obsession was there, and could not be denied. He desired her above all else already, and the anomaly was painful. Yes, the desire was there, but the fear of being consumed by it existed also. His entire future depended upon that stone beetle.

"Mr. Tyler," he said. "You have played out your hand. And lost. I want that scarab. Now."

"Why?" Tyler hissed, more with anguish than anger.

Teldaris studied him before replying. "Today, your sister lost everything. You owe her a new start—the scarab will buy that. Also, you owe me your freedom. Without me, you would now be in jail or dead. I repeat, you owe me your freedom, and the scarab will buy me mine."

"How?"

"That's not your concern."

"What will happen to me?" Tyler protested.

"We'll discuss that, *after* you tell me where it is."

"I don't know! I hid it at Sue's. I went back to look for it, but it was gone. Then, the fire—"

"Tell me!"

"It had to be Sue. She must have found it. That bitch stole it from me!"

Teldaris bent over the man. "Either you, or Susan, will tell me the truth by tomorrow. I don't care what it takes or who must give it up. There will be an end to this madness."

Adderson spotted the unmarked police car a half block from Tyler's duplex. He cursed for a length of time, then calmed. The duplex was dark, and there was no car in the driveway.

He walked back to his station wagon. This was but another variant in the night's drama, he told himself.

Susan stared at the carpet. Jason sipped a Coke, too weary to get up off the floor.

He wiped the bottle against his brow.

"I don't want you to return there without me."

"What's to return to?" she mumbled.

"I'm serious. There's nothing left."

She looked down at her only clothes. The acrid stench of fire lingered.

"You were right," she whispered, "We should have escaped . . . while we had the chance."

His jaw hardened. "Our chance passed us by."

Susan looked up fearfully. "You don't believe that, do you?"

"It sometimes happens that belief and reality are in accord." He pulled up a leg and draped his arm around his knee.

"Vern says you have the scarab. Do you?"

"No," she said, surprised.

He watched her closely. "I know you wouldn't lie, Susan. That's why I won't repeat my question." He almost whispered the last.

"I said I didn't have it," she replied irritably. "Should I remind you that I've just lost—"

"Death will come on swift pinions to those who disturb the rest of the Pharaohs," he recited without preamble.

"That was inscribed in gold as one of the many curses carved on the walls of the burial chamber of Tutankhamen. Howard Carter and his party found that out rapidly."

"Lord Carnarvon—"

"Was bitten almost immediately by an insect and died in three weeks. More than twenty persons connected with the opened tomb died under mysterious circumstances. That inscription next to the entrance continues to claim victims and their descendents to this very day."

"Why are you telling me this?" Susan's voice quivered. "The curse of Tut's tomb is common knowledge."

"To instruct. That scarab is dangerous."

Susan's eyes were downcast.

"Go to your brother. He needs a sister right now."

"Jason, I—"

"Go to him, then get some rest."

He turned, tiredly. "I'm going to shower, then sleep. There'll be linens and bedclothes for you on the couch. Tomorrow, one of you will produce the scarab, I don't care whom. By tomorrow night, the scarab will be in my keeping. Then . . . you *all* can go to the devil."

"Jason . . . ," Susan pleaded.

"I wish to be left alone." He went to the bathroom and closed the door.

Susan fought down an urge to huddle in a corner and cry.

Adderson drove the faded red Volvo up to the police barricades. The shell of the structure still smoked, despite the snow.

He hunched over the steering wheel, thinking furiously. He would have killed for a minute of Susan Tyler's time.

Susan laced up Jason's jogging shoes. She wriggled her toes in the extra space, and pulled on the oversized sweat-suit he'd set out for her. The sound of running water from the bathroom consoled her somewhat. She only wanted to be held. Just for one minute.

She looked at the closed door and knew it wouldn't happen that night. But, she vowed, the morning would witness better times.

She went to the secretary.

"Are you awake?" she asked.

"Where is it?" he growled.

"You're welcome. I'll think twice before I save your life again."

''Where is it!'' he bellowed, and raised himself up on his elbows with a grunt.

''What were you doing in my apartment? What were you looking for?''

''You know damn well! Where is it?''

''Don't you remember? You sold it, years ago.''

''Don't start with me—''

''How did it get there, brother?''

''I put it there for safekeeping.''

''So that if anything happened, I'd be a better target than you?''

''I had to hide it. It wasn't safe with me.''

''But it *was* safe with me?''

''Sue,'' Tyler lowered his voice, ''I've got to have it. They'll kill me if I don't hand it over.''

''But it was okay if they killed me?''

''Sue—''

''Who wants it? Why?''

He shrugged haplessly.

She balled her hands into fists. ''I want to know, or by God, I'll kill you myself!''

''Some people . . . occultists . . . magicians . . . Teldaris may be one of them. He knows too much. They want it or they'll kill me.''

''It's too late for that appeal, brother. You've shit on me one time too many.''

He tried to rise. ''My life depends on it.''

''It's not for you.'' She looked directly at him.

''It's mine!''

''You stole it!''

''You promised you'd get me out of this.''

''That's past.''

''You'll do it for me. I know you will, Sue. You've never had the heart to deny me what I needed—''

''Not this time, Vern. Not even for your life,'' she broke in. ''I suppose you can rest here. I don't know what the best answer is. Maybe turning yourself in to the police. If you're in danger, they can place you in protective custody.''

"I haven't done anything!"

"If you won't go to the police, I will. This has to stop somewhere. Mrs. Kelly died in the fire tonight. She was an invalid. She died indirectly because of you. I won't have another victim on . . .''

Susan shook her head slowly. "I don't understand you. I guess I never did. I've felt a loyalty to you, hoped that someday something good would come of it. But all I see is ugliness and more ugliness. You probably don't care that anyone's died.''

"You're damned right. I didn't even care when Janice died,'' he snarled.

"*You* should have died in that fire,'' she returned.

"I didn't start it!''

"What a twisted mind you have.''

"I'm getting out of here . . . out of Denver just as soon as—''

"You're not running away, leaving me here to face the consequences. This thing will follow you. I'm not stupid enough to think that you'll return the scarab to her.''

"Her?''

"Jason's ghost. Thea.''

"What the hell are you talking about?''

"We don't communicate very well, do we? I don't know what you and that . . . woman . . .'' She scowled in the direction of Cheesman Park. " . . . are up to, but you're not going to cause any more suffering.''

Tyler sat up despite the pain. "Give me your car keys, and the scarab. Now!'' His face twisted into a mask of fury.

"What in creation makes you think I will?'' she responded.

"Because I'm stronger than you!'' He leapt up, hands clawed at her. He caught her, brought her down to the floor. They wrestled on the concrete, and years of suppressed hatred erupted in both of them. Her nails dug into his face. He lay on top of her, bandages torn loose from his chest. She executed a quick knee jerk and he rolled over. A long agonized gurgle escaped from his throat. She used the opportunity to escape him, unmindful of the cut on her scalp, unmindful of her tear-blurred eyes.

She ran out of the basement to her car.

The Renault whisked across slick streets as snow fell with greater intensity. Snow trucks and sanding equipment stood unused in garages; it was too early to plow.

Susan gunned the car, causing it to spin in a forty-degree angle. She skidded through an intersection, and continued toward her destination.

Near the mansion she overshot the curb. The Renault stalled, headlights and blinkers on, two tires straddling the embankment.

She ran up the front walk, slipped once, rubbed her knee, then jumped up. She rang the bell insistently, and pounded on the door as well. Her hair was crusted with flakes, but she ignored the cold.

A light appeared on the second floor, another on the first.

"Stop it, stop it . . . stop it!" she shouted.

The snow was an effective sound dampener. Her words were lost in the uncannily still atmosphere.

At length, the door was answered. An exotic woman appeared, but said nothing.

"Stop it, damn you, stop it!" Susan yelled.

Joy looked at her intended victim.

"Come in, Susan Tyler."

"Who disturbs our rest?" Thea stood at the bottom of the stairs.

Susan waited in the entranceway. She looked at Joy, at

Thea, at the surroundings. Lush vegetation and a fountain made her think of a tropical rain forest. She looked down at herself. The heat quickly melted the snow from the bulky jogging outfit, soaking her thoroughly. Wet hair dangled around her shoulders. She swallowed, as the consequences of her rage caught up with her.

"Do I make you nervous?" Thea asked.

Susan felt the blazing challenge, found her will again.

"Yes. And I'm sure you wish to do so," she replied.

"Mistress, this is—" Joy began.

"I know who she is," Thea interrupted.

Susan came forward a step.

"Joy, serve refreshment. Our visitor is in need of drink."

With reluctance, Joy turned to obey.

"I won't be here that long. I have a simple message," Susan said.

"You are perhaps hurried?"

"Stop trying to ruin his life. If you can't have him, leave us alone."

"Your logic is as rumpled as your appearance."

"Stop it, damn you!" she shouted. "I'll go to the police, tonight if I have to, and tell everything . . . even what I can't prove."

Thea regarded her silently.

Joy reentered with a glass of wine, saw Susan's scowl, remained at a distance.

"Leave us in peace . . . I'm warning you!" Susan stormed out the door. Shortly, the car could be heard bouncing off the curb. The sound of the motor faded.

Joy closed the door and looked toward Thea.

"Apparently she was not home when I set the fire," Joy said slowly.

"It does not matter," Thea said smiling. "She is frightened, at the least. We are closer than I thought."

Thea turned, went back up the staircase. "Sleep well, Joy."

Joy peered out a window at the plummet of snowflakes and whispered, "I shall, Mistress."

Tyler breathed heavily. He hurt too much to move.

"Hiding there won't help you!" A sharp voice cut the air.

Vern's head jerked up. Adderson stood in the doorway, a flurry of white behind him. The man's silhouette loomed large.

He closed the door, slid the bolt home. "It's past midnight, Vern. Your time is up."

"How . . . did you find me?" Tyler trembled. The world seemed to unravel around him. He pounded a fist against his leg in utter frustration.

"Let's say I'm a hound. You're a rabbit. I followed your scent."

"I was getting the scarab, but the fire started."

"You lie again." Adderson walked forward. "Time's up. Where is it?"

"Sue will be back soon. She has it."

"Nice try. She just drove off."

"It's hidden in his place. Upstairs. We'll have to ransack it."

"Get your stories straight, Tyler." Adderson pulled out the revolver.

Vern heaved to his feet, cursing the fact he had no weapon. His eyes roamed over the darkened room in a frantic search.

"The scarab."

"I was getting it for you. Then I smelled gasoline, and suddenly there were flames—"

"Gasoline?" Adderson repeated thoughtfully.

"Sue must've stolen it and taken it to him. He's her—"

"Time's up, dead man."

In a desperate surge, Tyler lunged toward him. Adderson drew himself upward with a karate-like kick. His foot caught Vern in the rib cage. Tyler howled in pain, sprawled backward onto the cot. Adderson sprang onto Vern's chest, clamped his hand over his mouth. Tyler struggled briefly, then quieted.

At length, Adderson released his grasp.

"Get off, it's horrible, pain . . . I don't, I can't . . . ," Tyler blubbered like a child. "I don't have it, he does. Upstairs. You don't need me anymore." He bit his lip in anguish.

Adderson leaned close to the man's ear. "You're right," he agreed.

"Susan?" Jason called sleepily. He listened, heard nothing, looked at the clock. Two hours had passed since he'd fallen asleep. He felt alongside the bed for his robe, then switched on lights and opened the door. He called her again and got no answer. The couch was unmade.

She wouldn't remain with her brother this long. He slipped into pajama bottoms and pulled slippers over his feet.

Teldaris raced down the stairs, checked the parking lot. The snowfall had lessened, but clouds hung low in the sky, an indication of more before morning. Around front and in the rear, he saw no one, nor could he distinguish her car from the other lumps of white on the street. He spotted a station wagon double-parked on a side street. Its windshield was cleared, exhaust billowed upward. Jason returned to the building, ran the last hundred feet. Downstairs, he twisted the doorknob and thrust his weight against the door, but it wouldn't give. He decided to try the basement boiler door.

Inside, he crawled through a maze of boxes and over several cords of firewood. In the darkness, he stumbled on several loose bottles. He kicked four times at the metal door before it creaked open into the apartment. Instantly, he saw two shadows locked in combat. Teldaris flipped on the emergency boiler light. The man on top of Tyler flashed a startled look in his direction, and his hands released their grip from Vern's neck. Teldaris paused for a split-second; the face was somewhat familiar.

Then he leapt into the room. The stranger retreated to the front door. Tyler rolled onto his side and vomited.

Adderson spun around, thwarted by the door he'd bolted. Jason flung himself forward, and they grappled. Pressed shoulder to shoulder, each pressure-gripped the arms of the other.

"Run!" Teldaris called to Vern. Tyler rose and swayed slowly toward the metal aperture.

"I can't," he mumbled, "I . . . can't." He fell to his knees.

"Do it!" Jason shouted, and looked back. At that moment, Adderson shoved him against the narrow columns of steaming pipe. Teldaris's grip weakened. Adderson freed a hand, pulled the gun out of his jacket. Jason struggled to wrench away from the scorch of the heat as Adderson drove the revolver hard against his skull. He slumped against the wall and slowly sank to the floor. The wound bled freely.

Adderson turned to Tyler, who was trying desperately for the door.

Susan shifted gears viciously, which only pushed her car further into the drift. The wheels spun uselessly. She cursed.

On the periphery of her vision, she saw the approach of a dark figure. She pumped the accelerator and the engine flooded.

Before she could react, the right door opened and Joy slid into the seat. Susan panicked, but was powerless to act.

Joy held out a long angora scarf. "Take it. I brought it

for you. One couldn't help but notice your wet hair, and on such a cold night. You might catch your death."

Susan took it suspiciously. "How did you know I was stuck?"

"I didn't." The other's face was expressionless, as if frozen by the cold.

"Thank you," Susan said formally, and wrapped it around her hair.

"It was I who set fire to your building tonight," Joy offered blandly, as if discussing the weather.

Susan stilled, afraid to move. At last, she whispered, "Why?"

"Because I wished you dead."

"Vern." Susan sat back. "You nearly killed my brother."

"So be it."

Susan shuddered at the other's equanimity. "Why are you telling me this?"

"I wished you to discern my motive."

"My death?"

"Not necessarily. If so, you would now be slumped over the steering wheel."

"A woman died tonight, an invalid."

"Perhaps I released a soul entrapped in a crippled body."

"Perhaps you made yourself a murderess!" Susan accused.

"Or a liberator, depending on perspective."

"She never hurt anyone."

"That," Joy demurred, "is irrelevant. If she could not flee the fire, she was meant to die. Can you understand that concept?"

"I've never heard death-dealing described in such terms." Susan edged toward the door. "You are monstrous. . . . "

Joy drew closer, circumventing any easy escape.

"Do not attempt to flee, it would not be wise. I am quick. You, I recall, have no penchant for running."

"How . . . did . . . you—" Susan gasped.

"I collect information about certain individuals. I know much about you."

"*Too* much."

"My motive is simple. The man you know as Jason Teldaris belongs to my lady. It is he we seek. Not your destruction, nor the demise of your honorable brother."

"He has no honor." Susan sighed tiredly.

"I am well aware." Joy smiled. "I was being generous."

"Can't you understand that Jason doesn't accept this past-lifetime fraud, nor do I?"

"Admitting it or not, he remembers. You are afraid to concede the possibility, for this would leave you with nothing. You have bound your whole identity into one barren lifetime."

"Get out of my car!"

"In my own time. I am here to bargain." Getting no response, she continued.

"If I may, I would like to make what you would refer to as a business proposition."

"You *what*?"

"One million dollars. In cash or any other way you would prefer it. If you will leave Denver and swear never to see him again. You can have your laundromats managed through a proxy. With those, plus the cash, you will be able to live handsomely, may even be able to find another lover."

Susan thrust out a hand in outrage. Joy interrupted the blow casually. Susan inhaled sharply, then cried out. Joy brought the hand down with slow evenness. Her grip was painful and unbreakable. Her left eyebrow rose slightly, then she released Susan's arm.

"Do not attempt to become physical in my presence again. I am well-trained in old and deadly arts. You should not be offended by my bluntness, nor the candor that lack of time necessitates." Joy's eyes narrowed into hard scrutiny. "You are most unwise, as are many. There are multiple chances for affection on this earth."

"I mean to keep him," Susan said with conviction. "If I can."

"You will eventually find love. But it will not be with him."

"Why not?"

"He is bound to Mistress."

"He denies this."

"He denies it to himself, for there is fear. There was . . . an unpleasant conclusion to their first union."

"And what about you? Do you ever get lonely at night? Would your precious Thea even permit you to have a man? Are you totally dedicated to servility?" Susan automatically reached for a cigarette.

"Rancor does not become you. You are a severe woman; your features admit it. You should seek softness," Joy suggested.

"I'm not interested in your opinion. Jason and I are going to live together."

"Did he say he loved you?" Joy queried.

"Of course."

"I thought not. He never told the others, either."

Susan yanked the door handle.

"Our meeting is not yet concluded." A firm hand on her shoulder ended the attempt to leave.

"I'm going to report you to the police."

"I believe not," Joy predicted. "It is not in your best interests."

"If he chooses to live with me, there is nothing you can do to stop it."

"Mistress requires the Scarab of Amon. It is her birthright."

Susan remained silent, listened.

"With the scarab in her hands, she might be willing to allow him . . . to decide for himself."

"That's decent of you, since he already *has* decided." Susan unwrapped the scarf. "Thanks for the use. I won't bother seeing you to the door."

Joy prepared to leave.

"The scarab must be returned. Then we will depart."

"Without Jason?"

"If it pleases him." She shut the car door and quickly disappeared into a swirl of white.

Teldaris became aware of humming. Faint, distant humming that grew louder. His senses returned one by one. He realized that he was riding face down in the back seat of a car. His hands were bound, securely tied.

The car hit a bump, and he lapsed into unconsciousness once more.

TEN

Xeperu

FOR WE SHALL NOT STOP
AND NONE SHALL STOP US
OR OUR KIND—
FOR THOSE WHO ARE ALIEN
SHALL NOT SUBJUGATE—
AS WE PROGRESS FORWARD
WITH EITHER ADVANCEMENT
OR NON-CHANGING
CONTENTMENT,
UNTIL WE REACH THE
MOST DISTANT LAND OF
PLATEAUS AND VALLEYS.

THERE, WE SHALL PARTAKE
OF WELL-DESERVED REST.
AND, THEN, WE SHALL NOT
PERSIST IN OUR REST,
BUT WILL COME BACK TO LANDS
DISTANT FROM US AND SHALL
BEGIN OUR WORK AGAIN.

—Hymn to Hat-shepsut,
  from *Shadow of Khufu*,
  Cecil Rupert-Lewis, 1894

THE DOOR TO NUMBER FIVE HUNG OPEN. "JASON?" she called out before entering. The apartment was destroyed, had been ransacked completely. She ran to his bedroom. Clothes were strewn about, drawers emptied onto the floor, pillows slashed open. Every room was similarly gone through.

"Jason!"

Susan returned to the bedroom, stripped out of her sweatsuit, found a blue flannel shirt and a pair of jeans. She hitched these up, pulled two pairs of socks over her feet. She rummaged through the piles of clothes until she came across two matching boots.

There had to be a limit, she concluded, even if she were forced to draw the boundaries herself. She hobbled to the kitchen in the oversized boots, located a carving knife, hid it inside the right boot and left for the basement apartment.

A cold hand shook her.

"Wake up, damn it!"

Debbie blinked at her husband, then choked back a cry. "What happened to your face?"

"Fight."

Adderson threw back the covers and pulled her up. "Come help me. Hurry, we've got problems. It's starting to get light. Someone will be up early for sure, and if we're seen—damn it, I thought I'd never get up that road."

He pulled his wife outside as he spoke, ignoring her protests.

The snow stung her bare feet. "Let me get some shoes on," she protested.

"No time," he snapped. "Help me get him inside."

Adderson opened the car door. A dark-haired man, bound and gagged, grunted as he struggled to free himself.

Deborah put both hands to her eyes, unable to focus well without her glasses. Kevin took the man's shoulders and hauled him out. One leg caught on the door.

"Who is he?"

"Shut up! Just get his fucking feet out, will you?"

Debbie scurried past her husband, picked up the stranger's legs. He wriggled, and she dropped them in fright. "Pick him up! What'd you think, he's a sack of groceries?" She obeyed, glanced over her shoulders.

"Who is he?" she asked, once they were inside.

"Never mind that. Help me get him into the back bedroom."

"Kevin, kidnapping! This is trouble, real trouble."

A hand whipping across her face subdued Deborah. The bound man watched from the floor.

"We'll keep him till this afternoon. Then we'll let him go."

"To the police? Even I know better than that."

"Give me time to think! He's our only chance left to get the scarab. It's his life or ours."

Adderson pulled Teldaris across the carpet, down the length of the hallway. He motioned for Debbie to help.

After they'd tied him to the bed, Adderson poured himself a drink. Deb reached for one, also.

"No." He shook his head. "You have to stay sober and keep an eye on him while I sleep. I've got important things to do today. See that he doesn't yell or get loose."

"How will I know what to do?"

"Do whatever's necessary. Knock him out, pour booze down his throat, shoot him the needle. Just keep him quiet." He headed for their bedroom.

"But he looks so strong."

"Then keep him harmless."

Adderson fell down on the bed, wearily pulled off wet shoes and socks.

"Kev, what if he needs to go to the john?"

"You'll think of something," he said crossly, and kicked the door shut.

Susan stared at her brother's body as it swayed from a pipe. He had been hung with a thick extension cord. His legs, bent at the knees, were tied up behind him. Two rusted coat hangers joined his hands in front to another ceiling pipe. The eyes bulged, and purple-maroon marks covered his neck, but the tongue was worst. Its tip stuck out ever so slightly, protruding through whitened lips. A scrawled note was fastened to his stomach with a penknife.

"Man for scarab—the tree—noon today."

She read it with unnatural composure, wondering absently if Vern had already died before the knife had pierced

223

his stomach. She nearly touched the dried blood on his chest, but couldn't. A sour aroma, similar to curdled cream, hit her. She stepped back.

Waves of nausea and trembling threatened to overcome her. She felt utterly depleted. But she knew there would be no rest forthcoming. She would have to marshall resources she wasn't sure she owned.

Joy roused from a deep sleep. She tiptoed to the door, adjusted her robe, freed hair from inside the collar.

She looked out the call box, saw Susan Tyler in the snow, knife in hand. She opened the door immediately. Susan savagely hurled something at her and, at the same time, brandished the blade.

Unperturbed, Joy studied Susan for enlightenment. Finding none there, she looked for the object that had been flung onto the rug.

"The scarab!" she gasped.

"I didn't *know* which tree, nor would I wait till noon! Now, where is he?"

Joy frowned in confusion.

Susan walked forward. "I'll use this, I swear it." Stainless steel glistened.

"Haven't you disturbed us enough for one night?" Thea stood on the second-floor landing. "Put that knife away before you hurt yourself." She descended.

Susan felt disoriented. She'd anticipated different reactions.

"Where is he?"

"What are you raving about?" Thea asked.

"Where is he?" Susan repeated, less forcefully.

Thea looked at Joy.

Joy held out the scarab.

"Khepri!" Thea cried, taking it. She closed her eyes.

They ignored Susan.

"Where is Jason? What have you done with him?" she screamed hysterically.

"What ails thee?" Thea asked in annoyance.

"This!" Susan tossed the bloodied note in the air. Joy retrieved it, a moment later allowed it to drop. Bending, Thea read the message.

Her anguished cry confirmed Susan's worst fears. The knife slipped from her grasp, and she sank to the floor.

She viewed the scenario with a very cynical eye. Next to her sat a woman who'd tried to burn her to death just last night. By her side was a woman who was startlingly, extraordinarily beautiful—and who claimed to be a queen of ancient Egypt. Susan nodded in concession to the surrealistic tableau and sipped more sherry.

"Only one hour remains, Mistress."

"I cannot fathom this." Thea paced the length of a Persian carpet in anger.

"What about my brother?" Susan demanded.

"Nothing can be done, he is dead. If you had imparted the situation to us earlier, this would not have occurred!" Thea said.

"Mistress, there was understandable confusion."

"She can speak for herself."

"I can speak for myself."

Both ignored Susan's repetition.

Joy rose. "I must leave if I am to meet him."

"It is a trap, or he would not have used that location."

"Nephew knows . . ."

"Why do you call him that?" Susan questioned.

"He *was* her nephew, long ago," Joy informed her.

"Sure." Susan drank the last of her wine. She felt a tug of drowsiness.

"If nephew gets the scarab, he would be impossible to control. He is abler than we thought."

"Or more fortunate. Could this be an accident?"

"We have no choices in this situation. Somehow, he knows what I have done," Joy said somberly. "He has the upper hand. But still, Mistress . . . I doubt he yet knows fully who he is."

"Why don't you kill me now and get that bit of business over with?" Susan said, interrupting them.

"Because we might need you," Joy answered.

Susan looked bemused.

"When he . . . is safe, perhaps some arrangement can be made. I am liberal," Thea said.

"No. I think not. You are the ultimate conservative," Susan replied.

"Jason will decide, is that agreed?" Joy asked.

"We'll see," Susan said flatly, confounded by this strange alliance that was forming.

"We must conceive a plan," Thea continued.

"No time for plans," Susan said. And then, despite herself, she yawned sleepily.

"Mistress, I must go. I do so willingly."

"What if he does not honor the bargain?" Thea demanded.

"I shall return with him," Joy promised, "then we shall have our pleasure with nephew."

"What of her?" Thea pointed to Susan's limp form.

"The wine was drugged. See? She sleeps." Susan's head rested comfortably on a green cushion. Her lips were parted and looked parched.

"Slumberland thirst," Joy whispered.

"I thirst for blood."

"Your cup shall overflow," Joy predicted, and picked up the scarab sadly.

"Joy." Thea touched the woman's brow with tenderness. "He must return to me, at all costs. You know this."

"I know this."

* * *

Deborah moodily watched the clouds through her glass-paned front door. They hovered, uncertain, awaiting some silent command to snow or disperse.

She'd fretted for hours, afraid to make a sound. She glanced again at the rear bedroom door. She gathered her courage and ventured down the hallway. She peeked inside the room. Teldaris looked up at her.

She fought a compulsion to shut the door and run, instead walked slowly toward the bed.

"You're not gonna try to hurt me or anything, are you?" she asked in a whisper.

He shook his head from side to side.

"You're not going to try anything stupid, are you?"

Again he shook his head.

"You know I'm not responsible for this."

He nodded.

"It's between you and Kevin. I'm not involved. Well, I am, but not really."

He scowled.

Deborah looked at the thin pajama bottoms. "Are you cold?"

Jason shook his head.

"I've got to go. Need anything?"

He nodded vigorously.

She hesitated.

"If I pull out the gag, will you yell?"

He shook his head.

"If you try anything, Kevin'll beat us both up. Maybe worse."

Debbie bent over him cautiously. She grimaced when she saw the gash on his head. He grunted, urged her on. She pulled the red bandana from his mouth.

"I've got to piss."

"I can't untie you, my husband would kill me."

"Just help me to the bathroom."

"Can't you wait until you leave this afternoon?"

Jason winced, mouth sore from the gag. "You know

damn well I won't be leaving—I'm a dead man.'' Debbie shivered, would not face that thought.

"You look too sensible to get involved in something like this," he said.

Debbie looked around, startled. "No more talking." She threw a quilt over him.

"He killed another man, the one Janice—" His words were cut off when she pushed the bandana back into his mouth.

"That's enough," she whispered fiercely, "I don't want to hear any more." She rose to leave. She looked back once, thought about it for a moment, then relocked the door in haste.

"Woo-man, woo-man be free," Debbie sang. Kevin's sudden appearance made her choke on the bourbon. He yanked off her headphones.

"I told you to wake me up at ten!"

He snatched the bottle and tossed it away. The glass tumbled out of her hand, as she tried to stand.

"It's only eleven."

Adderson gave her a violent shake. "Are you drunk? What'd you do, let him go?"

"No, Kevin, he's there," she mumbled.

"Get us some coffee while I dress."

"Can't we let him go? Please, Kev," she asked on returning.

"Sure. I'll just make him promise to cross his heart and not say anything." He poured cold water into his coffee, then pulled a sweater over his shirt. "Think, for once. Meeting's at six. Get this place into shape."

He sipped half a cup, then stalked to the back of the house where he checked Teldaris's bonds. Still secure. The eyes of the prisoner revealed nothing.

As he returned down the hallway, Adderson tried to pinpoint why the man seemed so damned familiar.

Inadvertently, out of some nearly forgotten habit, he went to kiss Deborah good-bye, but stopped himself, surprised, and left the house quickly.

Back in the bedroom, Teldaris dozed and experienced another dream.

A gray mist filled his vision, then parted. He saw high white walls, embellished with a rainbow of images. A young woman fled from room to room, down stone steps, past a long cloister. A phalanx of guards blocked her path. Behind her, soldiers pursued. She looked back desperately, pulled off several bracelets, flung them at the men. They paused to retrieve the gold. In that instant, she pressed her full weight against a stone block beneath a wall sconce. The stone gave way, and she leapt through. The guards broke rank to stop her, but the stone had reseated itself. She crouched in darkness on the other side.

Teldaris saw himself run through a tunnel, to where the girl crouched. He grabbed her. "Nefari!" She shook her head hopelessly, exhausted. He took her in his arms, descended more steps into another underground passage. Behind them, the stone slid forward. Two soldiers pushed themselves through. "Sen-Mut!" the woman warned.

The girl he had called Nefari, he recognized as the woman called Joy. He saw her jump down, take his hand. They stumbled through the darkened vault, toward distant torchlight. The soldiers fell behind, delayed by the tortuous maze of the cavernous corridor.

At the entrance, a shaved priest's head showed itself. More guards waited at the only other exit. Teldaris and the girl clutched one another in horror. Soldiers with drawn swords ran toward them from either side.

Adderson surveyed the park, glanced into the rearview

mirror, and did a double take. For an instant the eyes gazing back at him had seemed alien, as if they belonged to someone else. He frowned, then turned another page of the battered book he had picked up while ransacking Teldaris's apartment. He checked his watch. It was past noon.

The last few pieces of this puzzle were missing. Nightmares. Dreams. Since childhood. The same ones, repeated time and again. The dark-haired mother-tyrant who did not in any way resemble his own mother . . .

He was a child sitting on the outer ledge of a tiered blue-tiled fountain. He squeaked in fear and held his hands over his face because. . . . A lovely young woman with long black hair approached. She smiled. He leapt up to escape, but was caught by her braceleted arms. He ducked beneath them, wriggled free. Running, he looked back to see her playfully splashing water. He stumbled over a step, fell, bruised his knee, as she refreshed herself at the fountain.

When she turned toward him, she was older, though lovelier than ever. Miraculously, he had grown to manhood. He stood before her solemnly. He regarded her with half-opened, suspicious eyes.

"Why do you send for me?" he asked.

"It was my whim." She laughed, but there was no mirth in her voice. "You have the cold eyes of a fish," she added.

He did not respond to her goad.

"I shall tell you myself why you are being banished. . . . "

"Why do you despise me?" he asked.

"Because you exist."

"What have I done to deserve your wrath?"

"You were born. That is enough."

He gestured toward the military insignia dangling from his belt.

"Have I not proven myself worthy?"

"You have proven yourself worthy of contempt. You are

an antagonist, a predator of the lowest order. You conspire inside Amon's very temples, it is said, with those power-hungry eunuchs.'' She stepped a pace closer. ''I suffer no intrigue against me. I have selected a remote post for you to command . . . before you are old enough to cause me serious grief. There the wind blows constantly, the sun never relents, each day the sand whips more bitterly.''

''I am your sister's son,'' he protested.

''The scorch of the desert should burn out any relation to me.'' She placed a hand upon his cheek. He flinched. The chill of her words transmitted itself through her fingertips.

''In ten or twenty years, perhaps, you will be permitted to return. By then you will have forgotten the lure of a woman's flesh, the aroma of her scent, the promise upon her breath. . . . ''

Her lacquered nails dug into his face. He fought for control and won. He did not move, nor display pain. A tiny trickle of blood crested at his jawline.

''That was for molesting my handmaiden.'' Her eyes bore the deepest, coldest fury.

''Nefari consented.'' His jaw tensed.

''Why, then, is she covered with welts and bruises?''

''She protested her love.'' His eyes looked past his stepmother, to the fountain.

''You lie, nephew.'' Her lips thinned.

''She wished thus to be taken.''

They studied each other in silence. Neither set of eyes wavered.

''The wastelands are too noble for you. Perchance humility will arrive with age.''

''Perchance. Am I dismissed, my queen?''

The blood on his face hardened under the rays of the sun.

''*I am Pharaoh!*'' she answered angrily.

He bowed slightly. ''Forgive my error.''

"I forgive nothing." She raised her head. "Leave me, before my anger does you great harm."

He executed a military salute, turned. A sneer appeared on his face. "Nor shall I forgive, stepmother," he whispered.

The scene faded. Adderson blinked.

A dark Bentley appeared. It slowed to a crawl, nearly stopped.

Kevin smiled. He'd guessed correctly. This justified the chance he took in the wording of his note. Only one person could have understood it.

Joy opened the driver's door. She emerged, wearing sable over black silk. Against the shining black car, backdropped by snow, she was an arresting image.

"Nefari," he murmured, thrown into a shocked sense of déjà vu. The woman no longer stood in front of an English motorcar. Instead, she lit oil lamps as flame reflections danced across her forehead. She watched, always watched.

Oil. Gasoline. Love. Betrayal. Passion. Punishment. Adderson felt far older than a man in his twenties. His eyes felt jaundiced, his mind world-wearied. "No more," he growled.

The sound of his own voice snapped him back to the here and now.

"Do not look upon me!" he commanded.

Joy's forehead wrinkled slightly, then a nearly imperceptible smile formed on her lips.

"To the tree. Back up against the tree!" he ordered, delighted in turning the tables on her.

Joy leaned against the car door.

"Obey me, you . . ." He waved the book at her, as though it was a weapon. He threw it down in the snow. "I've done a little reading."

"*Shadow of Khufu?* I doubt you would comprehend."

232

She betrayed no emotion at this proof of Teldaris's capture.

"What's the meaning of all this?" he spat.

"All what?" she asked coolly.

"What have you been doing to me?"

"I made you rich."

"I worshipped you!"

"You worshipped what I could do for you. You *feared* me, because I came to you out of the night."

He frowned.

"I jolted your memory, and your avarice."

"I don't understand."

"You might have lived your entire life without truly suffering. That would have been unforgivable."

"Make me love you, make me rich, give me power . . . Why?"

"It was difficult finding you, Kevin Adderson. It was another viper that proved your downfall.

"One from your own nest." Joy picked up the book, brushed off the pages. "Do you imagine veterinarians place classifieds in newspapers for months, only to hire the unskilled? Without state certification? Without references? Do you think a doctor would not notice missing entrails, animals, medicines?"

"That job . . . Deb . . . You set me up!"

"Your wife is a clumsy practitioner of the arts. Your fondness for specialized butchery is how I located you."

"All that money spent—"

"A score is not settled until it is *ultimately* settled."

"Enough goddamn riddles." He approached a step, Joy flung the book at him.

"I was the handmaiden Nefari, whom you chose for especial punishment because I was a favorite of the Pharaoh herself. You were most unkind. I have never forgotten. Thousands died by your cruelty. They await, too. The Curse of Hat-shepsut is upon you, Thut-mose."

He advanced another step. "Do I look like I'm cursed?"

"You fear!" Joy said defiantly.

"The scarab!"

"Well hidden until you produce him."

"All this fuss over one man?" Adderson laughed to himself.

"His architecture was unsurpassed for thousands of years in elegance, in lightness. So shall it be again. In creation lies beauty. Beauty is the *ultimate* power."

"*Dominance* is power."

"Dominance? Yes. Knowledge also. Wealth? Certainly. Strength in arms? Yes. Many things can be power, yet none can stand alone. Do you wish to know the secret of power, Thut-mose? It is this. Power is water in the desert. It is the thing that people need more than any other, and this ugly, grasping world needs beauty above all else. Beauty is the goal of power, whether the seeker knows it or not."

"The world is ruled by people who think like me. It always will be."

"Governed perhaps. Not ruled."

"I've no time for your games!" he shouted. "I want the scarab."

"I do not see him in your car."

"The scarab first." Adderson stuck a hand in his coat pocket.

Joy produced a handgun equipped with silencer from beneath her fur.

"I'll have it," he demanded.

"We have traveled beyond that point."

He kicked the snow in frustration.

"Take me to him, or you die." Joy aimed the gun.

He did not doubt her threat.

"Follow me."

Joy waited until he was a safe distance away, then lowered the gun, got into her car. "Have no fear—I shall do so," she whispered.

Adderson got into the Volvo, circled the Bentley, then

floored the accelerator. He smashed the car into the parked car's side. His windshield cracked. Blood oozed from his arm, his head throbbed, but he did not loose consciousness. He looked up and saw that his desperate plan had succeeded.

Joy lay against the dashboard.

Debbie held the straw as Teldaris sipped the soup.

"You won't tell him I did this?" She rubbed her cheek.

He thanked her with his eyes. She turned away.

"I was hungry," he said.

"Can . . . I get you anything?" She did not turn back to him.

"You could let me escape."

Debbie heard the sound of a car door, stiffened. She set down the soup.

"I was only kidd . . ." His last word was muffled as she replaced the gag.

"Be quiet!" she whispered. "He's back."

She scurried from the room. Jason strained to listen. Shouts, cursing, and a low-pitched female cry penetrated the bedroom walls. He stilled his breathing and heard a series of crashes, knocks, and thuds, punctuated by the staccato sounds of flesh striking flesh.

A half hour passed. The noise gradually lessened, then moved into the adjoining room.

The door opened and Debbie reentered. Her eyes were puffed, new bruises showed on her face.

"Your friend is here. The Oriental woman. She had a fight with Kev . . . ," she mumbled, and sat on the edge of the bed. "Do you know what he wanted?"

Teldaris nodded.

"The scarab, right?"

He nodded again.

"He found it in her coat. Kevin says you can't go yet. I mean, he wants to wait." She swallowed.

Teldaris stared angrily.

"I can't let you talk right now. He's locked himself in the next room with her." A suffering look passed over her face. A woman's muffled scream pierced the wall.

Debbie's back straightened. "Nothing's wrong . . . I mean, Kevin knows I'm right here in the next room. He wouldn't do anything . . . nothing—" A second scream silenced her. Her hands began to tremble.

The sounds from the adjoining room spurred him to a desperate struggle to free himself. Debbie seemed unaware of his movements. Teldaris groaned in frustration. He turned his head to one side. The noise increased. Joy was being raped by the monster in the next room. And, unless she was deaf, the monster's wife heard it, too.

Susan awoke. She sat up, startled.

"Another storm approaches," Thea said.

"What happened? What time is it?" Susan rubbed her eyes.

"You fell asleep. It's nearly four. Soon it will be dark."

"Four! Why did you let me sleep through . . ."

She looked at Thea with sullen anger. Her movements were slow and stiff. She spied an urn of coffee placed on the table before her.

"For me?" she asked warily.

"The coffee is for us both," Thea replied without much interest.

Susan offered her the first cup.

"You understand what their continued absence means?" Thea said.

"Couldn't there have been a snag?"

"A deliberate one."

"What time did—"

"I trust nephew was prompt."

"Didn't you follow them?"

Thea shook her head. "It was not wise."

"Why not?" Susan sputtered.

"Your brother is in my basement. Most of Jason's personal belongings are in the garage, as well as his automobile. All traces of your involvement are gone. I have been busy."

Susan uneasily scanned the floor, as if Vern could see her from below.

"I haven't cried," Susan said in astonishment. "My brother's dead and I haven't cried."

"There's time for that later," Thea said as she rose. "We must be on our way."

"Our way?"

"Clear your head," Thea said sharply. "Joy has failed. We must go to the location of their meeting."

Debbie cut the rope with pinking shears. She moved as though hypnotized. Teldaris flexed his legs once they were free, and motioned for her to untie his hands. He rolled his eyes in relief when she finally loosened his right arm. He turned over, unbound the left, removed the gag, and stood.

"I did . . . this . . . for Gail," she mumbled.

"*What* did you say?"

"Your picture . . . she showed me your picture once." Her words were slow, slurred. "I remember now. . . ."

"Where is she?" he whispered fiercely, taking her by the shoulders.

She lowered her head. "Gone."

"Where?" he demanded.

She spoke in a barely audible voice. "Dead. Kevin's group killed her." Deborah nodded toward the next room.

The news did not stun him. Jason had expected his search to end in this manner for some time.

"Stay here," he ordered.

She sank to the bed numbly.

He crossed the bedroom, opened the door a crack, and

listened. The noise had diminished. He searched for a weapon, found a plaster plaque representing some kind of country landscape nailed above the doorsill. He unhooked it just as the adjacent bedroom door flew open. Adderson, nude, stumbled past, headed toward the bathroom. Before he could turn around, Teldaris swung the plaque with great force. Kevin dropped to the floor, kicked once, then lay still.

Teldaris ran into the adjoining room. Joy was sprawled across the bed, tied with a cloth belt. Her dress lay shredded beneath her. He untied her, covered her with her fur coat. He picked up the revolver, checked it, returned to the bathroom.

He lifted his arm with deliberate care, took aim.

"No!" The sound came from the direction of the doorway behind him.

He spun around. Deborah was silhouetted against the light.

She had no weapon, so he aimed the gun at Adderson again.

"No." Her delivery was flat, an unconvincing monotone, yet it had more command than before.

"He killed Gail, didn't he?" Jason's voice rasped.

Deborah waited silently, demanding her husband's life as payment for Jason's freedom. He looked at Adderson, then at her, and relented.

He dashed back to Joy, lifted her along with a blanket, and carried her from the room. In the hallway, he saw Deborah again, still in the doorway.

"He wasn't always this way . . . ," she murmured.

"Are you coming?" Jason asked.

"I want to leave him . . . but I'm too scared. There's nobody left to go to . . . ," she whispered.

"Come with us."

She shook her head.

"You know what this means?" He shifted his weight and rested against the wall.

She nodded, gave him a feeble smile.

Jason started to speak, but decided further argument would be useless. He hurried out with Joy in his arms.

ELEVEN

Set

WE SHALL KNOW EVERY PLATEAU AS WE
HAVE CLIMBED AND REACHED IT.
WE SHALL KNOW MUCH WITHOUT
BEING SPOKEN TO.
AND, IF WE ARE SPOKEN TO,
WE SHALL KNOW ALL THAT
WE CAN UNDERSTAND
AND WE SHALL HAVE THE PHIALS
OF OUR MINDS FILLED
TO OVER-FLOWING.

—Hymn to Hat-shepsut,
  from *Shadow of Khufu,*
  Cecil Rupert-Lewis, 1894

ADDERSON ROUSED, STRAIGHTENED HALFWAY. HE forced himself to the bathtub, dowsed his head under the cold water tap, and swore in pain. Water streamed down his body. He stood, listened intently. Instinct told him that the woman was gone. He swayed into the back bedroom, confirmed that Teldaris, also, was gone. He saw from a rear window that the Volvo was not in the driveway.

He rushed into the living room in a murderous rage. Deborah was rocking placidly. He stopped short, noticed an empty medicine bottle at her feet. A few tablets were scattered across her lap.

"You let him go!" he screamed.

"Choose," she ordered.

"What?"

"Choose. I swallowed a bottle of pills when I heard

you get up. You can save me if you act now. Keep me awake. Call the paramedics. Or let me die. Choose.''

Kevin glanced at the counter. The scarab was gone.

He dashed to the bedroom, threw on some clothes, and came back to his wife.

''Choose,'' she repeated once more.

He hesitated, then darted out the front door. He bolted down the drive, already looking for a car to steal.

The muscles of her stomach began to contract. Deborah smiled. Kevin had chosen. She laughed, as tears ran down her face. Sleep started to gnaw at her awareness. She closed her eyes, grateful for a moment of peace. One last sweet minute of peace.

The Volvo coasted to a halt. Joy woke as the car stopped.

''Where are we?'' she whispered. The first flakes of a new storm had begun to fall. Teldaris peered apprehensively into the endless white that covered the foothills.

''Not quite where I wanted to put us. Can you see any houses?''

She did not answer.

''Probably only a little way to the nearest phone. Can you walk?''

''I believe so.'' She nodded.

''Are you sure?''

She nodded again.

Teldaris looked around. ''Surely a car will come along. . . . '' He trailed off.

''Why didn't you kill him?''

''You knew? I thought you were unconscious.''

''You fled without killing him. What if he pursues?''

''I don't know.'' Jason reached beside the seat, pulled out Adderson's revolver. ''Just in case, there are two bullets in the gun.''

''The scarab?''

Jason felt along the dashboard, produced the necklace, handed it to her. She smiled in faint satisfaction.

"It'll all be over, once we get to safety." He tried to start the motor. It whined, but wouldn't turn over. He looked back again, then opened the door. "Here comes somebody now," he said as he got out.

Teldaris waved his arms, unaware that the approaching Triumph was driven by Kevin Adderson.

The DeLorean raced into the storm, headlights on bright.

Thea hesitated, then asked for directions.

"Strange place for a rendezvous," Susan commented. "An older neighborhood of abandoned stores, tract houses, and heavy industry."

"Nondescript. Joy selected it for that reason."

"It was nice, when Vern and I were growing up . . ." Susan stopped herself. "You're going too fast, there's a speed trap up ahead—been one for years."

"Traps are meant to be eluded." Thea expertly careened through traffic.

"Whatever you say. . . . " Susan shrank back in her seat. They bounced over railroad tracks, past a huge tire factory. The scent of hot rubber filled the air.

Several turns later, the park appeared. Soon they stood next to the smashed Bentley. A moment later, Thea whirled back into the sportscar. Susan raced after her, barely inside before the DeLorean roared downhill.

The Triumph swerved toward Jason, veered up the road, braked, then reversed. He jumped back inside the Volvo.

"It's him!" Jason shouted. "The gun, where is it?"

Joy handed it to him. "It's useless at this distance. Where is mine?" She looked around the seat.

"I didn't know you had one."

"Then he has it." Joy rubbed her wrists in agitation. Teldaris noticed the broken skin for the first time.

"I'll hold him off. Can you run down the field to the nearest house?"

"No." She pulled him down as the car sped by. A bullet shattered the rear window on the driver's side.

Teldaris again tried to start the car. This time, the motor miraculously turned over.

"He's back!"

The Volvo built up speed slowly. The Triumph pulled abreast. Adderson sideswiped, tried to push the wagon into the canyon below, but an oncoming car's approach forced him back. Jason floored the accelerator. He steered to the left expertly. The car spun slightly on the slickness. They passed the sharp curve.

Moments later, they approached a straightaway. He inhaled deeply.

"I won't fail this time," he promised. "I'll get you away."

She touched his arm gently, showing that she understood his allusion to a long-ago miscarried escape.

At a public phone by the wayside, Adderson pulled a stranded commuter out of the booth without a word. The surprised man saw the blood on Adderson's face and wisely decided not to argue.

"What do we do now?" Susan asked, distracted by rows of glittering neon lights.

"Search."

"Shouldn't we return? Maybe they've—"

"You know they have not." Thea stared straight ahead.

"We should have gone to the police."

"I am faster, and smarter, than the authorities."

"What makes you so confident?" Susan asked in irritation.

"I always get what I'm after."

"I think we've eluded him."

"I do not trust this." Joy looked back frequently.

"In a minute we'll be on the freeway." Teldaris wiped the back of his hand across his lips. "God, I could use a drink."

"We must go directly to Mistress. Susan is with her."

He looked askance.

A renewed sputter from the motor cut off further conversation. Wisps of steam from under the hood blew past the windshield.

"You love her, don't you?" he asked quietly.

Joy nodded. "And you?"

Jason nodded also.

"Why do you hesitate so?"

"We're not going to make it." He ignored her question. "Look, the windshield's begun to crack, and we've got a damned leaking radiator. We'll have to go back to your car and use it."

"Turn left at the next intersection. Make a right before the trailer sales lot," she directed.

Another silent moment passed before she turned sideways in her seat. "Why are you afraid of Mistress?"

"There are several reasons that come to mind," he replied wryly.

"Please explain."

"Let's disregard driving nearly naked through a snowstorm, wrecked cars, and murder. Yeah, let's just leave those *incidentals* for a while. If I go to her, I'm certain that I won't remain myself for long, that I won't retain any identity at all. My God, *look* at her. *Nothing* about that woman is normal."

Joy didn't respond.

"Look at the source of her income: narcotics. That's the tamest part of her." Teldaris pointed to a snow-splattered sign. "Exit at Federal?"

"Yes."

"Don't you ever get weary of it?" he asked.

"No. As I breathe, I serve. I shall not sleep if something can be done to please her. I shall not spend for myself as long as a lira can be better used to further her ambitions."

"But she's made you lose your own ambitions."

"Thea Markidian took me off the streets of Istanbul when I was starving. Turkey is harsh to a girl fifteen and alone. I had no hope. Mistress took me by the hand when she could have had me arrested. . . . "

"Arrested?"

"No one buys an emaciated prostitute. I had turned to thievery."

"Why?"

"It kept me alive." Joy stated this without bitterness.

"Go on," Jason urged.

"She could have indulged herself in adolescent capriciousness," Joy recalled, "but she devoted hour after hour to teaching me."

"I'm . . . sorry for your childhood."

"You cannot be, unless you lived it."

He raised an eyebrow, thought of his own.

"I grew to learn that Mistress and I were brought together for an extraordinary purpose. *She* understood it all along. I gravitated toward her as you did. We were both predestined to meet and love her . . . again."

"I came here to look for Gail," he said bitterly, "and discovered instead how easily I've been manipulated."

"Do you always accept things as they are?"

"What?" He scowled.

"Does it not occur to you that Mistress may need a man who will fight her, who will lessen her ferocity?"

"*I* tame her?" He chuckled.

"You did it once before," she replied.

Jason paused.

"She would not permit me."

"Foolish man, she desires it."

He shook his head.

"Do you think so little of yourself?"

The station wagon began to shake violently.

"It's going to quit on us."

"We are close."

"That's encouraging," he said flatly.

"The future is never to be feared," she whispered, ". . . until it happens."

Susan watched Thea, loath to interrupt her thoughts. The silence continued.

Abruptly, Thea's foot hit the brake. Susan braced herself against the dashboard with an outstretched arm. The DeLorean skidded to a halt.

"We must return at once. I sense it."

Susan felt her hackles raising.

"To the house?"

"Yes," Thea said. "Yes. Immediately." The car spun into reverse, made a U-turn.

"Do you drive like this in Istanbul?"

"No, I do not possess a license."

"Great," Susan mumbled.

"Do you love him?" Thea asked bluntly.

"My feelings are my business, but I've made my position plain."

"I believe you think you want him."

"Is that so?"

"If you truly loved him, you would give him everything he could need, including his liberty."

"Why haven't you?"

"He doesn't need freedom from me."

"That doesn't make sense."

"Not common sense, certainly."

Susan inhaled sharply, longed for a cigarette.

"In the glove compartment."

"What?"

"Look in the glove compartment."

Susan did so, curious.

Inside, a cigarette case gleamed. She slipped it out, pressed a tiny button. Susan looked up gratefully, saw that Thea held out a light.

"How . . . did you know?"

Thea smiled, as Susan hesitated.

"Turkish tobacco, nothing more."

Susan drew deeply, regained a sense of clarity. She looked down idly. The winterwear she'd changed into was warm, the imported wool felt good against her skin.

"Yes, it is better than looking like a lumberjack." Thea seemed to read her thoughts.

"I must say, you've been very generous of late to your competition."

"I no longer regard you as competition."

"Why *doesn't* Jason need his freedom?" Susan backtracked.

"He is a very complicated man." Thea paused a beat. "Poetically expressed, a late-bloomer."

"So what is he *now*?"

"One given to ideals, rather than practical affairs."

"Reliving an Egyptian past is practical?"

"The mystic can be merged with the reactionary. He has a weakness, a flaw. . . . "

She held out her fingers for a cigarette. Susan lit another and marveled at the naturalness of Thea's autocratic manner.

"He would prefer to abandon his destiny," Thea completed.

"What do you propose his destiny is?"

"To create."

"Create what?"

Thea smiled. "A foolish question. To create that which cannot be surpassed."

"Which is?"

"You would be better-suited married to another."

"I don't see why."

"All the more reason you should see how wrong you are for him—in every way. He needs someone who can give him power, buy him a mountain if he wishes it. Someone who would force every drop of energy out of his flesh until he falls, exhausted from the effort of living." She nodded. "And I shall."

"I can give him peace, a sense of ease, and sharpen his mind and my own at the same time." Susan tilted her head back.

"I prod him to be what he must."

"Jason's not a spoiled child. I don't push," Susan countered.

"Would you spoon-feed him, too?"

Susan stared out the window.

"I remember how shy he was. Moderns are vulgar by comparison. Understand: if Pharaoh was approached, it was with great trepidation. He feared me then, as he does now." Thea seemed lost within memory. "But he changed, and will again. . . ."

Susan listened, fascinated.

"How he learned! Our enemies thought him a greedy schemer, yet it was *I* who pursued. He built some of the most beautiful shrines in antiquity. Beauty . . . such beauty. And, oh, how we laughed. Bright, with so much laughter, such gladness. That is what I miss most. Laughing." She quieted, cheeks indrawn.

"How do you know this is the same man?" Susan protested. "Isn't it one hell of a coincidence that you two were reborn at roughly the same time? Mathematical probability alone is against it."

"The gods do not tolerate eternally unfinished business.

We have been given another chance, and it must be cultivated carefully."

Susan considered this. Thea handed her the cigarette to extinguish.

"He surmises that I wish to live in the past . . . I do not. I wouldn't wish to recreate the splendor of Thebes, only the atmosphere. Only the relationship. Once you are whole, you can never again survive as half."

"I've heard that somewhere." Susan thought aloud.

"You have no knowledge of these things. I forgive you."

"Thanks . . . I guess."

Thea scowled. "It will begin to sleet soon."

"It doesn't sleet much here. Too dry," Susan said, correcting her. She paused, waited for rebuke. None came. "I don't remember anything from the past, nor could Vern."

"Ah, the charlatan brother?"

"Please . . ."

"I apologize. It was wrong to speak unkindly of the deceased in my basement."

Susan remained silent, bemused, wondering what they would do with the body.

Thea observed Susan's frown.

"Most likely, you've filled your mind with numbers, grocery lists, and skepticism."

"Why didn't your nephew remember?" Susan challenged.

"Not all can, unaided. Joy could not, until she was taught. Few remember past lives."

"What makes you so positive you're right?"

Thea only smiled in reply.

"Couldn't you once—just once—be wrong about something?" Susan goaded her.

"When it concerns the very core of my existence? No. Can you say the same for yourself?"

Susan left the question unanswered, saw ice begin to hit the windshield.

TWELVE

Àusàr

AND THOSE WHO ARE AT
THE BASE OR LOWER LEVELS
OF THIS PYRAMID
SHALL LOOK UPON US
WITH WONDERMENT,
CYNICISM, AND DEJECTION.
THEY ARE TO BE NEITHER
HURT NOR TAKEN SERIOUSLY
NOR IN CONFIDENCE, FOR THEY
HAVE MANY STEPS TO CLIMB
AND SHALL ONLY CONFESS OR ADMIT
THEIR WRONG-DOINGS AND DEEDS
TO ANGRY GODS.
THEY ARE TO BE AVOIDED
AND A RELUCTANCE TO LOOK
AT THE HIGHNESS OF OUR EYES
SHALL INDICATE WHO THEY ARE.
THE MOST EVIL OF THESE ARE
THE ONES WITH DECEIT AND
DESIRE OVER THEIR HEADS,
FOR THEY ARE THE ONES WHO
SAY THEY LOVE PHARAOH AND THEIR
BROTHER THE MOST,
BUT, IN TRUTH, SHALL HURT
HIM THE MOST AND HELP HIM
THE LEAST.

IT IS NOT WISE FOR US TO
SLEEP UNDER THE SAME CANOPY WITH

THEM, FOR WHAT WE DO INNOCENTLY
SHALL BE CALLED SIN BY THEM
AND WHAT THEY DO UNKNOWINGLY
SHALL BE THOUGHT SIN BY US.
AND THERE SHALL BE NEITHER CLOSENESS
NOR PEACE BETWEEN US.

—Hymn to Hat-shepsut,
 from *Shadow of Khufu*,
 Cecil Rupert-Lewis, 1894

THE BENTLEY SHOOK CANTANKEROUSLY AS IT EASED past the abandoned Volvo.

"I was at a disadvantage or he would have been killed for such a blatant trick," Joy explained. She wrapped the fur tightly around herself.

Teldaris switched on the wipers. Only one headlight worked.

"Funny, somehow I expected to see Susan here."

"I thought the same of Mistress."

"Let's hope I can drive this thing." He stripped gears, then stopped. "Everything's reversed!"

"Shall I drive? I'm accustomed to the car."

"No," he said huffily. "I can do it. You ride shotgun." The Bentley hit the curb twice.

"What will you tell Susan?" Joy asked at length.

"About what?"

"You and Mistress."

"She already knows more than she needs to."

"Pardon?"

"About how I feel."

"Then, why does she believe she has a future with you?"

Jason glanced at his companion in some surprise. "Because she has."

The car stalled on the railroad tracks by the tire factory. He changed gears, slowly rocked the Bentley back and forth. Two minutes later, they moved again.

"You said you loved Mistress." Joy found her voice.

"I didn't say I'd live with her."

"You said you loved her!"

"I never said I'd return with you to the Mediterranean, nor did I imply it." He felt anger rise within himself.

"I believe you play a delaying game: cat chase its tail," Joy surmised. "You shall come to Mistress because you enjoy not wanting to; you enjoy a mistaken sense of your independence."

Teldaris controlled his temper. "Once the scarab is safe, and Susan's affairs are settled—"

Joy seized his arm. "The scarab will be returned to Mistress. By you."

Teldaris shook his head.

"No one person may own it. Those who tamper with it for power or profit are doomed. That relic belongs to the Egyptian nation."

"Fool!" Joy erupted. "Which best typifies the ancient peoples of the Nile: Mistress, or a squalid military machine? The scarab must remain with those who worship the old ways."

"The scarab was—"

"Made in honor of Amon, but in Pharaoh's name. Thea Markidian now represents the royal house. She is the wind of Egypt, the voice of Egypt, the soul of the Egypt of the Pharaohs."

"What about the claim others might have on the scarab?"

"Like the monster following us?"

He nodded.

"For the sheer power. It lies untapped, waiting to be harnessed and directed."

Jason jerked slightly. "I don't understand—"

"Think of it!" Her eyes blazed with intenseness.

"Imagine the raw energy—the sweat and toil needed to survive each day by each person—from the Upper and Lower Kingdoms. Multiply that by the number of days passed since. That stone *is* Egypt." Her voice conveyed horrified awe. "No power equal to it exists on earth."

He fought against gooseflesh, shook his head adamantly.

"Worse, you would condemn Mistress, too. Only she may prevent the misuse of the scarab."

Teldaris fidgeted behind the wheel. "No more!" he shouted. "No more." He perspired heavily. "Just let me drive in peace!"

Sleet began to hit the windshield.

"Quickly, take this. Take it!" Joy thrust the scarab into his coat pocket.

Before the startled man could react, a silver Lincoln sideswiped them. The Bentley stalled.

"Damn this car!" Jason cursed.

Joy rolled down the window, leaned out, and fired the gun's two bullets. One caught the Lincoln's back tire. The automobile swerved, jumped a curb.

Jason put the Bentley into reverse as two men scrambled out of the Lincoln.

"That's why we lost him," Joy said, once they turned down a side street. "He was getting in touch with his cohorts."

"Cohorts?" He laughed. He wiped sweaty palms on the

seat's upholstery. "I don't think I've ever heard that word used conversationally—though I must admit it fits the situation."

Joy allowed a smile to cross her features.

He turned the car down a series of unplowed residential streets. Their progress slowed.

"Talk to me." He stared ahead.

"What do you mean?"

"Something to fill my mind. Something pleasant." Teldaris flexed his left hand. "Nothing about scarabs, or pursuit, or Egypt. Just talk to me."

Joy sat closer to him. "All right, I shall tell you about my bells."

"Bells?"

Joy nodded. "Ever since I have been able, I have collected small bells from around the world. My secret passion, bells."

"What kind?" he asked.

"All kinds. Brass bells from India, porcelain bells from Germany. Silver bells, cast iron . . ." She laughed to herself. "Late at night, when everyone else is asleep, I have a kind of ritual. I select one bell. Just one, from among hundreds. I hold the bell in the cup of my hand, imagine where it's traveled, what it's seen. I ring it softly, and listen. I hear the beauty of its tone, then conjure up appropriate images to match its sound. It helps me sleep peacefully, and . . . I never tire of it," she ended quietly.

He smiled.

The car wended down street after street, twice narrowly missed abandoned vehicles. Only when they returned to a plowed main thoroughfare did their speed increase.

"Look, we're nearly downtown—" Teldaris began.

Out of nowhere, the silver Lincoln reappeared, catching both of them off-guard. The big car pulled in front, slowed to a crawl. A bullet shattered the Bentley's remaining headlight.

"The monster is behind us!" Joy cried, as she saw the blue Triumph block the rear.

"Can we get to the left?"

A third car pulled alongside, blocked an escape.

"How did they find us? How in hell did they find us?" Jason swore.

"We fell into their trap—"

"They haven't got us yet!" Teldaris jerked the wheels to the right. The car shot over the curb, down a sidewalk, into an alley.

Tires squealed. The Lincoln roared forward, the Triumph following.

"If we can make it to . . . anywhere . . . ," Jason muttered.

Joy pointed to the State Capitol dome shining in the distance.

"Stop, I can run, serve as a decoy."

"No. Not this time, no matter what."

They dodged slower traffic. Ice began to fall in earnest. Vehicles skidded into one another on both sides of the Bentley.

"Great night for a joyride," he joked.

Joy smiled back. "Jason, I—"

"I'm the one who's sorry." He stretched a hand in her direction. "Listen . . ."

The Lincoln sped past them and stopped.

"Get down, damn it!" He shoved her to the floor. She promptly reappeared.

"Stop the car, Jason! I'll run, you pull into the right lane. Open your door, escape through the park to the house!"

"No!"

"Allow me this!" she pleaded.

"No. We're nearly there!"

A bullet hit the front left tire. The car slid counterclockwise before it smashed against a mailbox. Joy opened her door, pulling him by the arm.

"Run!" he shouted.

Joy raced up the street, Jason beside her. The Lincoln pulled back. A series of shots was fired from its rear window. Joy grasped her side, staggered, and fell.

Jason looked behind him, saw the crumpled figure in black. He dashed back and stooped down. She moaned when he attempted to lift her. The Lincoln rounded the corner.

Teldaris looked up and saw the Triumph bear down on them. In blind rage, he ran in the direction of the oncoming car. "Run, damn it, run!" he screamed at Joy. He turned his head back once, saw her motionless on the snow.

He made one long leap at the Triumph. It swerved and began an uncontrollable slide. He reached for the driver's door handle. A shot was fired, but it missed him. The face inside was frantic. Adderson shoved the car into low gear, but the tires spun uselessly in the snow. Teldaris wrenched the door open. Before the driver could move, Teldaris grabbed a fistful of hair and dragged Adderson, howling, from the seat.

The pair slugged and punched, as the car moved slowly forward. Oncoming traffic swerved to avoid them. The Triumph came to a halt next to the curb. Both men fell on the ground, grappled with each other.

Teldaris was astraddle Adderson when the Lincoln pulled up. Two men emerged, rushed toward them. He looked up, saw that Joy was gone. With a fierce grin, he punched Adderson twice in the mouth, and smashed the man's nose before they reached him.

They tackled him, pounded the butt of a rifle between his shoulder blades. Adderson rose, with their aid, and held Jason's head down in the snow until he struggled no more.

Thea released the steering wheel and put both hands

over her face. Susan dropped her cigarette and seized the wheel.

"What is it?" She steered the car onto the shoulder of the road.

Thea moaned once. Susan extinguished the cigarette, got out and crossed to the driver's side. She took Thea's hands and held them. Traffic on Broadway had totally stilled for several blocks.

"No," Thea groaned.

Susan pushed her aside forcefully and climbed in.

"Tell me!"

"My love . . ." Thea rocked back and forth in the car seat.

Susan set her mouth in determination, started the motor, and drove grimly toward the mansion.

Adderson's nose had been bandaged by the doctor in the group. He watched the others watch him.

"You may have done irrevocable damage to us," the leader lectured.

"I could be ruined!" the councilman stated.

"We'll end up in prison," cried another.

"The police may be here any moment," a woman complained.

"Why didn't any of you get the woman's body?" another cursed.

"Damn you all!" Adderson swore. "You're not worth pissing on!" He angrily shoved the doctor away.

He could barely stand, but he stood. Savage gasps came from his mouth. His eyes bulged with rage.

"Today I lost my wife, because I chose you over her. I let her die for this!" He waved the scarab at them.

"I killed, I maimed, I raped, and I boast of it!"

He thrust a fist toward the body of Teldaris. "I have severed the links to my past."

The leader leaned forward.

Adderson pointed a finger in his direction. "Tonight I must leave, a fugitive in a snowstorm. You can go back to your quiet little homes. But I will start again, with others less timid!" He held the scarab up.

Each listener reacted to his outburst with mixed emotions.

The leader thought for some moments. "Who, other than the Oriental, can trace you here?"

Adderson shook his head. "No one. We took the plates off the British job." He indicated the Bentley's tags. "So now we can trace the source of our trouble, and deal with it for the last time."

Two men nodded in confirmation of his story.

"Are you sure the Oriental was dead?" the bald man pressed.

They exchanged glances with Adderson, then with each other, fearful.

"She was dead," Adderson lied, "or we wouldn't have left." He stared hard at the two men from the Lincoln. They hesitated, then agreed.

"What about the car you stole?" the leader asked.

"I won't be caught." He produced the gloves he had worn.

"Did you leave any loose ends?" the leader repeated with suspicion.

"*I* did the dirty work." Adderson pointed to the two bodies. "Other than these, there are no loose ends." He paused, thought of Joy. " . . . that I can't handle tonight," he finished.

The leader looked him straight in the eye. "I retain the scarab."

"No."

"We could kill you now, blame everything on your psychosis, and still have the scarab."

Adderson considered this. "You won't."

"Why should we spare you?" growled the tall one.

"No more challenges," the leader ordered.

Adderson looked at the group. He was hopelessly out-numbered.

"Agreed," he lied.

"Swear it!"

"How!"

"Prove it!"

"How?"

The old man pointed to Deborah's body.

Kevin's lips curled in revulsion. "And I thought that Crowley was a monster!"

"I propose an additional test to see how powerful this trinket is," added the tall one. "Maybe it's not worth saving, or worth the trouble of protecting him." He regarded Adderson with undisguised hatred.

Susan drove in silence, with frequent glances at her passenger.

Thea stonily refused to speak.

Susan wished she would say something. The last blocks to the Cheesman area had seemed to take an eternity. She was afraid to ask, yet her mind screamed in anxiety.

"Are you . . . better?" she ventured softly.

Thea looked at her as though she were mad.

"We're nearly there."

"Are we?" Thea asked, a hand over her eyes.

The scarab was placed on a tall stand of carved rose-wood. The group sat on the floor around it. Adderson stood next to his dead wife. Deborah lay upon the couch, cleansed. Only her head was covered. The horrific gri-mace on her face from rigor mortis was hidden by a black cloth. Adderson was unclothed as well. A smattering of white bandages on his face and torso were proof of his ordeal. Long scratches from a woman's fingernails glistened like war paint down his back. The red streaks had an erotic quality about them.

An assortment of knives and syringes lay on a glass coffee table nearby.

"We, this night, invoke Darkness," he intoned.

> Darkness for the might of us,
> Darkness under cover
> Darkness to enter by,
> and Darkness to discover.

Moments later, lights throughout the city of Denver began to dim. The scarab appeared to move slightly. Any onlooker would have sworn that it lived.

Susan blinked. Thea shook herself back to clarity.

They exchanged quick looks as the entire area plunged into darkness.

Susan repressed a start at Thea's reaction. She made a sound akin to a cat hissing—fur raised, claws ready for anything.

"The ice storm," Susan mumbled.

"The scarab," Thea whispered hoarsely.

"The streetlights should come back on any time," Susan explained, "after the auxiliary power system—"

"This is not the work of a storm," Thea said angrily, "but of those assembled against me."

"There's the house. Perhaps they're back."

"No," the woman replied. She untied her hair. It fell long past her shoulders. She looked up, seemed to gaze through the roof of Jason's automobile.

Susan braked the DeLorean slowly. The sight of her Renault in the mansion's back drive comforted her.

"Thank you for retrieving my car."

"You will need it tonight."

"Oh, yes." Susan hadn't thought about leaving. Vern's

duplex or a hotel—the thought of either gave her a forlorn feeling.

"He will be avenged," Thea vowed. "The scarab must be recovered."

"What are you saying?"

"Look!" Thea cried. She leapt from the vehicle, ran toward the front walk. Susan saw a body lying prone in the snow.

"Jason!" she called, coming up behind.

"Joy," she amended, unnerved by the long thin trail of blood across the white yard.

"Help me!" Thea ordered. Susan helped pull Joy to her feet.

Once inside, Thea became lightning-quick, graceful, and efficient, resembling nothing less than a jungle cat on deadly business. Susan became a human machine, devoid of all thought, save one: is he alive?

They carried Joy to a sofa. Susan knelt before her and massaged the coldness from her limbs. Thea prepared medicines, poured a thick golden concoction down her throat, and examined the bullet wound. Susan saw evidence of rape.

Joy's eyes were soon open. Her face began to color from the drug's effects. Susan watched in surprise as Thea worked with the expertise of a practiced field surgeon.

"This must come out tonight," she whispered.

"No," Joy begged in a weak voice, cheeks flushed by the narcotic. "Bandage it, Mistress. And I will take something against the pain. They must pay. They must pay tonight!"

"Is he alive?" Susan cried haplessly.

Thea leaned closer to Joy.

"He succeeded, this time he succeeded," Joy gasped. "He wanted to give his life in exchange for mine. . . . "

"Does he still live?"

"I . . . do not know."

"Was he alive when you saw him last?" Thea pressed her.

Joy nodded gravely. "Gave him the scarab . . . he would need it more . . ."

Thea dropped her eyes. Susan burst into tears.

A sharp slap nearly knocked her over. She looked up in utter shock, for Joy had dealt the blow.

"Not while hope lives. Not if there is one chance."

Susan turned her head, brushed away tears.

Thea handed her a phial. "Drink this. Your strength will be needed."

Susan looked at the bright red vessel, then at Joy, who struggled to rise despite her wound.

Thea's eyes were filled with admiration when Joy sat upright.

Susan grasped the container with both hands and drank, no longer hesitant. Instantly, intensity rallied through her. She licked her lips hungrily.

Dressed in black, moving like three animals racing through a forest, the trio left the mansion. First they returned to the Bentley. It was encircled by a flock of tow trucks and police cars. All earlier traces of Joy's blood were obliterated by fresh snow that had followed the sleeting. Traffic had slowed to a standstill on Fourteenth Avenue.

Thea, Joy, and Susan communicated without words, seemed to share one mind and purpose. They abandoned the vehicle.

Thea sat behind the wheel of the DeLorean, Susan smoked in her Renault. They watched Joy procure a third car. As always, she was superbly efficient. The Mercedes probably would not be missed until after daybreak.

Susan glanced at the seat beside her. The collection of weapons there reassured her, seemed perfectly natural.

Her old life of tax records and laundromats seemed more distant than girlhood promises.

An image fleeted past as she watched Joy lower the hood of the Mercedes: her mountain lake. A sad smile crossed her lips. The one place she would have frequented during this upheaval was the placid lake. But she hadn't. The one person she would have shared it with was Jason. But she hadn't. Her thoughts were cut short. Thea signaled, led the trio. Susan followed Joy. This would be as great a tribute as sharing her favorite place on earth. She smiled grimly as the hunt began.

"What about me? My runoff's next week!" The councilman ran nervous fingers over a wisp of hair stuck to his forehead.

"We don't have time for that!" the leader snapped.

"If we don't quiet the mayor, I'll lose!"

Adderson stared into his bathroom mirror, dully overhearing the exchange from the living room. He touched his nose tenderly, glad the doctor could fix it tomorrow. He looked at his chest, sighed, then buttoned his shirt.

"What kind of man are you?" he whispered to his reflection.

"A snake man," his image answered.

A middle-aged woman appeared in the doorway.

He straightened. "What?"

"One more thing. Elliot needs to win. We might not convene again before the election."

"I'll be there," he muttered.

She waited.

"I'll be there!" Adderson snapped. "I'm still washing blood off my hands, see?" He held up puce fingers with crimson stains under the fingernails.

"You've been washing for twenty minutes," she tossed back.

"Yes," he hissed, "but my wife's blood doesn't come off easily."

Three cars wound their way up the darkened mountain. The glittering view was gone. The only illumination below was an occasional car's headlights. Candles flickered bereftly from a few windows.

Once, a hoarse voice attached to a flashlight broke the eerie silence.

Twice, frantic motorists jumped aside as the triad ignored their appeals for help.

The Renault fell behind, unable to make it further up the steep road. Thea ordered it abandoned.

Susan climbed in beside her.

Soon, Joy's vehicle slowed, stopped, reversed.

"Turnabout?" Susan broke the silence.

"Never."

"A swift exit?"

"Precisely. You *are* quick!" Thea complimented.

"What should I expect?"

"Everything."

"What if—" Susan experienced apprehension.

" 'This was for him.' When you must leave, say those words. Run for your car and don't look back. Return to my house."

"When must I leave?"

"When you can't take any more."

"And you?"

"Not until I'm finished." Thea switched off the motor.

THIRTEEN

Àuset

FOR WHAT WE DO NOW SHALL BE
REMEMBERED IN LIFETIMES LATER,
AND WHAT DOES NOT MATTER
SHALL NOT.

WE MUST WAIT NO LONGER.

TOO MUCH TIME HAS PASSED.
LET US START AND ADVANCE
FROM THIS MOMENT.

—Hymn to Hat-shepsut,
from *Shadow of Khufu*,
Cecil Rupert-Lewis, 1894

"SOMEONE'S NOT CONCENTRATING, I CAN FEEL IT! Concentrate, or we'll . . . that's better. See the heart: beating, quivering, pumping, failing . . .''

Wolfgang issued a low-pitched howl outside, followed by an excited muffled yelp. Then he was silent, but his master hadn't noticed.

Adderson glanced repeatedly at the scarab, plotting the best way to take it.

"Concentrate! Whose attention wavers?''

The Circle drifted in their communal trance.

Two bricks crashed through the closest window. A violent gust of frigid air extinguished the candles. The only light left glowed from the fireplace.

An excited babble erupted. All hesitated, except Adderson. He bounced to his feet, grabbed the scarab.

A large stone shattered a window opposite. Then a second, and a third. The excited babble hushed. They were surrounded.

Adderson ran for the front door. A steel pipe ripped through the glass. He was knocked to the floor, senseless. Glass lay glittering all around him.

The councilman bolted for the back door. The leader took his wife's hand and headed for the bathroom, where they locked themselves in.

The tall one went toward Adderson, hoping to reach the amulet. He fumbled when a cold liquid squirted through the open door. He cried out in surprise, then yowled. He fell against a wall in agony, screaming without pause. The cold liquid was sulphuric acid, and it covered his face.

The councilman leaped through a shattered window, ran across the yard, tripped, was struck by something heavy. His mouth was forced open and a thick mixture forced down his throat. He gagged, but was forced to swallow. The mixture was lye.

A younger man, the tall one's brother, climbed out another window and raised his eyes in time to see a steel garden rake swing directly for his face. It was his last sight.

A sobbing woman huddled in the corner with the doctor, who wielded a fireplace poker. Not knowing where to turn, they waited.

The real estate tycoon crawled on his belly to the kitchen, grabbed a steak knife, then wriggled his way to the back of the house. He sensed a light motion and raised himself slightly, trying to peer down the darkened hallway. A kick to his throat knocked him to his knees. Choking, he fell forward again, on his own weapon. Thea placed a foot on his back and pushed. The knife penetrated past its narrow hilt.

The other man who'd attacked Jason burst through the front door like a football tackle, headed for the Lincoln. He made it to the trunk, where he was shot through the shoulder by a silencer-equipped gun wielded by Susan.

Two ropes tied his hands together, two his feet. These were attached to the car's rear bumper. From without, the car was put into neutral gear, and his last ride slowly began. Susan quickly lost sight of the man, though his cries could be heard all the way down the sloping road.

Howls and screams resounded into the night sky. But no help came, could come.

Thea softly knocked on the bathroom door. The old man opened meekly, trapped and knowing it.

"You wouldn't hurt my wife, would you?" the leader pleaded timidly. "She's an old woman. . . . "

Thea displayed her handgun, then ordered the woman to get into the shower stall. The woman looked at her husband, then to the door. Thea placed the gun barrel against his right eye. The woman complied in terror.

Thea forced the man to his knees before the toilet, turned on the shower hot water tap full blast. She pushed the shower door shut with one hand. Cries for help went unanswered, violent thrusts against the door were useless against the strength of Thea's restraining arm. As the leader cowered, as though praying, before the porcelain bowl, with a hard thrust of her booted foot she shoved his head downward. His arms flailed, his legs jerked uselessly. She stood with casual poise as his movements lessened. He drowned in the toilet, then Thea turned, opened the shower door and casually shot his dripping wife.

In the living room, Joy appeared beside the fireplace holding an ash scoop. The doctor sprang up, swung the poker wildly. They clashed like duelists.

A woman reached for a poker.

"Look, the flames!" Joy shouted. The woman turned around, unprepared, as she bent for the metal utensil.

"I said *look*!" Joy kicked the woman in the buttocks, propelled her headlong into the fire. She rose, ran for several feet, hair aflame, before she collapsed next to the tall man. From her ghastly light, the doctor saw the tall man's face, the one who had been doused with sulphuric acid.

One lidless eye still visible, he now resembled multi-colored candlewax.

Nauseated by the grisly sight, the doctor spun around—too late. The shovel caught him on the back of the neck. He fell sideways, toppled over the stereo. Joy approached, one hand clutching her waist. She waved the heavy scoop ominously over him, like a flag.

In the firelight's glow, she saw the man stare up defiantly. He resembled a trapped rodent ready for one last suicidal spring.

"I'm going to nail you to the wall." Joy smiled widely.

"How?" he snarled, as strength returned.

"You'll see," she purred. "I was, of course, speaking literally."

Susan waited outside, lest anyone escape. A shadow shot from under the house. She blocked the retreat, Japanese sword in hand. A barefooted woman trembled in fear, then darted around and past her. Susan gripped the samurai weapon and rapidly overtook her.

She swung the sword twice. Several parts were severed. As the woman bled to death, Susan kicked snow over her body—and saw a gleam in the whiteness. She bent down, saw the scarab beside the premature burial mound. Susan clasped it tightly, felt an immediate response, then thrust it in a pocket.

Two shadows appeared from the front of the house, stiffly carrying a large bundle. She relaxed upon seeing Thea and Joy. The sword clattered to the iced walkway and she put a hand to her mouth. They held Jason on a bier of outstretched arms.

Susan ran up in horror. "It can't . . . no. . . . He looks like he's asleep!"

"The deepest sleep," Thea said evenly.

"No! He's only . . ." Susan touched his face and recoiled in shock. The cheek was cold, stiff, repulsive. She shook her head slowly. Total fury flared within her eyes. She headed for the house.

"No!" Thea commanded. "There is only one left. He is mine."

"I want revenge," Susan said, enraged. "I will have it!"

Joy spoke quickly. "It is not necessary."

"It *is* necessary for me!" Susan cried.

"He must be safely carried back. I honor you with that charge." Thea shifted her gaze from Susan to Joy, and saw that her breathing became labored as she bore her share of their precious burden and fought to keep emotion at bay.

"To be dumped in the basement with my forever-damned brother? No! I won't have it!" Susan screamed.

"This was for him," Thea repeated her earlier words. They had an immediate calming effect upon Susan.

"One day long, long ago, he commanded me to look into his eyes and repeat after him, 'I am gold, you are silver.' He first insisted that I promise to utter the words very solemnly, and so moved was I by his intensity, by his love, that I did as bidden. Do you know what those words meant?" In the frigid air, frost formed on her breath.

They eased Jason's body onto the seat of the sports car. Face lightly ashen, he appeared to nap.

Susan came up behind them. She pulled the scarab from her pocket. Both women watched as she placed it within his rigid fingers.

Thea reverently touched the scarab and whispered, "He who becomes . . . Become thou soon reborn with me, my love."

Thea turned, hoarsely spoke aloud. "He meant 'We are both precious, but you are more so than I.' I kept my promise, and, thanks to timely warning from Joy, escaped my Egypt."

Joy swayed, leaned against the car, but said nothing.

"Go with Joy, help her. The drug will soon wear away. If I do not follow, see that he is not left for the scavengers.

You will know what to do. Susan Tyler, in this task you are gold, I am silver.''

Susan broke into tears.

Thea gently placed a hand on Susan's head. "We are bound now . . . sisters . . . for we loved the same man.'' She brushed a strand of hair away from Susan's face. "Do not fail me, do not fail him.''

"Mistress, must I . . .'' Joy began to swoon. Susan ran in time to catch her.

Thea walked back to the house, did not turn around.

Down the road, Susan drove past the Lincoln. Blurs of red streaked down the middle of the snowy lane. Limbs ripped from sockets hung off the limousine's rear bumper. She avoided it with a gentle swerve, swallowed against nausea. Susan thought of her dead lover. "You are gold, I am silver,'' she whispered.

Joy moaned, sank against the door.

"We'll get you to a hospital fast,'' Susan said, trying to comfort her.

"No, not until Mistress returns. Promise me . . .''

She fainted.

Susan bit her lip, and continued the lonely, treacherous drive down Lookout Mountain.

When Adderson awakened, he found himself in bed. His arms and legs were splayed, each tied to a post with silky nylon cord. Automatically, he tested the strength of the thin cord, and it bit deeply into his skin.

A woman stood in the doorway. Adderson saw that she wore an open black robe, with nothing underneath. She walked to the bed and sat in a straight-backed chair beside it. All the while, she studied his face.

"What's . . . going on?'' he asked weakly. He looked frantically at the doorway.

"No, they won't help you. All are dead. Not butchered like your wife, but suitably judged and executed.''

"Who are you?"

"Hello, *nephew*."

Impressions of hot winds, a blue-tiled fountain, and cold, cold laughter wandered on the edge of his consciousness, but abject fear forced the images away. Panic leapt like a flame. He closed his eyes.

"Do you hurt, nephew?"

He opened his eyes to see a hypodermic descend. The woman administered the shot gently, so that he barely felt it. He watched her. She was beautiful, with dark blazing eyes, and darker hair.

She sat back in the chair. Adderson felt a slight euphoria overcome him, and guessed the shot was a painkiller. But soon he realized he had guessed wrong. His senses began to heighten to an unbelievable degree.

"Why are you doing this?" he asked incredulously, as she began to remove his clothes.

She twirled a pair of forceps lightly. She laughed softly and poked them against his face, to gauge the drug's force.

"So that every cell of your body will be as aware as possible." She cut away his shirt.

"Aware of what?" He squirmed.

"Pain, for as long as possible." She pulled his jeans from beneath him.

"Before what?" he stammered.

"You die," she completed.

His eyes widened in fear when she produced a gleaming silver scalpel. She tapped it lightly in her hand.

"What's that for?" he croaked, panic-stricken.

"Justice," she promised.

He stared at her, watched with bulging eyes as she drew a one-inch square in the center of his stomach with charcoal. Screams, then howls of excruciation filled the air when she began to trace the charcoal border with the scalpel. Evenly, meticulously, she lifted up the square of skin with the forceps, and slowly pulled it off.

Adderson sobbed in agony. She smiled, and waited.

"Why . . . are you doing this?" he cried, panting, stomach quivering like jelly. Thea leaned down, drew a second, identical, square—next to the first.

"I collect snakeskins, nephew."

Her lovely white hand reached for the silver instrument once again.

Epilogue For Silver

"THAT, WHICH WAS SO NECESSARY, PERISHED. AND with it, my strength. My will, indomitable and impoverished, quested—against all odds—for thee. And found a world so void, so negative, that my heart burst asunder.

"Loss, which came suddenly and spitefully, endured. Years passed. And, with them, that tragic thing called patience.

"Was I never meant to know happiness, nor find love in peace? I waited, knowing that somehow we would reunite. When you were but a small boy, I saw you laughing, walking down a street. My heart cried out, 'There he is, a child. What pain there will be when he is a man. Can I not spare him this?'

"Yet Wisdom, that counselor of the old, forbade by saying, 'No. Thou mayest not take the pain of another unto thyself. Watch him. Look, he is content. Do not spoil this moment with foreboding.'

"So I drew back, and smiled, knowing that one day you would be mine. Love endures all, triumphs over ego, conditioning, pandering, squandering—all the vices man can accumulate. And love contains it. Love contains the future.

"When we are one—united, at peace, at ease, with unburdened heart and single mind—hands, spirits, souls intertwined; laced with love, devotion, caring—all those futile worries and agitated nights will pass into the folly of all that ever was. For all that endures, is love.

"Love is all. It is the universe in a soul—it is the universal soul. The greatest power, the most sublime imagery, lies in the meeting of two loving minds. Use this, if you will, to find peace. Already you have found love.

"It is here with me."

ISIS LEARNED OF THE DEATH OF OSIRIS BY THE EVIL SET AND HIS AMBUSHERS. SHE SEARCHED THE LANDS RELENTLESSLY WITH HER HELPERS, ENDURED MUCH HARDSHIP THROUGH HER LOVE AND DETERMINATION. DEVOTED WIFE AND MOTHER, SHE DISCOVERED THE REMAINS OF HER BELOVED, SORROWED, THEN RETURNED HOME. THERE, WITH POWERFUL MAGIC AND IN-CANTATIONS OVER THE BODY OF OSIRIS, SHE IN-ITIATED THE FIRST RESURRECTION.

ISIS SPOKE AND TRIUMPHED OVER DEATH, TO RESTORE HER LOVE TO ETERNAL LIFE.

The following is a transliteration from the Egyptian.

Chapter One:	SĀT	— Slaughter
Chapter Two:	Ā UAA	— Destroying Goddess
Chapter Three:	PET	— Heaven
Chapter Four:	BA	— Soul
Chapter Five:	SET	— Fire
Chapter Six:	ḲERḤ	— Night
Chapter Seven:	ḤEḤ	— Eternity
Chapter Eight:	MĀU	— Cat
Chapter Nine:	ĀBA	— Battle
Chapter Ten:	XEPERU	— Kheperu (Scarab God of Rebirth)
Chapter Eleven:	SET	— Set (The Eternal Adversary)
Chapter Twelve:	ĀUSĀR	— Osiris (God of Blessedness)
Chapter Thirteen:	ĀUSET	— Isis (Goddess of Magic and Blessedness)

Author's Note

THE MILITARISTIC ENTERPRISE OF THUT-MOSE III HAS been vilified for dramatic purposes. All references and information regarding Queen Hat-shepsut and her favorite minister, Sen-Mut, are based on historical fact. The outgrowth of their characters is conjecture.

Cecil Rupert-Lewis and *Shadow of Khufu* are creations of the author.